THE MAN WHO NEVER WAS

"All right," said Port Commander Forgues, "let's get to the bottom of this. Who are you, anyway?"

Pearsall exhaled, hard. "Sir, I am Commander Harwood Jay Pearsall, First Officer of *Hawk Flight*. You've known me for years. Is my identity in doubt?"

"It certainly is. Whoever you are, you're not Woody Pearsall, and what you were doing on *Hawk Flight*, I don't know. But I intend to find out. So you might as well tell me the truth. Now."

"Damn it, sir, I *am* Woody Pearsall." He shook his head to clear the cobwebs. "Who the hell else would I be?"

Forgues grinned tightly. "Well, in that case, we do have a problem. Because, you see, you're dead. . . ."

ALL THESE EARTHS

Ξ

F. M. Busby

BANTAM BOOKS

TORONTO · NEW YORK · LONDON · SYDNEY · AUCKLAND

ALL THESE EARTHS

*A Bantam Spectra Book / published by arrangement with
the Author*

Bantam edition / December 1985

ISBN 0–553–25413–8

Published simultaneously in the United States and Canada

---

*Bantam Books are published by Bantam Books, Inc. Its trade-
mark, consisting of the words "Bantam Books" and the por-
trayal of a rooster, is Registered in U.S. Patent and Trademark
Office and in other countries. Marca Registrada. Bantam
Books, Inc., 666 Fifth Avenue, New York, New York 10103.*

PRINTED IN THE UNITED STATES OF AMERICA

O   0 9 8 7 6 5 4 3 2 1

To Vonda,
who got it off the ground.

CONTENTS

PART ONE:

Ξ

PEARSALL'S RETURN

The door was locked so Pearsall rang the door chime—who carries a housekey light-years down the Galaxy's arm and back, eight months by Skip Drive? It was long enough, he saw, for the white paint to begin flaking off the door. Pearsall had applied that paint, slowly and lovingly after sanding down the roughness, only a few weeks before *Hawk Flight*'s departure. The industrial fumes were getting worse.

His wife opened the door. "Who—? *Woody!*" She flung herself to him, arms tight around—but only for a moment. Then she recoiled and staggered back, face contorted.

"No! *No!*" She backed away toward the living room, hands clenching and unclenching, gray eyes wide and mouth gone slack with shock.

He followed, but didn't try to touch her. "What's the matter, Glenna?" Everything was happening too fast—he couldn't believe her reaction, let alone understand it. "You heard the ship was in, didn't you?" Her face was pale, the fine cheekbones standing out from the faint hollows below. She shook her head; her mouth worked but no words came out.

"You've cut your hair," he said. She had always worn it long and straight; now it was a mass of short curls, tinted a lighter red-brown than he remembered. One curl hung loose over her right eyebrow, near the tiny black mole at the corner of her eye. Almost as tall as he, still slim, she stood rigidly defensive, angles of bone accenting her loose beige robe.

"Who are you? What do you want?"

It didn't make sense. He tried to smile but the smile died—he suppressed an impulse to reach out to her. "Well, who do I look like?" His tone was gentle. "Have I changed so much in only eight months?"

Her hands, fists, stood out a little from her sides, shaking. "Whoever you are, it isn't funny! It's a cruel, *cruel* joke!" Now he felt the edge of panic—sweat prickled at his armpits.

3

She turned and ran to the bedroom, paused in the doorway. "Get out! You get out of here! I have a gun. My—my husband's. So you just better get out of here!" She disappeared behind the half-open door—he heard her rummaging through drawers.

To Pearsall, his mind stalled at dead center, the chime of the picturephone came almost as a relief. Automatically he set his bag on the floor and crossed the room to flip the answer switch. The thought came that he'd never heard of anyone being shot while answering the phone, and he almost grinned. But not quite—a bullet wasn't what he feared.

The chubby-faced man on the screen was familiar by sight but not by name—a junior member of the spaceport commander's staff. The picture's bluish tint did not aid recognition.

"Yes," the man said, "we thought you might be there." He waved Pearsall to silence. "We've pinpointed the discrepancy in the records, that was noted when *Hawk Flight* landed. Admiral Forgues wants to discuss that with you. Meanwhile, a John Laird urgently requests that you call him at his home. One of your navigation personnel, I believe. The young man seemed almost hysterical."

Forgues, the port commander, moved into the picture. "I'll take it—I'll take it." Peripherally, Pearsall saw Glenna in the bedroom doorway. She'd found the old automatic pistol but her arm hung slack; the gun pointing at the floor as she watched Pearsall and the screen.

"All right," said Forgues, "let's get to the bottom of this. Who are you, anyway?"

Exasperation drove out fear. Pearsall exhaled, hard. "Sir, I am Commander Harwood Jay Pearsall, First Officer on *Hawk Flight*. You've known me for years. Is my identity in doubt?"

"It certainly is. Whoever you are, you're not Woody Pearsall, and what you were doing on *Hawk Flight*, I don't know. But I intend to find out. So you might as well tell the truth. Now."

"Damn it, sir, I *am* Woody Pearsall." He shook his head, briskly to clear the cobwebs. "Who the hell else would I be?"

Forgues grinned tightly. "Well, in that case, we do have a problem. Because, you see, you're dead."

The viewscreen, as Pearsall maneuvered *Hawk Flight* to its final descent, was spattered with random moving dots. He jiggled a tuning knob slightly, but saw no improvement.

The knob was sticky. He made a mental note to tell young

Laird that if he absolutely had to eat on watch, for God's sake to wipe his hands before touching the equipment.

The landing area showed clearly enough, but the flashing dots were a distraction. The viewing equipment was due for a full overhaul—but then, so was the entire ship. And so was Pearsall.

The spaceport looked unfamiliar, somehow. To his right toward the nearby city he remembered a soaring tower, topping a white, shining building. Surely it couldn't have been torn down in the eight months he'd been away—the building had been almost new. Perhaps he was confusing one spaceport with another—perhaps an overdose of Skip Drive was fogging his memory. He put full attention to landing the ship. The impact was barely noticeable.

"Nice grounding, Woody." The voice over the intercom was Captain Vaille's. "Give the watch to Laird and report here to my quarters, would you, please?"

Pearsall acknowledged. "All yours," he said to John Laird. "See you next on the ground, probably. The maintenance crew will be here to relieve you as soon as our landing blast cools. When they arrive, call the captain's quarters for clearance and you're home free."

"Yes, sir," said Laird. "Now remember, Commander, I want you and your wife to meet my family, have dinner with us, as soon as you can. You have the address?"

"Right." He tipped Laird a mock salute and left.

The captain's quarters were one deck below. Halfway down the narrow ladder Pearsall's heel caught on a torn edge of plastic; he almost fell, but caught himself. "Damned old crock really needs some work," he grumbled. But he patted the bulkhead beside him, to soften the curse, before proceeding to the captain's cabin.

Vaille was big, taller and heavier than Pearsall. On his deck were a bottle and two small glasses.

"A toast, Woody? It's been a hard trip, but a good one." They raised their glasses, then sipped. The liquor was an offworld product, a brandy from Harper's Touchdown. Golden flecks hung in the dark fluid; its aftertaste was tart fruit.

"You're right, skipper—a good, hard trip." Eight months on high Skip Factor, never landing, only slowing a few times for fly-by reconnaissance of new planetary systems, took a lot out of men and ship alike. But the odds had been good to

them—*Hawk Flight*'s unmanned one-way probes had discovered
two new habitable planets, potential colony sites.

"We should be able to disembark in an hour or two," said
Vaille. "All the tapes and solar wind samples are boxed to go,
and I imagine everyone has his own stuff packed, or nearly. I
can throw my gear together in five minutes."

Pearsall grinned. "Me, too. Or leave it—and good rid-
dance." Vaille laughed with him. It was good to be home;
even the normally reticent captain was affected.

In due time the maintenance-and-repair crew boarded. Its
chief brought clearance papers, thus accepting responsibility
for the ship—red tape was minimal. Spaceport personnel
began the unloading of cargo. And finally *Hawk Flight*'s crew,
fifteen men and nine women, trod the catwalk to the outside
gantry, rode the elevator down and touched shoe soles to
Earth's concrete rind. As always, that moment gripped Pearsall's
throat.

Port Commander Forgues no longer greeted returning
crews personally. Many ships came and went now, and Forgues
had other duties; procedures had been streamlined. Even the
newspersons stayed away, making do with official handouts
unless a real news item were involved. Announcement of the
two new colony planets, Pearsall guessed, would soon bring
them running.

He didn't recognize the subordinate who was preparing to
do the honors. The man struck him as a bit of a fussbudget,
with his clipboard in one hand and pencil shifted awkwardly
back and forth between handshakes.

"Captain Vaille? Yes." Checkmark, shift pencil, handshake.
"Welcome. Honored, sir." End of handshake. Shift pencil.
"First Officer Frantiszek?" Checkmark. Shift pencil.

"No. I'm First Officer Pearsall." No handshake. The pencil
wavered.

"Pearsall? Must be a mixup. Where's Frantiszek?"

Pearsall looked for Vaille to answer, but the captain was
talking with someone else a few feet away. "I replaced
Frantiszek when he broke his leg skiing, a week before we
left. Funny you didn't get the correction." The mishap had
boosted Pearsall to First Officer a year or two before he had
expected the promotion.

Erase checkmark, scribble note. "All right; we'll check it
out," the man said, and moved along to the next person. No

handshake for Pearsall. Bored, he withdrew his attention
while the man checkmarked and handshook his way down the
list.

A tone of exclamation broke his reverie. "*Laird?* My roster
shows no John Laird. What is your position on this ship?"

"Junior Navigator, sir," the boy answered. "On Commander Pearsall's watch."

"Pearsall, eh? Neither of you on my roster." He harumphed.
"We'll check it out." No handshake for Laird, either.

They were escorted to a nearby building for a quick,
perfunctory medical check. Orin Teague, *Hawk Flight*'s own
medical officer, had made thorough examinations and certified the ship's complement as free of alien infection, but the
minimum formality was still observed.

Then they were free, the two dozen, to go where they
would and do what they could. "Report back Tuesday morning," said the man with the discrepant list. "0800 sharp. That
gives you seventy-two hours, less a few." By Tuesday, Pearsall
thought, their reports would be analyzed—the reports they
had prepared during the past in-flight months. Until then,
Hawk Flight's crew was superfluous. That suited him just
fine.

He shook all the hands he could find, waved good-byes and
left to catch a city-bound tube train. On arrival he used his
spaceman's priority card to rent a ground car. He checked its
fuel cell reading and set off for Fisher's Landing, the small
neighboring town that was home. He didn't call first; it had
never been his habit.

During his absence some street routings had been changed.
He found his usual access to the throughway was one-way in
the wrong direction. Rather than taking time to solve the new
layout, he settled for an older, secondary arterial and soon
made his way out of the city into a countryside of rolling hills.

It was the time of autumn when leaves turn color but have
yet to fall. One small maple, half yellow and half red, so
entranced him that he pulled over and stopped—just to look,
to make it part of him.

He left before he was done with his tree, because now he
was so near that he could no longer wait to see Glenna.
Married almost twenty-five years, more than half his life—
still she brought all his senses alive. First, to see her . . .

Either the signs were changed or he'd daydreamed—he
missed his turnoff. But he circled, found an unfamiliar road

with the proper designation. Soon he was back on his homeward route, and entering Fisher's Landing. Until he turned into his own street he didn't realize he had been driving faster than usual.

He parked in front and paused a moment to look at the house, savoring the weathered wood. Ivy was growing to cover the bay window again; it needed cutting back. A brick, maybe more than one, was missing from the chimney top—he tried to remember if he'd seen it before. He couldn't be sure. No matter—he'd have to fix it, anyway.

He got out of the car and locked it, taking only his bag, leaving his other luggage for later. He strode up the flagstone walk, finally giving his impatience its head.

By habit he reached into his pocket for the house key. Then he laughed and rang the door chime.

"Dead, sir?" Pearsall stared at Forgues' blue-tinted image and shook his head. "One of us has to be crazy."

"That's possible," said the admiral. "Why else would you pretend to be a man who was killed more than a year ago? Tube train failure—you must have seen it in the news. The propelling field collapsed; cars smashed out through the girders. At least seventy dead."

"Not me, though." Now he remembered the disaster. "I missed that train."

"Obviously," said Forgues, "but Pearsall didn't. You look like him—or like his twin if he had one—but you *can't* be Woody. I attended the funeral myself, damn it! So, who are you?"

To Pearsall, none of it made sense—but somewhere there had to be a handle, a place to apply logic and twist hard.

"Ask the captain," he said. "Captain Vaille—he can vouch for me."

Forgues shook his head. "Can't locate him. He and his wife went off somewhere, left no word."

"But, any of the other officers—or the crew?" The admiral's head still moved side to side, his face stony in negation. "Or even—the fussy fellow with the clipboard. *He* saw me come off the ship—"

"But he didn't see you get on. Or *where* you got on." Abruptly, Forgues' face went stiff, his eyes wide.

At first Pearsall didn't get it—and then he did. He laughed. "*Hawk Flight* made no outworld landings, Admiral. We had no occasion to use the airlocks, even. Run the telemetry tapes through your computers." Faced with questions that had answers, he felt his mind coming alive, working surely.

The admiral's grin was sheepish. "All right; that's easy enough to check. We can scratch the suggestion that you're some kind of alien. But that doesn't tell me who you are. So *you* tell me!"

Pearsall shook his head. "I've done that. Sir, with all due respect, we're wasting time. There's a mistake somewhere—I don't know what it is. I'll report Tuesday as ordered. Meanwhile I have a couple of personal problems to attend to—urgent ones." Before the admiral could reply he hit the cutoff switch. He caught himself worrying, with one fingertip, the spot at the crown of the head where his hair was thinning, and took his hand away.

And what of Glenna? He turned and saw her standing near the bedroom doorway, the old handgun hanging loose in her hand. She stared at him, but now in puzzlement rather than outrage.

"Well, Glenna? Am I me—the man you married?"

"You can't be." He could barely hear her words. "Woody is dead—I saw him buried." She winced. "Oh, you look like him, talk and act like him—but you can't *be* him." The gun dropped to the carpet. "I wish to God you could. But you can't." She put her hands to her face—leaning back against the wall she slowly sank to the floor and sat there, sobbing.

Knowing he must not touch her, Pearsall moved to squat facing her, not close enough to threaten. Quietly, he spoke. "Glenna—Glenna." Again, "Glenna." Repeating slowly, until she raised her head and looked at him.

"I am Woody," he said. "Woody Pearsall. I look and talk and act like him—and love like him—because I *am* him. I'm me, Glenna, nobody else. A long time ago we married each other—remember?" Blankfaced, her head shook slowly.

"The tube train didn't kill me, that night, because I missed it. I was late for dinner; you were really angry when I finally got home, until we saw the news of the wreck.

"I've been gone eight months, on *Hawk Flight*. Before we left, you and I had a champagne dinner—more champagne than dinner, I'm afraid. Then we took a boat out near the middle of Lake Fisher and made love there. Don't you remember?"

"I'd like to. Oh, I'd like to!" Then her voice went dull. "But I can't—because it didn't happen."

"To me it did. And you were there; you were all of it. Try to remember!"

"I'd like to," she said again. "But I saw my husband dead." Facing him, she was like a blank wall.

"I'm dead and I'm not dead." He spoke more to himself than to her. "We made love on the lake and we didn't. I was on the ship but I wasn't. The admiral helped bury me—but I'm not buried!

"Glenna!" His voice rang, jarring her alert. "I don't know what's wrong, but if there's any way I can, I'll find out." He sighed and touched her hair gingerly, as though it might electrocute him. "I have to leave now, for a while. But try, just *try* to know who I am. Will you?"

She could manage no words but she nodded, then fled, crying. Gently he shut the bedroom door behind her, then moved again to the phone.

John Laird's line was busy. Pearsall calculated—it was less than an hour's drive—best to go now, without calling ahead. And better, he thought, not to stay in one place too long— Forgues might decide to have him pulled in, rather than wait until Tuesday. The front door key was on its usual hook in the kitchen; he took it.

Dusk had come, the time of beauty that is dangerous to drivers. Pearsall drove fast but with full concentrated alertness— officially he might be dead but factually he was alive and determined to remain so.

He passed an apartment high-rise; it loomed gray, square and ugly, but the massed upper windows reflected the last of the day's sun as molten copper. The glow fit his mood; he watched until it passed to the side of his vision.

The Laird home was hidden in a semisuburban housing cluster, a puzzle piece of contrived curving streets that changed names at every jogging. By backtracking and persistence Pearsall found the address he sought.

In the dim light the house both sprawled and soared; its style of architecture had bloomed rapidly and dated almost as fast. He parked in the double-width driveway and approached the huge, oval front door. Finding no pushbutton, he knocked.

An older, heavier version of John Laird opened the door. "All right, what do you want?" The man sounded as harassed as he looked, with his rumpled hair, high color and heavy breathing.

"I'm looking for John Laird."

"You found him. What do you want with me?"

"The John Laird I know is younger. Your son, perhaps?"

"No—Christ, no! But maybe you'd better come in, at that. You might be able to help."

"Help? How?" But Pearsall thought he knew.

"A young man came here. He says he's my son, claims to be named John Laird. I came home this afternoon—my wife was half-crazy, this boy we never saw calling her 'mother,' and then me, 'father.' We never saw him before, I swear!"

"But how do you think I can help you?"

"Sounded as if you said you knew him. If you do, maybe you can get some sense out of him for a change. He locked himself in the bathroom and won't come out. Come on—I'll show you the way."

Pearsall was led into a large living room, past a wide-eyed plump woman, a boy about twenty and two teenaged girls— he was introduced to none of them—along a hall, to a door. Closed, it was—closed, and inscrutable.

Laird, Senior, nodded. "He's in there."

"All right." He raised his voice. "John Laird! This is Pearsall."

"Commander!" The voice was muffled. "Thank God you're here—someone who knows I'm real. I thought I was going crazy. Or that everybody else was . . ."

"I—think I know how you feel, John." Pearsall grinned briefly, a ticlike twitch. "Why don't you come out now, and talk it over? See if any of it makes sense—all right?"

"You won't let them send me away?"

Pearsall thought—he couldn't speak for the Laird family. "If you can't stay here, John, you can come with me. Will that do?"

"I guess so." The door opened; young John Laird, looking both sheepish and defiant, emerged. His reddened, puffy eyelids hardly befitted a junior navigator. Pearsall ignored those signs and shepherded the two Lairds to the living room, where the others sat stiffly, as though posing for an old tintype.

"I'm Commander Pearsall," he said, "First Officer of the ship *Hawk Flight*. As you may have heard, we've just returned from an eight-month mission." He turned to the older man. "Would you introduce me?"

"All right, Commander. You know my name. This is my wife, Bonita—my son Charles—my daughters Mildred"—the older girl—"and Irene."

Pearsall smiled and performed the ritual courtesies. "And now," he said, "may I introduce this young man, who for the past eight months has served as my junior navigator? He is listed on the ship's roster as John Laird, Jr.—of this address."

"I can't believe that," Mr. Laird said.

"The roster isn't classified; I can get you a photostat, if you like." Impatiently, Pearsall shook his head. "But right now— Laird, men on watch together pass the time by talking—and they talk of home. Young John here has spoken often of you. He has described this house to me, and many pleasant recollections of it.

"Tell me," he said, "do none of you recognize him at all?" He saw only blank stares. "Are you saying that it's some kind of delusion, that he believes himself to be your son and brother?"

Bonita Laird spoke, her voice low. "I have two sons: James and Charles. Two daughters: Mildred and Irene. There would have been a John, but . . ."

"*I* have two brothers," said young John Laird, breathing in gasps as though at high altitude. "Two brothers—James and Charles—and a sister Mildred." He turned to the younger girl. "I don't know what you're doing here—I don't have any sister Irene." She shrank away.

He reached a hand toward her. "Oh, wait; I'm not saying you shouldn't exist—I won't do that to you. You're here; I don't understand it but I won't tell you not to be here, the way dad's been telling me—"

He frowned. "I just don't know *why* I'm not supposed to be here; that's all. Because I *live* here. I've lived here all my life, with all of you—except Irene. And James was here, too— where's my brother James?"

"Your brother James," Mr. Laird began, "I mean, my *son* James—was married last spring. He and his wife live north of here about forty miles, in the Horizon Hills complex."

He hunched his shoulders for a moment, let them relax again. "I don't see what this has to do with your barging in, claiming to be my son. *I* should know how many children we have!"

Pearsall was gutted empty by pity for them all—and some for himself. "Mrs. Laird, you said a moment ago that there would have been a son named John. Could you explain that, please?"

Color flooded her cheeks. For a moment he could see the pretty girl hiding behind the armor of fat—the ultimate disguise for beauty afraid of itself. "Mr. Pearsall—Commander Pearsall, I mean—it's not really any of your business, but if it will help this young man—well, when my James was two, I had a son born dead. And his name would have been John."

"But James was two when *I* was born," young Laird protested. "And I grew up here, and we all—you don't *know* me? You don't know me at all?" Five heads shook as one.

Gently, Pearsall said, "Don't any of you see a family resemblance—a possible relationship? Couldn't you start as cousins or something, and work up?" He knew he was pushing too hard on something he didn't understand, but his own needs were eating him. So he laid it on the line and hoped. "Can't you try?"

He lost. "We can't take a stranger into our home," said Laird, Senior. Bonita Laird's mouth twitched but she did not speak. Of them all, it was Irene who protested.

"*I* wouldn't mind if he stayed," she said. She shook back her fair hair, fallen forward over one shoulder. "I like him."

"Out of the question." Her father's face showed fear. Fear of what?

Pearsall knew when to cut his losses. "Let's go, John." He gave the obligatory handshakes.

Young Laird looked at each person in turn; he paused at Bonita but shook his head. Only to Irene did he speak. "Thanks," he muttered, and touched her hand briefly. Pearsall took his arm firmly and led him away. The boy's luggage was by the front door; Pearsall picked it up and got the two of them out and safely away.

In the car, before starting it, he said, "You're not insane, John. You're up against a problem that's totally new, that's all.

"And so am I."

Pearsall had nowhere to go but home—and there, only if Glenna allowed it. If she did, he supposed Laird could stay also. What effect the boy's presence might have, or his story, he couldn't guess. To learn that the Universe held other confusions, other mistakes—it might help her.

Driving now in night, his headlights carving a dark-walled tunnel as the road skirted a swamp, Pearsall explained his own problem.

"So, to her," he finished, "I'm an impostor. I have to be—she saw me dead." He made a sound, half snort, half chuckle. "I suppose I should find my grave and pay my respects."

"We're in the same boat, aren't we?" said Laird. "Except that your wife knows, at least, that she was married to you. *My* family simply doesn't believe I exist—or ever did. I can't understand it—what's happened to everybody?"

"*We* happened to them. Otherwise they're all perfectly sane, sensible people."

"Then we're what's wrong? Or has the whole world gone crazy?"

"No, we're fine, John—just fine. So far, anyway. And as worlds go, this one is sane and good."

"Then what *is* wrong?"

"Don't you get it yet? Well, I'm not sure I do, either, in detail. But one thing's clear—this perfectly good world isn't *ours*."

"You mean this isn't Earth? But—"

"Of course it's Earth! But—different, somehow. Probably more so than we realize yet."

"You mean, my family back there—it isn't really the one I grew up with?"

"Almost, but not quite. They had a son born dead, so they're not the same people they'd be if he had lived. The difference isn't much—except to you, who happen to be that son. You see?"

Silence for a time, then, "Yes, I think so. Do you suppose they'll ever accept me?" The voice trembled.

"Eventually, I imagine, when they understand what has happened—when they're told by someone who can speak with authority. Keep your hopes up, yes. But be patient—it may take a while."

"I'll do that," said Laird, "and thanks. But what *did* happen?"

"I'm afraid that's the question of the century. I wish I knew."

They were silent then, the rest of the way. An unfamiliar car was in Pearsall's driveway; he parked at the curb. He took his remaining luggage from the car and motioned for Laird to bring his, also. This time, at the door, he used his key—once inside, luggage and all, his position would be stronger.

As they went through the hall to the living room, he heard conversation that broke off as they entered. Pearsall recognized the small, dark woman with Glenna.

It was Glenna who spoke. "You're back, I see." Her voice was stiff and forced, close to the breaking point. "Well, maybe you can explain to Ludmilla here, where her husband is. She's been asking me, and of course I don't know."

"I don't understand," Pearsall began—but suddenly he did understand, and realized he should have foreseen the complication.

Ludmilla Frantiszek rose and faced him. Her hands clenched tightly across her chest. The heavy black braid, that fell forward over her left shoulder to her waist, swayed with the slow agonized shaking of her head. "Where is Miro?" Her voice was low and ragged. "What have you done with my husband, you dead man who walks?"

Pearsall tried to answer, but could say only, "Milla—"

"Ah, you know me, do you? I knew you, too. And Miro knew you. We grieved at your funeral. And then Miro left with *Hawk Flight*, to be gone a long eight months. I waited, but I was not here when *Hawk Flight* returned—I was with our troupe in London, dancing. You remember that I am a dancer?"

"Yes, Milla. And a very good one."

"Yes." She nodded. "That is true; I am. When I heard, I returned. To the port. *Hawk Flight*'s crew was gone, scattered to reunite with families for three days. They will be back on Tuesday, the fat-faced man said." Pearsall nodded; he knew the one she meant.

"But Miro, that one said, has not come back. Instead there is you, who are dead. Tell me—you must tell me! How can this happen?"

"Milla—Milla, I don't know. Miro was not on *Hawk Flight* with me; he'd broken a leg skiing and was grounded while it healed. I took his place—he stayed at home. And somehow I have returned to a world in which you've seen me dead and Miro, not I, left on *Hawk Flight* as First Officer.

"That's all I know, Milla. It's not much, but it's true."

Black eyes wide under furrowed brow, she gazed as if trying to memorize him cell by cell. Finally, she nodded. "I believe you. I don't understand all you say, but I never knew you to lie, Woody, while you were—alive." She was trying not to cry, but could not stop her tears.

"I will go now." She turned away, Pearsall moved toward her but Laird waved him back and took her arm, guiding her out. He did not return immediately; Pearsall decided he was making sure she was in fit condition to drive before letting her go.

"Then I was right," Glenna said, suddenly breaking silence. "You're not my Woody at all, are you? You're some kind of a Woody Pearsall, all right, but you never saw me before today. Nor I, you. You're a close match. I can't see any differences yet—maybe I never can. But you're simply not—*my* Woody!" Tears welled; it was Pearsall's night for weeping ladies.

"Oh, I wish you were!" she cried.

He passed off the thought that her wish, literally taken, would make him dead—he knew her true meaning. "So do I, my dear," he said. "You have no idea how much I wish it."

She ignored his words. "I should have known—I *did* know—when you said I'd cut my hair. Because I haven't worn it long for nearly six years. I cut it when I had the role of Helen in that play—what was the name of it? I can't remember—" Pearsall couldn't recall her ever acting in any play at all. "And somehow I never got around to growing it long again. Though I should, really...

"But you didn't *know*. So you can't be my Woody, can you?"

She asked the question as though it had an answer, so he gave her the best he had. "No, I'm not," he said. "And you're not quite my Glenna, either. But—" and now for the first time he moved and touched her, took her by the shoulders to hold her facing him—"we are each the best—the best Woody and the best Glenna—that either of us is ever going to find."

She came to him and clung, sobbing, but by the feel of her he knew it was still no good between them.

At least, he thought, she had accepted him as a friend.

Pearsall and Glenna shared the same bedroom that night—Laird had the guest room—but not the same bed. Lying awake, he heard her slow, sleeping breath. He had steeled himself to being aroused and frustrated by her nearness, but within him no excitement stirred—he was as much disappointed as relieved. The thought came that the need to establish identity was stronger, even, than his need for sex.

When on a mission he schooled himself to celibacy. Some men and women formed shipboard liaisons—he did not. Early on, he'd considered the idea—but apart from Glenna's unorthodox Monogamist convictions he felt the pleasures did not compensate for the risk of jealousies and impaired morale. He took no moralistic position, but felt that as a ship's officer it was unwise to invite possible trouble.

At home, though, his urges were strong and frequent, not much diminished by age. And so were Glenna's—in the world he remembered, they were well matched.

He had to get away from that thought. Instead he considered what Glenna had said when Laird came back from seeing Ludmilla Frantiszek safely on her way.

"Admiral Forgues called," she had told them, "just before Milla came here. Everyone from *Hawk Flight* is to report back to duty tomorrow morning."

"Sunday?"

"Yes. He said it's important."

"I'm sure it is. I wonder—" *if it's really everyone,* he thought, *that he wants there tomorrow—or only me . . .*

"What, Woody?"

He shook his head. Anything he could say would sound as paranoid as he was beginning to feel.

Now, lying alone as though he were on the ship and Glenna light-years away instead of a mere few feet, he still wondered.

Sleep came eventually, much later than he wished.

Next morning Glenna was cheerful in an impersonal way, as she served the two men breakfast. "I'll expect you both home for dinner," she said, "so call me if you can't make it. And do let me know if you learn—well, anything that explains anything, won't you?"

"Of course, Glenna." He wanted to say more, but it was no time to crowd his luck. Besides, Laird was there.

The latter looked more at peace with himself now; the night's sleep must have helped. He said little, but smiled occasionally.

One bathroom among three people did not help two of them set forth as early as Pearsall would have preferred. Once on their way he drove fast.

At the spaceport he took a shortcut to the Administration Building—rather, to where he remembered it to be. The building wasn't there. In its place stood an old, dilapidated warehouse.

Now he remembered—the soaring tower he'd looked for and hadn't seen, when he was making his landing approach, was the new Admin Building. Before he'd ever touched ground, he should have known that this was not his world.

He stopped the car and searched through memory.

"What's the matter?" asked Laird.

"Nothing. Well, yes—there is, in a way. John, do you remember the Ad Building, and its tower?"

"Of course. Why?"

"Well, this is where it was. Now it isn't. Let me think a minute. We'll have to find the old building, the one *our* Space Services tore down."

Laird's face went blank; abruptly, the rhythm of his blinking eyelids increased. Pearsall shook his head—just now he couldn't afford to worry about Laird.

The old building—Admin had vacated it two or three years ago—he should be able to remember. Yes, he knew where to go.

He was right; the building he had seen razed was where it had been. He parked, and used an elbow to nudge Laird. "Come on, John—the admiral doesn't like to be kept waiting."

Inside the building, Pearsall said *"Hawk Flight"* at each checkpoint and was passed through to Forgues' receptionist without having to show identification. One desk removed from the admiral's presence he repeated the name and added: "Where do we go?"

"You are . . . ?" The girl was blonde, and pretty. The blue eye, her left, that aimed slightly outward, accented her piquancy. It would be unwise, thought Pearsall, to correct that defect.

"First Officer Pearsall," he said. And pointing a thumb at his companion, "Navigator-Third John I-forget-the-initial Laird. We're a little late. Where do we go, please?"

"Oh—yes, sir. The small conference room just off the admiral's office, to your right. You know it?"

"Yes. Thank you." He guided Laird along; they entered the room.

From his seat at the end of the long table, Forgues peered up at them. At first look his head always seemed too large for his small frame, but Pearsall was accustomed to the discrepancy and adjusted automatically. A quick count told him that he and Laird were the last to arrive. The dead, stuffy air of the drab room was heavy with anxiety.

"Sorry we're late, sir," said Pearsall. "No excuses. But I think I have part of the answer to some of the questions you'll be asking."

"No doubt," was the dry-toned answer. "You're an intelligent man—you must have reached the same conclusions we have."

"I don't understand. I thought—"

"You thought you were the only odd fish in the soup. Please find a seat, Commander—you too, Laird—and we'll get down to it." Confused, Pearsall sat.

"Let's not waste time," Forgues began. "I've heard some of your stories, I believe them. We'll get to your individual problems a little later.

"About six hours after you disembarked I knew as a certainty that your ship was not the *Hawk Flight* we sent out eight months ago. Unfortunately, Commander Pearsall, I did not have this knowledge when I spoke to you at your home.

"The maintenance crew ran into a few problems—some of their testing procedures wouldn't work. It took a while to find out why, but when we did, the answers told us a great deal.

"Shortly before *Hawk Flight* left this port, the Labs sent us a new set of modifications to improve control efficiency. I put crews on overtime and got the work done in time for liftoff. Our repair crew's problem turned out to be that on your ship, these changes had *not* been made. We checked and found that the departure date in your log is three days earlier than our own records show. It is not the same ship—you are not the same people. There have been a number of repercussions..."

Pearsall saw a small, iridescent green insect crawling along the upper edge of the admiral's collar, never quite touching his neck. Unable to look away from the little tightrope walker, he felt akin to it—he wanted it to survive.

"We have," said Forgues, "three gross anomalies. Commander Pearsall, who was dead before *Hawk Flight* undertook its mission, is now returned alive to us. My congratulations, Commander. Commander Miro Frantiszek was first officer of the *Hawk Flight* I knew—your records show he was never aboard. And ours make no mention of Navigator-Third John Laird, who is indisputably present.

"The remaining twenty-two, many of you, have encountered problems of your own. If you wish to discuss any of these, now would be a good time." He looked around the table. "Prentice?"

Second Officer Miles Prentice rose—a tall man, stooped and lean—and spoke in a low, intense voice. "I went to my address—someone else lives there. When I found my wife, finally, she said we've been divorced more than three years. She's remarried and has two new children. I don't know what to do." Shaking his head, he sat again.

Forgues looked at him but said nothing. He acknowledged a raised hand. "Chandri?"

"I was married, too. But now I find that my wife—I said good-bye to her only eight months ago—has been dead nearly five years. It's insane, that's all. Or I am . . ."

"You're not," said the admiral. "Only . . . misplaced."

The testimony continued. "Gehring—Lena Gehring. I was a widow with a son in boarding school, a married daughter and a grandson. Now I'm a childless spinster. I'd rather be dead."

"Cheng here, Second Pilot. Last year my wife and I moved to a new house—but somehow it turns out we didn't. Nothing else is much different."

"Johnson. I was a bachelor, but now I seem to have a wife and two kids. I'm not complaining—I like it."

"Lightfoot. I drew good cards. My husband was a hopeless drunk—and I do mean hopeless. Here, he's been dry for the last four years."

"Ramirez. I went home. It wasn't my place and never has been. My wife's folks never heard of me and she's married to somebody else. So I looked myself up in the Directory. I have a wife I never saw before. It's a little scary but I think it'll work out okay—she's pretty nice."

"Timon—Aldred Timon. There are some minor differences but nothing serious. It doesn't bother me any."

"Parelli, it says on the roster. I have a different husband but I probably would anyway by this time, even if I'd stayed home. I always seem to marry the same type. I think maybe this one is a little better than average."

"I'm Red Sarchet, Drive Tuner. I live with my folks, like always. But down at the corner bar they all let on I was one of the gay guys. I'm not—I don't have anything against them, but I'm not. I had to fight one fellow. I'm not going back there."

"Gerard, communications. I didn't have anybody before and I still don't. I live in a new place. What's the difference?"

"Vaille, Captain. I found some problems to be worked out, but nothing insurmountable."

On and on it went, all through the twenty-two. One short, fat man said only "I pass." Looking at him, Pearsall recalled his name, Crawford, and his job, Supply Clerk. Nothing more came to mind from eight months on the same ship. *Poor Crawford...*

The consensus was almost evenly divided between those adjusting successfully to the changes and those finding them distressing to intolerable. What could anyone do for Chandri or Gehring?

Forgues muttered into the intercom—the pretty, blonde girl came almost immediately with a big pot and a tray of cups. As the coffee ritual began, the admiral spoke again.

"Your attention, please." The green insect was gone. Pearsall hadn't seen it go, didn't know whether or not it was still circumnavigating the admiral. "For what help it might be, I'll tell you as much as I understand, of what has happened.

"It seems we didn't know enough about the Skip Drive. Of course the press stories, that it beats light-speed by going through hyperspace, are a lot of horse puckie—there's no such thing as hyperspace. But all *we* had to know, in Operations, was that it works. It took us there and it brought us back. For ten years, on the shorter hauls our power sources could handle, we had no trouble. So last year when we got the Krieger power units, we pushed performance as high as we could.

"Now, I had a two hour lecture last night, by a top man from the Labs. I won't take two hours to tell you, because I didn't understand that much of it. But I'll tell you the parts I did get."

The little bug reappeared, sitting like a tiny épaulette on the admiral's left shoulder. Pearsall was glad to see it.

"The trick is that space and time are quantized. If you don't know what that means, wait and ask me later. Mainly, the Universe doesn't exist continuously. It pulsates—appears and disappears at a rate much too high to measure. So when you move, you do it by vanishing at one point and reappearing at the next—normally.

"Ordinarily, in moving we hit every point along the way. Skip Drive suppresses our appearances at most of those points; we beat light-speed because it's the ins and outs that use up time and energy, not the motion itself."

"Excuse me, sir." It was Captain Vaille who spoke. "Was it explained, how the relativistic effects are avoided? That's one thing I've never understood, and it bothers me."

"I can't give you the math for it, Captain"—Vaille smiled and shook his head—"but the way Dr. Kunda from the Labs put it, velocity has to do with the number of appearances, not the distance between them. So at a Skip Factor of ten your theoretical limit is ten lights, not one. And of course we never push that limit—our instruments are redlined at ten percent time-mass variation, which we've found acceptable.

"Nice, isn't it? We thought we had the Universe by its short hairs. So we sent you out at top Skip—well over a thousand, I believe—and instead of coming back to where you once belonged, you came here instead.

"Kunda told me why. There are more worlds than one—more than we could count, I expect. There have to be, to explain what's happened. They run side by side in time—in the ordinary way you'd stay in your own rut—no way to get out of it. But on high Skip Factor, with the checkpoints fewer and farther between, so to speak, you can drift into a new world, a different set of probabilities. The higher and longer you Skip, the farther you may drift from the world you know. That's why you're here instead of there."

"And you can't get back."

"Huh?" "Why?" "Why not?" Several people were shouting at once. Pearsall, though, remained quiet. And the little green insect had vanished again.

"You could try," said Forgues, "—go out again and take your chances. But you'd probably find circumstances even more strange to you. Effects on any one trip appear to be random, but may well be cumulative. You *might* come closer to your original world—then again, you might not. The odds aren't at all favorable."

"Then where do we stand?" someone demanded. "What are we supposed to do?" Suddenly everyone, nearly, was shouting, releasing pent emotion. Forgues beat his fist on the table like a gavel, and eventually the room quieted.

"I don't know," he said. His voice was flat, deliberate. "When I do, I'll inform you."

Pearsall spotted his small green friend. It had flown, while he wasn't looking, to a window ledge. He felt himself released from an anxiety he hadn't consciously noticed.

"Sir," he said, "is there anything more for us to do here, now? Or may we leave?"

As Forgues began to answer, the door opened. The fey-eyed receptionist failed to block the entrance of the aide Pearsall had seen on his picturephone. The chubby man spoke.

"Admiral, sir, a ship has landed."

Pearsall thought Forgues would explode into harangue, but he said, level-toned, "Thank you, Abbott, for the information. But ships land here quite often, I believe. This is an important conference. Why did you interrupt it?"

"Sir, I thought you might want to know immediately, about this particular landing. The ship is *Hawk Flight*."

"*Hawk Flight?*" Forgues broke the intent silence. "Is it ours this time, do you know?"

"It seems to be, or as near as makes no difference. At least the roster checks out, and the time of departure."

Forgues sighed. "My friends, it seems we have a whole new ball game. I have no idea how to cope with it; I welcome any suggestions."

"Just a minute, sir," said Pearsall. He turned to the chubby newsbearer. "Are all the crew members alive and well?"

"Yes, they are," the man said. "Why?—"

"Excuse me, Admiral." Without waiting for a response, Pearsall walked into the receptionist's office, closing the door gently.

"May I use your phone?" The girl nodded. He punched the remembered number; after a few seconds the picture lighted.

The woman's eyes were swollen, but dry now. Her long, black mass of hair swung loose; her right hand held a brush.

"Milla!" he said. "The other *Hawk Flight* has landed, the one that belongs here. Miro has come home!"

The brush dropped unnoticed. Her eyes filled—she smiled like a very young child seeing the antics of clowns. "Miro? *Miro!* Oh, how wonderful! You have just learned?"

"About thirty seconds ago. I called you, first thing."

"Oh, thank you, Woody—thank you! You have seen him?"

"Not yet. But all crew members are reported alive and well."

"Shall I come there?"

"I—don't know, Milla. Does Miro usually call from the port, when he lands?"

"Yes. Always."

"Then I'm sure he will now, as soon as he can. Why don't you wait for his call, then decide between you, where to meet?"

"Yes, that is best. Though waiting will be very hard."

"Yes, Milla—I know. But it's not for long, now." *My God,* he thought—*she looks ten years younger.* "Look, Milla—I'd better get off this line, so Miro can get through to you as soon as he has the chance. And I'm very happy for you."

"Yes. Thank you. I hope also for *your* happiness. And now, good-bye."

Shutting off the phone, Pearsall thanked the receptionist for its use and returned to the conference room. It stank of desperation.

"Has anything been decided?" he said.

"Where the hell have you been, Pearsall?" Forgues snapped.

"Telling Ludmilla Frantiszek she has her husband back, sir. I thought somebody should."

"Oh, yes—yes, of course! Sorry, Pearsall. Glad you thought of it."

"It's all right, sir. Does anyone know what comes next, now?"

"Not so you'd notice it. The other crew should be through Med Check before much longer. I'll have to talk to them, explain the situation—I suppose they've heard a garbled version from someone and are feeling anxious, to say the least.

"I should have thought of that and issued instructions, but it's too late now."

"When?" said Pearsall. "Begging your pardon, but none of us anticipated this landing until it happened—and then the first people to talk with the ship would naturally let the whole story out."

"What?" The admiral's preoccupation was evident. "Oh, yes, you're right." He rapped on the table for the group's attention. "Well, I'd better give the situation readout as I see it."

He looked around at all of them. "For some of you, this

new development must be one blow too many. Having to
readjust to living someone else's life was bad enough, terrible
in some cases. And now the someone else has come to take
up his or her own life and you must live with that, too."

He sighed and shook his head. "One thing is clear—your
Service careers are secure. You're all competent people in
your own right; despite the fact that someone else now shares
your name, there will be a place for you. We'll find a way to
straighten out the records, if I have to kick the computer
myself until it believes us. So you needn't worry about any of
that. I'll take care of it."

He frowned. "Now, your personal lives. Each case will
need its own unique solution, I expect. Some of you may
have to give up your families—and no help for it. Or your
alter-ego may want out of his current life situation and bow
out in your favor—it's not impossible, but don't count on it.
Or some of you, and your doubles and families, might agree
to share your lives—multiple marriages aren't common, but
they are legal. And it could be arranged for any pair of
doubles to ship out alternately, if that would help. The
Service will make counseling available to any who feel the
need for it; don't hesitate to ask. I'll see that the red tape is
bypassed."

Forgues looked at his watch. "Please remain here while I
speak to the other crew. I'll arrange for lunch to be brought
in. Then I want to be present at the first meeting of each pair
of doubles, in privacy—maybe I can help you accept each
other's existence, a little more easily.

"I realize the procedure will be time-consuming, but at the
moment I can't think of a better one. Your welfare is my
responsibility, and I intend to discharge that responsibility as
best I can.

"That's all I have to say at this time. I'll have somebody
hustle that lunch for you."

"Sir," said Pearsall, "Laird and I have no doubles to meet.
But we do have personal problems of our own. May we have
your permission to leave?"

"What? Oh, yes. And Frantiszek, in the other crew. I'll call
and have him released, if Abbott hasn't thought to do so—
which I doubt." The admiral turned to go. As Pearsall and
Laird followed him out, they paused to wave restrained
good-byes. In a way, Pearsall felt like a deserter—but what
more could he do here? He hurried to catch up with Forgues.

"When do you want us back here, sir?"

"Tomorrow morning. No, make it after lunch—1300 hours. I may be up most of the night with those twenty-two pairs of doppelgängers—and I need *some* sleep."

They parted. Outside, Pearsall noticed a new gouge along the side of the drab little rental car. Some things never change, he thought—he remembered his grandfather complaining about "damned idiots in parking lots." And throughout most of his childhood, young Harwood thought "idiots" were strange creatures who lurked in parking lots and lived only to ravage the cars of innocent grandfathers.

The vagrant memory eased his tension. He found himself smiling.

The morning drive had been hectic. Homeward bound he drove more leisurely, wondering what he could do or say to help his cause with Glenna. Not much, he decided—she had all the pieces and would have to put them together herself. Neither he nor Laird spoke during the drive; he didn't know what the boy was thinking and, just then, he didn't want to know. He'd think about Laird's problem later, and help if he could.

Before they got home he was sweating—the morning had been cool, but now it was past noon and Indian-summer hot. He'd have to take time, he thought, to turn in this underventilated rental contraption and get his own car out of storage.

Glenna greeted the two men cheerfully enough; she wore lightweight halter and briefs in a colorful print pattern. Pearsall went straight to the refrigerator and was pleased to find a pitcher of daiquiris cooling, as in earlier, happier times. He took a little in a glass and sipped it, before taking a cool shower and changing into shorts and sandals.

Glenna, when he rejoined her, was setting out cold cuts and salad. The sound of running water from the basement shower indicated that Laird was also cooling off. Pearsall poured himself a full glass from the pitcher and sipped from it, between bites of cheese, liverwurst, salad and crackers. He kept the silence until she broke it.

"Woody—Laird told me what happened."

"*Hawk Flight* coming back? The one that belongs here?"

"Yes. Why didn't you tell me? And what does it mean—what happens now?"

"I wanted us to take our time talking about it. And I needed that cold shower first. Mind?" She shook her head. "Well, first it means that most of my crew have doubles, and may be excess baggage on this world." He summarized Forgues' conclusions, then added: "Tomorrow, after he's talked with all the pairs, we'll have a better idea of how they're reacting. It's not going to be easy for most, I'm afraid."

She was rubbing a knuckle alongside her nose, looking steadily over it. "But, then Miro Frantiszek is back! Does Milla know?"

"I called her immediately, as soon as we heard."

"Yes—you would. You were always thoughtful . . . in my world."

He had to speak. "It seemed that I—that my *Hawk Flight*—ever since we landed, had been doing nothing but make people unhappy. I guess I jumped at the chance to make somebody happy for a change. I think it did me as much good as it did Milla."

He touched his cold glass to his right ear; the chill was refreshing. Changing hands, he gave the other ear the same treatment and grinned at Glenna. She began to smile back at him. The door chime interrupted.

"I'll get it." She rose and went to the door. From where he sat, Pearsall couldn't see who she greeted.

"Yes, he's here. Please come in." What did they want with him now? But into the room Glenna ushered Bonita and Irene Laird.

He stood and saw them seated, offered and served drinks, and returned to his own chair.

The two Lairds weren't talking, so Pearsall took the plunge. "You've come to see John? He should be here soon—he's been showering, but the water stopped running a minute ago."

Mrs. Laird leaned forward. "It was my husband, you see—not me. It's like a superstition or something, with him. I wouldn't have turned young John away—he needed us, I could see that." Slowly, she rubbed her hands together.

"But my husband—he's John, too, of course; I suppose I'd get used to that—he wouldn't have it. Charles and Mildred never could stand up to him—any more than I can, except just once in a while. James and Irene got all the family spunk." She smiled tentatively and fell silent.

"Yes, Mrs. Laird?" said Pearsall. "Go on."

"Well. After you left, Irene wouldn't let it go. She just kept on—didn't you, honey?" The girl blushed and nodded. "I agreed with her, we should have taken the boy in, but John—*my* John—never listens to me unless I throw a fit and a set of dishes. Well—not quite that bad, really. Usually things aren't important enough, and I let him have his way.

"This time, though, I stood with Irene. Any time she ran out of steam, I came in for her. But still my John wouldn't have it." Now she sat upright. "Then James called on the phone; it was late, by then. He'd seen on the news—about *Hawk Flight*, and the John Laird who wasn't on the records. They showed a picture of him and told his address on the ship's books—our address. So James called us, even that late."

"What did he say?" If he could keep her talking, Pearsall thought, sooner or later she'd get to the point.

"He said, had we seen the news? My John said we'd seen more than that—the man had come here, saying we're his family. James asked, well, where is he? John said he'd sent him packing. And James called his father some names—very disrespectful, James was."

Pearsall raised his glass to hide a grin. "And then what happened?"

"James said he didn't understand it, but when he saw young John's picture, his spine went cold. That he knew he couldn't ever have seen him before, but he felt he recognized him. Then he said, if we didn't take the boy in, he would."

"And I said, good for them." For the first time, Irene spoke. Her voice was low and clear. "And I asked James, did they have room for me, too?"

"That's right, honey—you did. And right there I had enough. I love my John, but sometimes—I shouldn't say it, though it's true—he's a pigheaded fool! I'd carried a son nine months, I said, and lost him—a woman never gets over that. Now somehow I had a chance to get him back alive, and be eternally damned if anyone was going to take that chance away from me!

"We argued late, to daylight—didn't get up until noon today. John missed work, the first time in years. But he finally agreed last night and stands by it today. He still complains a little but that's just show—he does hate to lose

an argument. So here we are, Irene and I—if the boy still
wants anything to do with us..."

Pearsall stood and walked back along the hall, to the
basement door across from the kitchen. He shouted down the
stairs.

"Laird! John Laird! Get your lazy carcass up here! You're
going home."

"Yes, I know." From the kitchen behind Pearsall the voice
sounded thick, as though from a constricted throat.
"I heard."

The Lairds, all three, had gone. Pearsall felt wrung out like
a dishrag. In a short glass he poured bourbon over ice—
daiquiris were all well and good, but at the moment he
wanted a little more bite. He sat again, facing Glenna.

"Well, that's two happy endings today." His voice and smile
were gentle. "Care to try for three?"

She stiffened—not much, but noticeably. "Woody, I can't
take that—not just now. Couldn't you have waited? I was
coming to like you—I *do* like you—but now you've brought it
all back. That you're not my real husband..."

"Your real husband was killed." Maybe a little shock treatment? "You saw him dead—you told me so. Tell me—hadn't
you thought of remarrying? Were you going to waste the rest
of your life mooning over a rotting corpse?"

Visibly, she shrank into herself. Her face paled; he could
see, across her nose and cheekbones, the light dusting of
freckles normally masked by her healthy coloring.

"I—I might have remarried. I had no one in mind, but of
course I've thought of it. But not like this—you're asking me
simply to let you move in here, in place of my Woody. That's
not remarriage."

As if puzzled, she shook her head. "You know my beliefs,
my Monogamist upbringing. You accepted all that when you
married me. Didn't you?"

He overlooked the gaps in her logic. Yes, he thought, he'd
accepted her views—perhaps more thoroughly than she knew.
All right; he'd play it her way.

"Well, then, Glenna. Will you marry me?"

"No, I won't!" Instant anger. "You're making fun of me!"

He took a deep breath and exhaled carefully, stifling the
words that would estrange her beyond recall. In his mind he
rephrased what he would have to say next—win or lose.

"Glenna—isn't this all a bit pretentious? I mean—it's not as though there'd never been anyone else for you, besides the Woody who is dead."

"What do you mean?" Gripping the arms of her chair, she rose. "Of course there was no one else. I came to you virgin—don't you believe that, now?"

"You're mixing up your Woodys, aren't you? Yes—certainly I believe it. That's not what I'm talking about."

"Then just what *are* you talking about?"

He sighed. "All right. I'd never intended to throw it up to you—never thought I'd have to—how you broke your own special rules after I'd come to accept them. But I knew about you and Piers Carlton, when he was directing the Little Theater in Spring Harbor."

She stood frozen, mute—he had to go on. "It's no matter now, Glenna. After the miscarriage, I could understand—you needed something I couldn't give you. And I judged that Carlton wasn't the sort who would ever be unkind to you. So I endured it, and never held it against you—until now, when you turn me away."

Wide-eyed, she shook her head. "But I didn't, Woody—I didn't. No, listen—let me talk, I thought of it, yes—I played around with the idea. In a way it fascinated me. You're right, that I needed something—all the years of hoping, and finally I was pregnant. And then the miscarriage, and the doctor said I couldn't ever have the child I'd come so close to having.

"I think I was a little crazy, Woody, for a while. And I did flirt after Piers Carlton—that's true. But he got me interested in the Theater, instead. So I found what I needed—but on the stage, not on the casting couch."

It was Pearsall's turn to shake his head. "Glenna, don't bother to lie to me."

"Lie? I'm not lying! Why should I lie to a man I'm rejecting?"

"I have no idea. But, you see—I caught you—came home and found you together on the bed. You didn't see or hear me—I went out again, and stayed away until he was gone. Afterward, until I was sure it was over, I took care to give fair warning of my comings and goings, and to make it easy for you to find excuses to meet him."

She was frowning, intent. "Why would you do that?"

He shrugged. "I'm not sure. I suppose—I thought you'd be

having enough problems with guilt, without piling shame on top of it." He was getting off the point—oh, yes! "But, another thing, Glenna—you were never in a play, on the stage, in your life. Why do you try to tell me such things?"

Silently, she stared at him. Then she laughed—and laughed, and laughed! Finally she stopped and wiped her eyes.

"Oh, Woody! To paraphrase you—you're mixing up your Glennas. *Your* Glenna may have done all you say—since you say it, I'll believe you. But I didn't. And I did act on the stage. I have my keepsakes, the theater programs. Would you like to see them?"

He was trying to comprehend, to absorb what she had said. "I'd like to, later, yes. But not now—I'll take your word for it. Though . . . it's hard to understand.

"But right now, Glenna, I'm interested in only one thing. Where do we stand, you and I?"

She frowned, a vertical crease between her brows. "Separately, I'm afraid." She paused. "You can sleep in the guest room tonight—now that Laird's gone—but tomorrow you'd better go somewhere else. Or I'll leave, if you insist. But I need to be apart from you."

"But *why*?"

"Because we do mix up our Woodys and our Glennas. You think you know me, but you don't. And every time I come to feel that I know you, I find I don't, at all. How many more pitfalls are there in our separate pasts, that we'd find if we tried to make a future together? I don't know—and I'm afraid to find out.

"No, Woody. It won't work, for us, together."

Frustration bit at his muscles like electric shock, bringing him perilously near the edge of violence. He took a deep, gulping breath. Then, sitting, looking at his not-wife, he said, "All right. In the morning I'll leave; I'll take my luggage and I won't be back. You can ship the rest of my stuff—anything that's still around here—when I have a place for it. I'll let you know, and pay the freight.

"You can file the divorce papers."

Then he thought, and said, "No—of course you don't have to file for divorce. I'm dead; you're my widow. This place is yours. It was silly, Glenna, to say that you'd move out."

"No. It's only legally mine. You have as much right to everything as I do."

"But not to you?"

"No—not to me."

There was nothing he could say. He looked at his watch—it was midafternoon. Suddenly he couldn't face staying in this house through all the hours until tomorrow. He stood.

"I might as well gather my travel gear and go now, Glenna. It can't be too comfortable for you, having me here. It's not for me, either."

She stood, also. "What do you plan to do?"

"Ship out again, I suppose." He could still muster a grin. "Next time I may come back to a world I'm better suited to."

In a very few minutes he was ready to leave. Awkwardly, encumbered by his three pieces of luggage, he paused in the living room where again she sat. Silent and withdrawn, she looked up at him but did not speak.

He made no move to set down the luggage, or to touch her. "Good-bye, Glenna."

She made no answer; he started to move away. Then she said "Good-bye, Woody," and looked down again.

Outside, he stowed his gear in the car. He looked up at the broken chimney top that someone else would have to repair. Then he got in and drove away toward the city.

He registered at a hotel near the spaceport. He could have taken quarters at the port itself, but he didn't feel up to mingling with Service personnel—he needed to be alone.

He had dinner, but didn't eat much. He bought a book but, back in his room, didn't read much. He had a bottle, also, but didn't drink much. He went to bed early...

It was the longest night he'd ever known.

He got up dull-brained and heavy-eyed. A shower helped—the automatic routine of morning soothed him. He rummaged for clean clothes—in some cases he was down to his last item, and a few things were missing. Glenna must have laundered them, he thought, and forgot to tell him—so he'd left them, unknowing. He dressed as best he could.

In the hotel's restaurant he had breakfast—steak and eggs, with more black coffee than his nerves needed.

Outside, walking, he felt the sun's warmth, though it shone vaguely through ground haze. Two blocks away he found a store that carried clothing of the style he preferred, and bought a few things he needed. He walked back to the hotel, got his duffle together and checked out.

Through mists that lessened as the sun burned them away,

he drove to the port. He registered for quarters and moved his luggage into a clean, featureless cubicle. He placed his shaving kit and some other trivia on the dresser top, to identify the room for him, next time he entered it.

He looked at his watch: 1040. The Ad Building was less than two miles away—it would make a nice walk, he decided, and headed in that direction.

At 1115 hours, wide awake now but not overheated, he approached Admiral Forgues' office. He rated a smile from the blonde receptionist with the entrancingly offtrack eye. She wore an electric-blue dress; with her pale skin and hair, it made her look like a child playing grownup. Pearsall liked the effect—momentarily, he wished he could shed half his birthdays.

Through the thin office door the admiral's phone voice rumbled unmistakably. Pearsall raised his eyebrows toward the sound. The girl nodded, and he entered the admiral's presence just as Forgues said, "Well, *do* it, then!" and shut off the phone.

"Morning, Pearsall. You're here early."

"Yes, sir. I'm anxious about some of our people, and wondered how the interviews came out. If you're not busy—"

"Not especially. Most of the talks went faster than I'd expected. I got almost enough sleep—as much as I usually get, anyway."

"Congratulations, sir." It wasn't sarcasm; the admiral grinned, too.

"All right, then. It's not as bad as I feared, Pearsall. To begin with, at Captain Vaille's suggestion I had as many spouses and other family members brought here as I could reach on short notice, and brought them into the interviews once the initial meetings were over. I think their presence, in a number of cases, helped a great deal.

"Vaille himself was no trouble—either of him. When the two met, one said, 'Do you suppose our wife will agree that you can't have too much of a good thing?' They both laughed; then Mrs. Vaille came in. At first it bothered her that she couldn't tell them apart, so *your* Vaille took scissors and trimmed his mustache short. Then she relaxed, and rapport between the three was good. In fact, I prevailed upon them to stay for the rest of the interviews, and I think their example was of help to others who were less secure."

"Yes, sir—that's the captain, all right. He doesn't talk much—stays out of the limelight—but he's never at a loss."

"True. Well, then—not to bog you down with details— eight other triangular households are launched successfully, including three with the wife duplicated. I must confess, that *did* surprise me—I'm not sure why.

"Then in six cases your shipmate was displaced by his or her twin, and in three the other crewman was displaced. Leaving—let me see—" he referred to a scribbled list "—four pair of 'twins' who all, for one reason or another, are quite adrift in this world.

"So we have seventeen who are effectively 'displaced persons'; I hope we can find some way to help them."

Forgues scowled. "No, I forgot—make that sixteen. During the night, your version of Lena Gehring killed herself. I'm sorry—did you know her well?"

Shaking his head, Pearsall felt a pang. He hadn't known her at all. If he had, could he have helped?

"But you'd better make it seventeen again, sir," he said. "I qualify."

"Oh?" Forgues raised his eyebrows, started to speak, but shook his head and began again. "Sorry to hear that. And how about young Laird?"

"He'll be all right. The family decided to give him a try."

"Good—good. And Frantiszek's in safe harbor, too. The only problem is that I can't reach him—he's disconnected his phone."

Pearsall laughed. "I can't say I blame her."

"What? Oh, yes—of course. Well, that's the wrapup. Unfortunately I can't do much about the loose ends just now—they've saddled me with *another* insoluble problem."

"Another, sir?"

"The courier ships—were those on the boards in your world, before you left?"

"Hmmm—yes, sir. Little two-person cans, weren't they? With Skip Factors into five or six figures—the idea was to provide faster communications between here and the colonies. And expedite high priority small cargo."

"That's right. Well, the ships are built—almost ready to deliver. We put a lot of money into that project. And now we can't use the damned things!"

"Can't use them? Oh, of course—I see."

"Yes. Who'll pilot a ship that can't come home again? And what good are messages to an alternate world? You see?"

After a moment, Pearsall did see. Oh, God, *how* he saw! "Sir—I think—your two problems solve each other!"

"How's that? What do you mean?"

"The difference between one world and another may be important to *individuals*, sir, but on the larger scale—politics, economics, commerce—it would be minor, even unnoticeable. Every version of Harper's Touchdown is going to need new counteragents against the cyclic insect mutations, for instance. And—well, draw your own examples, sir; you have more data on the colonies than I do. And communications dealing with overall problems rather than individual ones will still be valid—especially if the first messages explain the multiple world concept, to alert everyone to be on the lookout for discrepancies.

"If our thinking is careful, sir, the courier ships can do almost the job they were planned for."

"But who will run them?"

"I will, for one—and probably most of your other displaced persons, too. You see—it's our only chance to find a world we can live in."

"But, Pearsall—you *know* how little chance you have, of finding what you have lost!"

"Yes, sir—I do know. But, what about a world in which I *have* no illusory ties, that don't really work? Where I never met Glenna and never will? In a world like that I could feel free to make a new start. Here, I can't."

For a time, Forgues was silent. Then, "Yes—I see. But how do we run a courier system with seventeen people—seventeen who will work at it only until they find a place to call home?"

"How many other ships, after *Hawk Flight*, went out long-haul at high Skip Factor—and aren't back yet? And from how many worlds? I'm afraid our seventeen are only the first of many.

"And think of this, too—the possibilities, of exchange of information *between* worlds. It will be random, but over the long haul the law of averages will make it work.

"And I expect you'll find people attracted to the program *because* of the chance of seeing new worlds—for the adventure of it. Younger men and women, particularly."

"Hmm—it might work. It just might, at that. For a time, at

least, until someone comes up with a better idea." He paused.

"Pearsall, before you go looking for your better world, I want you to help me get this thing organized." He stood. "Now, let's get on with our next conference. At least, thanks to you, I have something to say there—besides a lot of platitudes."

As he followed Forgues, Pearsall felt almost good. It wasn't every day, he thought, that a mere commander heard two sets of problems from an admiral and handed him the answer to both—on a platter, with an apple in its mouth. Yes, he felt almost good.

The cute cockeyed blonde, as he passed her desk, smiled and nodded. He returned the smile absently and continued in the admiral's wake, but she called after him.

"Commander Pearsall?" He turned. "I have a message for you—please call your wife. You may use this phone, if you like."

He called to the departing admiral. "Sir? Excuse me—I'll be along shortly." Forgues waved assent.

What, thought Pearsall, could Glenna possibly have to say to him now? It had all been said—what further excuses, rationalizations, would she need to offer? He punched out the number and waited, numbly, until the screen lit.

"Woody?" Her robe hung awry; her hair was tousled.

"More or less," he answered. "What do you want?"

"I have to ask you something. After—after Carlton, were you and your Glenna happy together?"

He thought about it. "Yes. Yes, I think we were."

"You were able to forgive her? You didn't resent what she'd done?"

"Of course I resented it—at first. Then I accepted it, and after that it didn't count any more, either way—it was over and done with. But why do you ask? What difference does it make?"

"I couldn't sleep last night . . . . thinking. *My* Woody—he was kind, like you, but not easily forgiving—I don't think he could have done what you did. That may be why I—*didn't*, after all—you see? For I might have lost him. Do you understand?"

"No, Glenna. I don't think I do. What do you mean?"

"I mean, come *home*, Woody! You were right—we're the

best Woody and Glenna we can find. Maybe an improvement on the originals—we can *try*, anyway!

"If you still want to...", and he saw her tears.

At first he couldn't breathe—and then he could. "Yes, Glenna. I may be a little late for dinner, but I'll be there."

Her smiling lips quivered. "I can wait," she said, and on the screen the picture died.

For a moment he stood, his mind worlds away. His own Glenna—there had never been any real chance of returning to her, but this decision made it final. So she was widowed. But this Glenna—*she'd* survived that...

How many worlds? How many Woodys and Glennas—some with the "right" mates, some with the "wrong"? Some with none, and maybe some with two. But for him and her, here—he shook his head and came back to one framework of time and space.

The blonde looked quizzically at him, but Pearsall merely winked at her as he left. In the conference room a discussion was under way. Unceremoniously, he cut into it.

"Excuse me, Admiral," he said. "Your displaced persons roster—you'll have to cut it back to sixteen." Forgues' raised eyebrows wavered between surprise and annoyance at the interruption—then he grinned. Pearsall smiled back.

"I'll be glad to help initiate the courier program, sir," he said, "but I'm afraid I can't ride in it. I'm taking no chances of losing this world of yours.

"I seem to have found a home here."

PART TWO:

Ξ

SEARCH

Still outside Pluto's orbit, young Jay Pearsall dropped the Courier Can through c-interface. His Skip Factor, he saw, was falling nicely but still a bit high; he reduced it further. To the woman beside him, he grinned. "Does it look about right, Raelle?"

She nodded, short brown hair swaying with the motion. "Much better than at Harper's Touchdown. You'll make a Courier pilot yet."

His first planetary approach, Jay reflected, had hardly done him credit. Attempting a least-time pattern he had waited too long to cut down on Skip, had overshot and been forced to backtrack. On this, his second try, he gave himself more leeway. Now on the screen Earth bloomed from bright dot to the familiar bluish disc, half shadowed; planetary motions slowed toward normal pace.

"I wonder," he said. "How far have we Drifted? What kind of Earth will it be?"

She reached to touch his hand. "Why don't you say what you mean, Jay?"

He shook his head. "Maybe I'm afraid to. I might jinx it."

Her dark eyes widened. "That's foolish. This Earth is what it is."

"No, it isn't—not until we get there and find out."

Now she pushed his hand away. "That's solipsism—like saying it's not raining until you look outside to see. Either they'll be there or they won't."

He felt his face tighten, and consciously relaxed it. "Yes—after all, this is only our first try."

"Of course, Jay." She patted his cheek, then clasped her hands together.

He said, "Raelle? When are you going to tell me what it is *you're* looking for, back and forth between worlds?"

"When I find it."

41

He had to be content with that. Shrugging, he prepared for his first landing on another Earth.

Jay Pearsall was sixteen when a freak boating accident killed his parents. Miro and Ludmilla Frantiszek—the Pearsalls' closest friends, and childless—took the boy to live with them. Slowly, through his shock, young Jay came to appreciate their solicitude.

His father had been a spaceman and so was Miro Frantiszek; for himself Jay never considered any other career. He was well into midshipman's training when Miro left as First Officer on *Hawk Flight*—the first ship to carry the new Krieger power units, and a Skip Factor into four figures. *Hawk Flight* was also the first starship, in more than a decade, that did not return.

Suddenly, by necessity, Jay Pearsall became adult. Seeing Ludmilla begin to change from beautiful woman to dry, haggard crone, he obtained permission to move off the base and stay with her, and changed his own role from foster son to admiring squire. The two were not lovers, ever—from his mother Glenna, Jay had accepted the beliefs of the Monogamist minority. But Ludmilla was no Monogamist—and he realized she should never be one. A noted ballerina, she had many admirers. When she began turning down both professional and personal engagements, and to neglect her appearance as well, Jay took a hand. His efforts combined the chores of manager, wardrobe superintendent and chaperone. For months, while Ludmilla seemed to take no interest in herself, he tended her, nagged her and encouraged her.

And one evening, after he had helped arrange her long, heavy hair into a dark shining crown and sent her off to a contract meeting for a proposed world tour, the news came.

A ship had landed—a very small one, carrying only two persons. They called it a Courier Can. Jay had heard of the Cans; they were in the building stage but none had yet been launched—from this Earth. Now the project would have to be reconsidered.

For there were billions of Earths, the Couriers said—in parallel continua, separated by Drift. And between one Earth and another, events *differed*.

As soon as Jay Pearsall realized the implications, he volunteered.

* * *

The lower echelons rejected him out of hand; he had to go to the top. But he had an advantage and knew it; Admiral Forgues, the port commander, had been a family friend from the time young Jay was small enough to ride horsey on the admiral's knee. Now, in the hot, stuffy office, Jay looked at the old man—his head too large for his small body—and thought of what he must say.

The admiral spoke first. "Come here, come here—shake hands." That accomplished, he said, "Damned sorry about Woody and Glenna. I was in space when I heard; did you get my message?" Jay nodded; the admiral continued. "So you want to go Courier, do you? A little young to make such a jump; I see you've been turned down, so far, for that very reason. You sure you know what you want?"

"I think so, sir." Jay chose his words carefully. "I *miss* my parents; I'd hardly grown up enough to appreciate them as *people*. Oh, sure, I adjusted to the loss. You have to."

He pulled a chair nearer the admiral's desk and sat. "My only other close relatives—my aunt and her family—emigrated, you know, while my parents were still alive. So the Frantiszeks were all I had. And then Miro didn't come back and it looks as if he never will—and now we know *why*, of course—and I saw what that's done to Ludmilla."

"I know, son. I tried to talk to her a couple of times, but . . ."

"Yes, sir; I've tried, too. And I think now she's coming alive again. I hope so. She's older, but—"

"And you're younger, Jay. So why can't *you* put up with this world?"

"I could; I *have*—but with the Courier Cans I wouldn't need to. I was just starting to know Woody and Glenna as *equals*, you see—when the freak cyclone dipped down on Lake Fisher and killed them. Killed them and cheated me. Sure, I'd live with that—but now it looks as if there's a way not to. And so, sir, that's why I'm here."

Forgues looked long at him, then said, "Do you understand how Drift works, between the universes?"

Now Jay smiled. "Enough to know that you can't pick what you want; you take what you get. And that no Courier can ever expect to come *home* again."

The admiral nodded. "On that basis I'm approving you for

Courier training. Conditionally. The condition is that we have another talk before you ship out."

"Yes, sir—thank you, Admiral." Jay knew his salute was clumsy—training was long on performance and short on military formality—but Admiral Forgues returned it.

Ludmilla prepared for a year's tour with her favorite ballet troupe. The night before she left, she insisted Jay share her bed for a time. They only held each other and kissed, but she said, "I do wish so, that I could be your first lover; you have helped me much. But I respect your beliefs, that were also Glenna's—and I will not urge you."

As he went, later, to his own solitary couch, Jay felt certain doubts.

Courier training was more practice than theory. Ginith Claare, Jay's first stage instructor, said as much. "All you have to know is that your Skip Unit suppresses most of your normal *appearances* in the physical universe, and those are what take the time, when you're moving. So with Skip Factor ten, which was all we had at first, your theoretical limit would be ten lights. Then we worked up to sixty and eighty, and of course well over a thousand with the Kriegers. You're redlined at about forty-two percent of Limit, though, at *any* Skip—so as to keep time-dilation down to ten percent. Changing worlds is enough problem, without losing your own time, too."

Claare ran a hand over her stubbled scalp; the cut was not mandatory among Couriers but had become customary. "The reason you Drift from your own continuum to some alternate is that on high Skip you simply don't touch base often enough to keep traction in your own time line." She shrugged. "That explanation's not physically accurate, of course. If you want to know more, go ask at the Labs. They'll tell you all of it, in Math."

Jay raised his hand. At Ginith Claare's nod, he said, "You've been out, yourself? As a Courier?"

The tall woman's grin showed widespaced, large upper incisors. "Once. That's enough." She shook her head. "I want you all to know, you may not like some of the changes you find."

With the rest, Jay nodded. But he thought, *I'll take my chances.*

* * *

The training Cans, all identical, were tiny compared to the ships Jay knew—the bare essentials needed to carry two in relative comfort, plus limited cargo space. Controls were simplified and concentrated; replacing the four manned control positions on *Prodigal Son*, where he'd trained for midshipman, were only two—and in most functions they were duplicated. In a pinch, one person could fly this Can.

He looked to see what was omitted. First, gravity and air pressure controls—both conditions were fixed, set at eight tenths Earth-normal. No override, to allow the Can to exceed the redline figure. And many niceties of control, seldom used even on the larger ships, were also missing.

He already knew that Cans have no airlocks and do not carry suits. "There's nothing to need outside maintenance," the instructor said, "and if you end a run, out of fuel on an airless rock, you're dead anyway. So why waste mass and ship space?"

Living arrangements were ingeniously simplified. The sleeping couches opened out for either combined or separate use; sanitary facilities folded away when not needed. Skel Harmiger, the flight instructor, gestured toward the bare, gray plastic bulkheads. "On your own Cans," he said, "you'll have soft-textured stuff to cover this—floor, walls and overhead. Even pick your colors, once you're teamed."

Short and wiry, past first youth, Harmiger believed in fast teaching and fast learning. On the short, low-Skip training flights he took his students by groups of five—each in turn seated beside him while the others sat on the couches and craned necks to see what he demonstrated.

Waiting his turn at control, Jay watched and listened. "Each advance we've made," said Harmiger, "required new instruments, especially sensors. Starting with the old sublight ships, then the first Skip jobs, the Krieger-powered models and now the Cans. Actually you have four sets of inputs, one for each range of speeds—the screen circuits are set to switch automatically. If they don't—well, there's your alarm light, though if you haven't noticed your indicators blurring I'll have made a mistake in passing you. The alarm shows which range you're in and *you* know whether you're on accel or decel; the switch here works up for up and down for down—

couldn't be simpler. Now then, I'm going to simulate—" And
the trainee beside him—a tall girl named Nila Romalle—
handled the problem well enough to merit a grunt and nod.

In his own turn, Jay maneuvered skillfully but did not draw
approval for his timing—adjustment of Skip Factor—in rendezvous exercises. "Now look, Pearsall—watch your time-
distance integrator; keep that third-derivative window spitting zeroes. I swear, you act like you're trying to match it off
the visual." Jay tried again, and improved enough that the
reproof was not repeated.

The next student wanted to know why there was no redline
override. "I mean, if our Skip unit blew we'd *never* reach safe
landing; we'd starve to death. I don't see why—"

"Then I'll tell you." Harmiger paused a moment. "Fact is,
override's useless on a Can. Mass limits—to get the high Skip
you need, we can't give you drive power for more than about
half of Limit. And if you pushed *that* for very long you'd blow
the whole Can, anyway." Against the young man's protest he
raised a hand. "What you do have—which is better because
it's all lightweight components—is a backup Skip exciter. You
plug it in *after* you're sure you've cleared the trouble. Then
what you do is stay down around Skip ten-fifth the rest of the
way—regardless of schedule." The student nodded; Harmiger
went on to his next lesson.

Jay enjoyed flight training and was sorry, in a way, when
the next period of groundbased classes began.

Raelle Tremona joined the training group a month late—by
special dispensation, Jay suspected. Perhaps five years older
than he and nearly as tall, she was certainly no conformist—
in contrast to the closely clipped hair of most of the group,
hers swung at waist-length. That brown mane and the inde-
pendence it implied first drew Jay's attention; then her wide,
dark eyes and slow smile attracted him further. He tried to
fight his growing fascination for her—and he had his reasons—
but he lost.

One day at lunchtime he asked, "Raelle? Why are you
going Courier?"

She did not look up at him, to answer. "My business. I
have no family to keep me here, for one thing. And I've
never asked *you* that question."

The truth drove him. "I lost my parents too soon. Somewhere I may find them alive."

Now she looked at him; her sleek, arched brows raised. "And what if you find *you* there, too? How about that? What would you feel?"

He shook his head. "It wouldn't matter; I could stand that. In most ways I'm not awfully possessive."

But in love, he found, he was totally the Monogamist. Raelle returned his affection, but—he explained to her, one evening, why he could not accept her. After a time, she nodded. "All right, Jay. If it's what you need, then I won't have anyone else, from now on."

Still it was a breach of Monogamism for him to accept her at all. But he did—he did—he joyed and laughed and learned, and well-nigh exhausted himself in the learning, and begrudged none of it. After all, they were married, weren't they?

Admiral Forgues presided at the wedding, and his presence kept the following reception relatively decorous. The charivari later, an impromptu offering of the other Courier trainees, respected Jay's Monogamist principles—bride and groom were not bedded separately by their friends, even symbolically. "We're missing something, you know," said Nila Romalle, but settled for his kiss.

Later, the newlyweds alone, Jay finally had to say, "Raelle— that's all there is, there isn't any more."

She laughed. "And quite, quite enough—and you always will be. All right?"

"Sure. It's just that you know things I don't."

She touched his face. "Never worry about it."

"All right. I won't."

Now he and Raelle were teamed for Courier duty, and Jay could concentrate more thoroughly on his training. He thought to study the reports of the two who had brought their own Can to this Earth. One day in class he said, "It's hard to tell exactly how different it might be—where *they* came from. Social customs may differ a lot—it's not stated clearly—but technology's about the same. A little ahead some ways, behind in others." He gestured. "Even the Table of Organization for their spaceport—some names changed, but not all that many."

Before Ginith Claare spoke, he knew what she would say. "That's true, Pearsall. But sometimes it's those few who make all the difference."

*   *   *

When he found himself and Raelle posted for a Courier run to Harper's Touchdown, Jay felt both thrill and apprehension. After that evening's celebration the days went fast. And three days before their scheduled departure, Ludmilla returned from tour.

She called Jay. "I will visit you at the port, when you are free. Would this evening be suitable?"

"Well, sure. But—"

On the screen he saw her blushing. "I would have you here, of course. But—perhaps it is that I am embarrassed."

He shook his head. "Whatever *for*, Ludmilla?"

"You see, I am not alone now. And he—he is younger than *you* are."

Jay laughed. "What's the difference? Milla, you're ageless and you know it." And as near as he could tell, judging by her looks and the vitality of her voice, he spoke the truth.

But when she met with him and Raelle she came alone. The three dined at a restaurant just outside the port. At first Ludmilla said little, and looked mostly at Raelle. After dinner, over coffee and liqueurs, she said, "News of your marriage lagged behind my travels, until I was home again. Tell me—what can one give Couriers for a wedding present?"

Jay grinned. "Not much room on a Can, for personal belongings."

Raelle said, "I'd like to take along your approval, is all. I know how important you've been to Jay."

"And he to me. You seem . . . very mature."

Raelle pushed back her hair. "I'm five years the elder, if that matters—twenty-four to his nineteen. And I hadn't been a Monogamist, before Jay. I am now, though."

Ludmilla nodded. "But not subservient; you could never be that, I think, nor would he want you to be." She smiled. "Honesty. On whatever terms we live, there must be that. You have my approval, Raelle—even on such brief acquaintance. I wish it could be longer."

The younger woman reached and squeezed Ludmilla's hand. "And so do I. Maybe someday—"

Ludmilla shook her head. "No. I have been told. If ever you come here, it will not be the same you. Similar, of course—we could explore old memories and see how nearly the same. But not you—or Jay. As, should Miro ever return, he will not be *my* Miro."

Jay spoke. "And if that should happen?—"

"How can I know?" Ludmilla shrugged. "I would meet with him, of course. And then we would see. But the chance, by now, is most unlikely, and I am resigned to the fact. As I am resigned to losing you, Jay, knowing that you do what you must."

She joined the two in their quarters for more talk, then a nightcap and good-byes. When she had gone, Raelle held Jay tightly. "Promise me—that *never* shall one of us risk Drift without the other!"

"Sure not," he said. And although he was impatient to hold her in another fashion, until she stopped trembling he did not release her. Then he waited, expectant, for her smile.

Admiral Forgues' summons, the day before takeoff, startled Jay; he had forgotten until now, the second interview the admiral had specified. "You don't suppose he's decided to wash me out, after all?"

"Of course not." Raelle put both hands to his shoulders. "He said he'd want to see you again; that's all. As an old family friend, certainly he wants to say good-bye."

But remembering the word "conditional," Jay approached and entered Forgues' office with taut nerves. He saluted; the admiral returned the gesture. "Here, Jay—shake hands and sit down. Wanted to talk with you a few minutes, before it's too late."

Seated, Jay said, "There's nothing wrong, is there?"

"That's what I wanted to ask *you;* far as I know, you're doing fine—good reports all around. And a married team has good basis for stability, carries its own security from world to world. Your partner's a bit of a rebel some ways, I hear—but for Couriers that's not all bad. Followers seldom seek the unknown. Now then—any doubts?"

The young man shook his head. "Oh, there'll be regrets now and then, I expect—a kind of homesickness—the Earth I know, people I may not see again even as alternates. But we're trained to be braced for that—and there's always the motto to fall back on."

"Yes." The admiral grinned. "Wait 'til *next* return."

"That's right, sir. Infinity gives you infinite chances."

Forgues leaned forward. "But don't forget—only the tiny fraction of those chances 'closest' to this Earth are likely to suit you much. The Can that first came here—the couple who brought it had been out more than twenty times, and said that nearly every Drift took them further from their home line. This world's quite alien to them—they're still having trouble adapting, which is why you trainees haven't met them—but they're afraid to try again."

"I thought Drift was supposed to be random. Is there any theoretical reason why it shouldn't be?"

"Nothing scientific—only a metaphysical formulation our 'immigrant' couple told us; no math will hold it. Something about local cross-continua entropy eddies, if that tells you anything."

Jay shook his head. "Not me."

"Me either. But here's a tip, until we know more if we ever do—any time you end two consecutive runs on Earths that suit you less than the previous ones, think carefully before deciding to go out again. That kind of losing streak, don't get stubborn and try to buck it; swallow your losses and stay put."

The statement sounded final; Forgues was reaching for a folder. Jay stood. "I'll keep it in mind, sir. Well . . . I guess this is good-bye?"

The admiral pushed the folder aside and stood also; the two shook hands. "Just one more thing, Jay. If you do find Woody and Glenna—and I judge your odds are good—give them my love from *this* Earth. I miss them . . ."

A pause. Then, "What's your Can named?"

"*Search*."

"Yes. That's good enough."

"Tremona and Pearsall—one hour to takeoff. Board within thirty minutes, please." The intercom's distortion rasped in Jay's ears; he acknowledged quickly, before the call could be repeated.

"All set, Raelle?" He tucked the last few essentials into his duffle, looking around to see that all he left was expendable.

Hefting a packet in one hand she shrugged and set it aside, then nodded to him. "Yes. Our first home, this place; I'll remember it." She picked up her own bag. "Let's go, shall we?"

They found *Search* brightly painted with ribald comments and cartoons, the traditional whimsy of training classes. Take-off would burn the paint away, so they circled the Can and looked at all of it. Raelle laughed and took a picture of one amateurish mural. "I don't quite understand it," she told the cheering group, "but we do appreciate the sentiment. Maybe we can puzzle it out eventually, but now it's time for takeoff—or almost."

As they started to board, Ginith Claare approached. She handed Raelle a small package, slim and light, and grinned. "Put this where you can find it in a hurry. Open it when you need something you don't have—or find you have something you don't need." With one hand she tweaked Jay's earlobe; with the other she stroked Raelle's cheek and hair. "Now get in there, both of you—and go find yourself some good worlds."

Takeoff. Raelle sat pilot and Jay navigator; during practice flights they had alternated positions. Now the low-Skip training redlines were removed from the instruments. Quickly, Skip Factor went past two figures to three, then more slowly to four, five—and finally six.

And then all hell broke loose. Roving electrostatic fields filled the small ship, jarring the two with unexpected shocks. Raelle gasped; Jay saw sparks leap from her fingers to the controls and felt the burning jolts to his own hands, near but not touching the knobs and levers. Static repulsion spread Raelle's long hair and whipped strands against the control board, the overhead, and sparking against Jay's face and head—then, discharging, back at her—and repeatedly, almost too fast to follow visually. Blue ionization haloed her head; her eyes widened and turned upward.

As she slumped back into her seat, Jay reached over and pulled Skip Factor down to five times ten-fifth; the sparking diminished and died away. Raelle shuddered and sat up again. Jay checked the control settings—they were on course, well enough; there was time to take a break.

She said, "How do we handle *that*, Jay? We need that extra Skip exponent, part of the time at least, to keep schedule. But—"

"I've worked in high-static environment before; a driveroom, on the big ships, gets pretty blue and spitting when the exciter's recharging. There's a trick to it—any time you take hold or let go of something, you do it quick and firmly. But you—"

"Yes." As she pulled her long, heavy mass of hair to one side, almost to armslength, her grin was rueful. "Now I see why this has to go."

He nodded. "Too bad, but I'm afraid you're right. What's to do it *with*, though?"

Now she chuckled. "If Ginith's farewell gift isn't a pair of scissors, I miss my guess."

When Raelle again eased Skip up to ten-sixth and the remnant of her hair flared straight from her scalp, Jay evened the raggedness of his first quick cutting. The result, ignoring a few dips here and there, stood out about four centimeters with shorter trimming around the edges. At a slowdown for course change, with static charges in abeyance, she inspected herself in mirrors. "I'll pass it, Jay." She sighed. "But I wish they hadn't built these Cans to fly at ten-sixth."

Quickly he touched her—hands and face and hair, then a brief, more intimate caress. "Maybe later we can hold out for slower skeds."

Until *Search* reached "clear space" the two stood watch-and-watch; then they could relax and settle into routine. Jay had agreed to Raelle's preferences in the matter of the Can's interior decor—"any colors you like," he'd said, "so long as they're not this drab gray." He liked the result; deck a very deep red, overhead pale green, aft bulkhead white, left chartreuse and right a dark orange. At front, the border around the ensemble of screens and controls was flat black. He had to admit, *Search* looked like no other Can he had seen—and that suited him, just fine.

Schedule to Harper's Touchdown gave *Search*'s capabilities considerable leeway; the port's agenda for the routines of living was guideline, only. Sleeping in high-static was neither easy nor refreshing—but since navigation in clear space meant only occasional course checks and even less frequent corrections, the answer was simple. On "dayshift" they ran full out; at "night" they pulled Skip down into the ten-fifth range and ran on automatic.

The cargo couldn't care—bacterial counteragents to fight the fantastic genetic ingenuity of Touchdown's ever-mutating insect hordes, antifungals to protect humans from the shocking fungoid mutilations—and often death—that had befallen most of Harper's original group. Each shift Jay or Raelle checked the cargo compartments' temperatures, pressures, atmospheric consistencies; the Can's computer and its mechanisms kept all readings within approved limits. Jay said, "You know, Raelle? I think they really built us a good one, here."

She laughed. "If you didn't think so to begin with, why did you come along?"

"Simple answer." Skip was below ten-sixth; *Search* needed no attention. He went to her. "Because you did."

Just once, in clear space, with the Can on automatic, they tried lovemaking in high ionization. At first the added sensations stimulated, but very soon they distracted instead, and finally became uncomfortable.

There was no question of trying the experiment again. "But anyway," said Raelle, "we learned something."

In Harper's day, Touchdown had been five years from Earth. *Hawk Flight*—any Krieger ship—arching toward Galactic North to avoid major stellar distributions, could make the run in perhaps four months. *Search,* were a straight course possible, could have reached its goal in less than two days—with most of the time taken by initial accel and final decel. As it was, *Search* lifted directly outside the Galactic arm, described a partial helix in clear space, then drove straight in to Harper's Touchdown. The longer route took nearly a week.

Raelle had piloted for takeoff; Jay did so for landing. First, too slow in reducing Skip Factor, he had to pass the planet and circle back. His second approach was perfect.

From high above, the colony appeared as a group of irregular clearings in a vast sea of fernlike trees. Dropping closer, Jay saw buildings and realized how large those clearings were. Also there were several more than his map showed—but in one, confirming his choice of landing place, stood a ship.

He called down for clearance and received it in digital code, indicating that an automatic responsor had identified his signal pattern.

He landed without a jar. Then, per regulations, they worked through the shutdown checklist and waited for colonial officials to approach the Can.

* * *

They had not long to wait. Within ten minutes a ground car, towing a cargo flat, came toward them. "An open car," said Raelle, "and they're not suited up, either of them. It looks as though we've missed sporing season."

"Or maybe this timeline's developed a really dependable immunizing treatment. Now *that* would be a goodie, to take back for distribution to other lines. But either way—"

"Yes." She nodded. "We stay sealed, of course, until someone tells us otherwise."

The car arrived and stopped. Seeing no sign of radio equipment, Jay activated their outside microphones and speakers. "Hello the car. Courier *Search*, with cargo as follows." Referring to the voucher, he read code numbers and quantities for each item. "I hope it's what you ordered."

From the car it was the woman who answered. "Pretty close, at that. You must not have Drifted much."

"We brought the usual Earth-status sheet," said Raelle, "so your computer can probably give you a fair idea. And do you know if any timeline's had success in *mapping* the continua? Putting some kind of quantitative measurement on Drift?"

"Not so far. Anyway, I guess we can unload you now. You got here lucky, by the way—it's at least a month before next sporing, so you won't need suits and shots and protective ointment."

"We've had shots," Jay said. "Maybe not as good as yours."

The woman laughed. "Or maybe better. Another chore for the computer. All right—you'll be out soon?"

"If not sooner. Checklist's complete. How's the temperature?"

The woman gestured toward her own light jacket. "Like this."

"Fine," said Raelle. Jay turned off the sound system and they disembarked.

The brisk air smelled like moist, unripe wheat. After a moment Jay realized the scent came from the great fern forests and, at this season, must pervade the entire continent. By the time they reached the car, he no longer noticed it.

Both the man and the woman got out of the car to greet them. "Andrina Kaile." Shaking hands, Jay evaluated her—medium height, slim to thinness, firm grasp, crisp voice. Pale skin, nose almost too large but the gray eyes and full, wide mouth saved it. Black hair coiled at the nape, unusually high forehead . . .

"And Carling Hennison." A big man, redfaced, nearly bald—his hand engulfed Jay's but he did not exert his obvious strength. "Glad to see you, both of you," and now he shook hands with Raelle. "Ever been here before?"

"No," said Jay. "This is our first run."

"Then you won't know anyone yet," said Andrina Kaile. "May Carling and I offer you both our hospitality, this first night?"

"You're together, are you?" said Jay.

Hennison laughed. "Not lately—maybe again sometime; who knows? No—Andrina has her own house, and my rooms are comfortable enough, so—"

"And you've been cooped up all by yourselves," said Kaile. "I imagine you're ready for a little variety. Of course you may want to meet others first and then decide, but our invitations are still open."

Jay shook his head. Before he could word an answer, Raelle said, "Thank you; we're flattered. But you see, we *are* together, Jay and I. That is—we're Monogamists."

"Oh." Andrina Kaile gave a startled laugh, then cut the sound short. She looked puzzled. "I've never known any Monogamists very well—met a few, of course. Well, certainly I respect your right to your own beliefs. It's just that the whole idea seems such a *waste*."

Raelle's arm went around Jay's shoulders. "Not to us."

Hennison smiled and spread his hands. "Well, now—we're none of us offended, are we, by needing to reach this understanding? Still friends?" One by one the others smiled and nodded. "Then let's do our unloading and get in the car and go find some drinks." And as they entered *Search* he said, "I have a sister who's Monogamist. Backslides a lot, though, she does. Not that I'm suggesting anything."

Jay met the man's eyes. "Of course not." Then the work proceeded.

The population of Harper's Touchdown was barely out of six figures; the spaceport, such as it was, was administered directly by Colony Headquarters. Jay and Raelle were assigned a small suite—transient quarters—in the Admin Building itself, then joined Kaile and Hennison in the building's lounge.

As they sat, Hennison poured beer from a large pitcher.

"Whatever you're used to drinking, you have to try our local product first."

Jay sipped it. "Very good," he said and Raelle agreed. The four talked of the disparate Earths they knew. Jay and Raelle found few acquaintances in common with the other two, and those casual. Jay did not mention his parents, or the Frantiszeks.

A squat, muscular man approached the table. "Reyez Turco," Andrina said quickly, lowvoiced. "Captain of *Star Dragon*, the ship out there." And in a moment Turco, one hand on the back of an empty chair, introduced himself.

His voice was husky. "You're the Courier people?" Names exchanged, they shook hands and Turco sat. In his fist the beer glass was almost hidden. Without speaking he looked from one to the other, his large wideset eyes shifting beneath shaggy brows. The black stubble that covered his rounded skull grew low on his forehead; along with his thick neck and hulking shoulders it almost gave him a brutish look. But the eyes, Jay decided, and the wide, sensitive mouth, contradicted that effect.

And finally he spoke again. "You're how long out from Earth?"

Jay answered. "Six days, a little over."

Turco gulped his beer; Hennison refilled the glass. "And I'm almost two years. Not all in one hop, you'd know—not with the Krieger power systems. And I've had stopovers. I shipped for Eden As Amended; round trip, I thought. But there I found Haakon Aarnstaad and his old *Muspelheim or Bust*, stranded with cargo for Death Warmed Over. Long thought lost, that ship and captain—Skip Factor no more than eighty at best, and he'd been out . . . oh, I forget how long. But all it was, his Skip Unit failed and he limped in on plain drive and override, slow and eating time."

Turco tapped his glass on the table, swirling its contents. "So—Death Warmed Over was never any prize; maybe they needed Haakon's shipment to stay alive. I had room; we transshipped the cargo onto *Dragon* instead of the scheduled return load."

Hennison spoke. "What about *Muspelheim* and its people?"

"We worked on the ship—my engineers did—not much luck. Haakon took it—I offered him a lift, and did take on as many of his crew as there was room for—but he said no, that now it was *Earth* or bust. Next century, he may get there."

Raelle frowned. "Captain, this is all very interesting—and

moving. But how does it tie into how long you and we have been away from Earth?"

Turco smiled like an angel, but his eyes held a fixed stare. "At Death Warmed Over we fought plague; when we were done, my ship wasn't crowded any more." Raelle tried to speak; Turco waved her silent. "I and the colony together couldn't scrounge up the fuel to get me direct to Earth. But here, I could get to. And here's where I—I found that Earth's not there any more."

"*What?*" For a moment, Jay stood.

"*My* Earth, I mean." Slowly, Turco nodded. "A shock, that was. No way of knowing, you see—only a few Krieger ships out when we left, and none due back yet. I guess my Earth lagged behind some others, a few years. Anyway, off we lifted with good old *Dragon*—Skipping near two thousand, no mere sixty or eighty. We've got the Galaxy, I thought! But then I get to here—" The huge shoulders slumped. "And find I've lost my world."

"Captain Turco—" Hesitantly, Raelle spoke. "It may not be that bad. Sometimes there's very little difference—there aren't any rules; it's unpredictable, so far. Maybe you'll be lucky."

Turco sipped from an empty glass. "Maybe—maybe not. It's four hops I'll have had, not a mere two. But it's the *waiting*, now that I know what to worry about." He shook his head. "Fuel's low here, too. Lots of traffic lately; the stockpile's wiped out. And I landed near to empty—it's more than a month, nearer two, to synthesize what I'll need. And then at least three more to get home, whatever that turns out to be." The man's face clenched into strain patterns. "Fighting plague, chancing death—that was easier!"

Jay said, "I know, Captain. And if I could help, I would. But we can't go find out for you—even if we reached the same Earth you will, we couldn't come back *here*, the same. You see, sir? Sometimes questions just don't have good answers."

From under lowered brows, Turco looked at him. "Maybe. But that doesn't mean I stop asking." He stood. "Thank you for the company. Good evening." And with his quick, massive stride, he left them.

Turco's story cast a pall over the group. After a period of silence, Hennison said, "Is anyone else hungry? The kitchen's quite good here." Relieved, Jay nodded; the others agreed, and when the waiter delivered a fresh pitcher of beer they ordered food.

Dining raised Jay's spirits—the meal lived up to Hennison's recommendation—and the others seemed more cheerful also. Afterward, over liqueurs, Hennison told of variant Earths reported by previous Couriers. None of them, Jay thought, sounded alarmingly different.

Then Andrina Kaile said, "Something I always ask Couriers—I guess I'm just nosy, so don't answer if you'd rather not—is *why*. Why leave the Earth you know, when you can't get back to it?" She shrugged. "*I* wouldn't have, if I'd known the risk."

Raelle was silent; Jay thought carefully, then said, "Let's just say I lost something and hope to find it again."

Hennison nodded. "A good enough reason—so long as there *is* a fair hope. And you, Raelle?"

Jay did not expect her to answer, but after a pause she spoke. "I haven't even told Jay yet—and I won't, until I *know*. But this much, yes—I haven't lost anything. But there's something I never had and always wanted. *That's* what I'm looking for." Puzzled, Jay watched her, but she smiled and shook her head. She touched his hand, and said to the others, "I'm afraid I'm tired early. Our shifts on *Search* weren't geared to your days here."

Kaile and Hennison excused them, and the two went to their quarters.

Couriers were supposed to wait at least two weeks between high-Skip flights. "If at all possible," the admiral had added. "Very high Skip disorients memory for a while. A few days' rest and you settle down as good as new. But if you jump too often *without* that rest, the damage can be cumulative—and permanent." Jay had noticed no gaps in his memory, until over the next few days he detected *improvement*. Raelle confirmed the phenomenon.

"The scary part," she said, "is that you don't realize anything's missing, until suddenly you remember more than you did yesterday."

"Yes. Well, now we *know* we'll follow Forgues' instructions."

With Andrina Kaile guiding, they explored the fern forest—as far into it as an hour's walk would take them. The giant cycads grew as high as fifty meters; beneath them, only scattered shafts of sunlight reached the ground. The deadly fungi, now dormant, ringed the base of each trunk. Andrina said that windstorms came a few months later, but now the air hung still. Jay remarked on the ground cover—low, sprawling plants with leaves like broadbladed grass, scattered in almost geometric precision but avoiding the immediate area around each fernlike trunk.

He thought he saw a flicker of movement but it did not recur. The meat and dairy herds from Earth stock, he knew, did not venture here. "How about animals, Andrina? Something moved, over there."

She nodded. "Small creatures, only, here in the plains forests. Several species, but all obviously related. Mostly they stay up in the big ferns, and they're well camouflaged." He waited, and she said, "Coldblooded, smoothskinned vertebrates—viviparous hermaphrodites. About the intelligence level of a rat, the largest species, but not destructive. And a very odd skeletal structure—three legs on one side and two on the other, staggered, and half of them are lefthanded, so to speak, with respect to the other half. Now the really strange part—" She paused a moment. "All mating, I'm told, is between complementaries, never between similars."

"And the creatures," said Raelle, "pose no problem to the colony?"

"Quite the opposite. They're helpful in controlling each year's wave of mutated insects—eat their weights, daily, in eggs, larva or adult bugs. The pentapods are even edible in a pinch, if you could catch one when you needed it. Not tasty, mind you, but edible. Actually they're fairly easy to trap. Be sure to cook them thoroughly, though—they're spore carriers, though not themselves affected by the fungus."

"For a headquarters type," said Jay, "you know a lot about the local fauna."

She laughed. "I should—part of my job is correlating reports to weed out duplications." She looked at her watch. "About time to start back. The time matches my appetite."

After so many sedentary days, Jay enjoyed the walking.

The day before scheduled departure—*Search* was fueled, and loaded with small cargo and the inevitable stack of reports—Jay and Raelle were summoned to the colonial governor's office. "Governor Makchuk's just back from the sea mines," Hennison told them. "He didn't want to miss you entirely, of course—but he sounds as if he has something more on his mind, too." He opened the governor's office door for them but did not enter.

The governor stood—a slim man with smooth gray hair and dark complexion. "Greetings—belated, but sincere. Come sit down." After shaking hands, they did so. "Coffee?" Both accepted. "Now then—I've seen the cargo manifest, your Earth-status sheet, all the reports. Quite satisfactory. And how do you like Harper's Touchdown?"

Jay grinned. "Fine—*now*. I'm glad we missed sporing time; in training we went around for a few days wearing the skintights and goggles over a coat of antifungal grease. The necessary fittings aren't the last word in comfort, either. How you stand it for a solid month . . ."

The governor laughed. "We get paid for putting up with it, so we manage."

"Whatever you're paid," said Raelle, "you earn it."

They talked a few minutes longer; then the governor glanced at his desk clock. "There's another matter. Captain Turco has . . . a request. I'm not sure it's in my jurisdiction, but for the record I wish to be present. The captain is due here shortly."

Jay looked at Raelle and she at him; before either could speak the door opened. Reyez Turco entered. He nodded to the governor. "You've told them?"

"I left that for you, Captain."

Turco brought a chair over to sit near the others, and declined the offer of coffee. He stared at Jay, then at Raelle. "I've thought it over," he said, "and decided. I'm delegating command of *Dragon* to my First Officer—and returning to Earth in your Courier Can."

While Jay was still finding words, Raelle said, "If *Search* could keep three of us alive from here to Earth—which it can't—you'd still have a poor idea there." Turco began to speak; she shook her head. "Do you know what *range* of Drift means? It's the term for how *much* different you'll probably find Earth to be when you get there, and it depends both on Skip Factor and duration of travel. If you're worried about change, you'd be making your odds worse—about six times worse—by riding a Can. If you could, and I've pointed out why you can't."

Turco glared. "I wasn't done talking. And I'll *take* those odds, just to find out next week instead of months from now."

"But—" Jay did not continue; Turco cut him off.

"Your Can carries two; I'll be one of them."

Jay's hand slapped the desktop; startled, Turco watched him. "You're out of your authority, Captain; Couriers are under direct, separate command of Admiral Forgues. That's for the record only—I realize you could commandeer *Search* and count on losing Raelle and me, and Governor Makchuk's report of your act, in Drift." Turco's mouth opened but Jay's outthrust pointing finger silenced the man. "So you could get away with that part, and leave us to return on *Dragon*, *if* you have a trained Courier pilot. Though going with only one pilot—that's a bad risk, too. But otherwise—" He shook his head. "Your chance of reaching Earth alive—or anywhere else—is about as good as surviving naked on this planet through sporing time."

Grinning, Turco shook his head. "*I* know all this—you think I got my job by being ignorant? None of my people can pilot a Can, including me. *Dragon* would get me to Earth sooner than I could learn. I accept this. But that's the point—*you two* are trained. And I'll take that extra risk you cite, so all I need is one of you. Either one, though to a man of my tastes the young woman would be better company."

Raelle shook her head. "Forget that plan, Captain. It's the one thing Jay and I will never agree to."

"No? What's the problem? Young love?" Turco shrugged. "Well, that comes and it goes—but *I* go to Earth."

"You don't understand," said Jay. "We're Monogamists— and vowed that Dirft will never separate us."

Turco's fist clenched. "*I'll* have to settle for an alternate—if at all, but never mind that part. Now look—" He spread his hands. "Probably you won't even notice the difference, you know that? Keep at it until you make the right lucky hops—if you still want to bother, by that time. Once I'm home, that's up to you."

The governor cleared his throat. "Captain Turco—I must tell you, I cannot give countenance to such high-handed action."

Teeth bared, Turco said, "Let's see you try and stop me! Sure, you've got your hand on the fuel spigot for *Dragon*— but the Can's fueled, ready to go. My armed people outnumber yours, here, and they still take my orders. You understand me?"

While the governor drew a shocked breath, Raelle spoke.

"Turco!" And to Jay, "No, let me say it—though I know you're thinking the same." Deliberately she inhaled, exhaled. "Turco—you won't ride *Search* to Earth. Here's why. If *you* try to fly it you'll kill yourself. Agreed?" The man nodded. "And if I fly it, leaving Jay behind, *I'll* kill you."

"You?" Turco laughed. "I think I can handle you—or him, for that matter."

"Can you?" She almost whispered it; to hear, Turco leaned forward. "I'm trained, yes—can you force me to *use* my training?" She shook her head. "You wouldn't live past Skip ten-fifth—neither of us would. All I'd have to do is . . . decide which mistake to make."

Turco looked from her to Jay. Jay said, "You're right, Raelle—I'd have said the same thing. Probably not as well, though."

Again Turco's gaze went from one to the other. Hope left his face, and his voice came flat. "You're insane, both of you—but you've beaten me. I could make you pay for that, I suppose—smash your Can and leave you stranded."

Raelle shrugged. "If you're that small, that spiteful, I suppose you could. I don't know what drives you, Captain—and it's none of my business. But if you have to smash *Search* to salve your ego, I suppose we can wait for another ship—commanded by a sane captain."

For a moment Jay thought Turco would strike her; he tensed for action—but the man drew a shuddering breath and even tried to smile. "You're right," he said. "My troubles aren't yours, and I've let them push me too far." He shook his head. "I'm not like this—not like what I've been saying, here. It's just that—oh, never mind." He stood. "You're free and clear of me, by your own guts and doing. Governor—I'd appreciate it if you'd forget this discussion."

Makchuk looked up at Turco. "You have a good record, Captain. Sometimes, under pressure, people go overboard; I think you're back topside now. The record stays clear."

Turco grinned. "Thanks. I won't ask anyone to shake hands. But one thing, you two Can riders—I think your example's going to help me some."

He left the office. In the remaining few minutes, before Jay and Raelle left also, no one mentioned Reyez Turco.

They saw the captain once more—next day as they prepared to board, he approached. He held out an envelope. "I know it's against rules—but could you take this and try to see that it's delivered? It's to my wife. Please?" The man spoke softly.

Jay felt pity, and heard it in the tone of Raelle's answer. "Captain—do you know *why* there's a rule against sending personal messages by Courier?"

The man nodded. "Sure—that the odds are, the message may not apply where it arrives." His voice raised. "But that logic's wrong—listen, you'll see." He gestured. "If there's a hundred—thousands, maybe, of us three having this same argument—what if you *all* take the message for me? *Then* the odds are that on a number of Earths you can stop a lot of sorrow. You see it?" Anxiously, he frowned.

Raelle hesitated; Jay said, "Ships' captains don't get their jobs by being stupid, either, do they? I hadn't heard that thought before; it's a good one. But another thing—you know your situation, and what's in that envelope—and we don't. Think, now—think carefully. Are there alternatives of your problem, in which this letter could make things *worse*?"

"No." Without hesitation Turco answered. "I've thought of all of it; I had to rewrite my letter four times. It can't hurt—but it could help."

"All right." Jay took the letter, and now he and then Raelle reached to shake Turco's hand. "I hope it helps for *you*, on whatever Earth you reach."

"Thank you—thank you both." Turco nodded and turned away.

Only when the two were aboard *Search* did Raelle say, "He still drives himself too hard. He had to get well away from us, before he could start to cry."

Slanting outside the Arm again, building Skip for the vast arc of helix and then cutting it back for the clear-space plunge toward Earth—*Search* performed without fault. Now familiar with deep space procedure, Jay and Raelle became more confident. They adapted quickly, this time, to the periods of high ionization; their routine became settled and easy. When, six days out from Touchdown, *Search* neared the Solar System's outskirts, Jay saw that Skip was close to optimum for constant decel to Earth. Moments later they dropped through c-interface and watched the universe slowing to match them.

And this time the landing felt, to Jay, like a practice exercise.

*   *   *

Lieutenant Commander Glynn supervised inspection and unloading of *Search;* within the hour she cleared the Can for routine overhaul. After another hour for debriefing, Jay had the chance to ask his question.

Glynn laughed. "That's part of the package now—*all* returning Couriers want to pump a computer terminal and get a sighting on this Earth before exposing themselves to it. And that's fair—you're the ones risking loss of valuable aspects of your lives—what you feel you have to know is none of our business. So we've installed some terminal booths near the transient quarters. Feel free to use them; they're not monitored."

Despite his own needs, Jay frowned. "I—well, aren't you being awfully trusting?"

The tall woman shrugged. "You trained under Admiral Forgues—or whoever holds his job on your world. What we trust is the system that puts people like Forgues in charge."

"I see. And with us, it *was* the admiral—yes."

"Fine. Then other things should be about the same, too; you'll know your way around the port all right. Do you want quarters on base?"

"I'd think so," said Raelle. Jay nodded, and Glynn gave them an assignment slip. "You'll find the computer terminals easily enough; there's signs posted. So—welcome then, and good luck."

As the two left, carrying their personal baggage from the Can, Jay said, "Well, on one thing they're ahead of us. Making Couriers feel at home."

Again they had to adjust from ship's time to planet's. Not until the next morning did Jay and Raelle enter adjacent terminal booths, to learn what each needed to know. Jay ignored the larger issues—politics, the lot—and punched immediately for data concerning his parents.

Commander Harwood Jay Pearsall. Born—the date was correct. But—*died*? Had this trip been for nothing? Quickly he scanned. Killed in a transportation disaster, not by freak storm—and months later than Jay's own father had died. Something else nagged him, a discrepancy below the conscious level; he ignored it and punched for the facts about Glenna DeLais Pearsall, his mother.

Born? Right. Married? Right. Died? No. Relief made him

shudder. But something didn't fit. Married now—but not remarried. And again he felt bafflement.

Back to his father's dossier, and now he saw the anomaly—the coding was not for a deceased spaceman, but for a man on active duty! Jay scanned ahead...

Next entry: two years after his death, Harwood Jay Pearsall landed on Earth as First Officer of *Hawk Flight*, Captain Vaille commanding. All right—he knew of Vaille. Let's see...

And then the readouts, all of them, made sense. There were two *Hawk Flights* here.

Well, of course. At moderate Krieger speeds the odds for a simple round trip were close to even, returning to one's own Earth or to another. Here, both had happened—and from another continuum, Glenna's husband had been returned to her.

Jay frowned. His mother's strict views—would she have accepted an alternate? Yet apparently she had done so. He shrugged. When he joined his parents—in happy anticipation, he shivered—either they'd tell him what had happened or they wouldn't. What did it matter? All was well now, and would be.

But was it? His mother's file—he didn't know what he'd seen that disturbed him, but it *felt* wrong. He looked again.

No. Of course he hadn't seen it; it wasn't there, and that was the trouble. *He* wasn't there; on this Earth his parents were childless, and Jay Pearsall did not exist.

When he could think again, he scanned the readouts fully, including personal details he was surprised to find available, and began to revise his plans. Completely.

When he left the booth, Raelle was waiting. He spoke first. "You find what you wanted?"

"Maybe; I don't know yet. But *you* look bothered, Jay. Let's go get lunch and you can tell me about it." At his look, she shook her head. "My problem's on ice; for a few days there's nothing I can do about it. So let's work on yours."

"All right. Oh—I forgot about Turco's letter. Did you think to post it?"

Raelle grinned. "An illegal message, through official channels? I sent it by private messenger. The address was right—I checked it with the computer terminal."

"Good. And I *am* ready for lunch."

At a nearby snack bar they ate lightly. Over coffee Jay told her what he had learned. "So I can't just go to see them, the way I'd intended."

"Why not? Wouldn't they be happy to know you?"

He shook his head. "You don't understand—it's too risky. Glenna—this Glenna—wanted a child, badly. When she finally got pregnant she miscarried. And the complications—she couldn't try again. The fetus was probably me; the timing's right."

"Jay—on this Earth, you're *dead*?"

"Never existed, let's say. The problem, though—Glenna never really adjusted. The balance may still be wobbly; I can't risk what the shock might do. At least, I'm not going to."

He reached to clasp her shoulder. "So here's what I plan to do instead, so that I can *see* them, anyway. Help me work the bugs out of the idea, will you? So that we can keep our stories straight, before I call my—" His breath caught. "My *home*."

Glenna Pearsall opened the door, and Jay thought, *but she's not my mother!* He looked again; she was three years older, of course—and so was he. Now he could think. Slimmer, this one—more angular, not so rounded. His mother's chestnut hair—long and straight, usually coiled atop her head—was cut into short curls. The smile—less relaxed, more wary. The gray-eyed gaze, still level and alert.

She reached to take his hand, and one of Raelle's. "So the Courier Corps brings me a nephew, when I've always had only nieces! Tell me—how *is* my sister?"

This was safe enough—in both their worlds, Janine DeLais and her husband Cimber Tanneha had emigrated to Earth's first and most successful colony, Second Chance. That fact, and Jay's strong resemblance to his mother, had dictated his choice of assumed relationship.

"They arrived safely; that's the last I'd heard. Don't ask me for details, yet—we're still suffering from high-Skip blur."

"Of course." As Jay stared around him, seeing familiarities and differences, Glenna led the two inside. "And I realize that some things must differ considerably from what I know—for you on your own world to replace my niece Leonie." She saw them seated in the cool, pastel living room and left to bring an iced pitcher and glasses. "I hope you like daiquiris. I always make them up for when Woody comes home—he should be here soon—so I simply doubled the recipe."

"Daiquiris will be fine," Raelle said.

"And you're Jay's wife? Or is it freemate? Customs vary so much..."

Through the shock that still hazed Jay's thinking, he heard Raelle explain that they shared Janine's—and Glenna's—Monogamist beliefs. Glenna smiled and said, "Well, I'm sure I'd welcome you just the same if you followed other ways— but I must admit I'm pleased that some of the family stick to our traditions." She gestured toward the pitcher; Jay shook his head—he had sipped barely a quarter of his frosted drink, and Raelle was in like case.

They continued to talk. Jay sensed a nervous tone in Glenna's voice, though she showed no other sign of tension. After a time, observing her, he began to see past the differences to the basic Glenna—not quite the mother he had lost and mourned, but another version she might have become. And here, of course, she had... He watched—small gestures; quirks of expression—the smile that began, paused, then fulfilled itself. *I am glad I came here*.

Before an hour had passed, a sense of familiarity that he knew to be false had so comforted him that now he had to be on guard, to remind himself that here he was nephew and not son. When the picturephone chimed, the interruption came as a relief.

Glenna went to answer. "Woody—guess who's here!" Then she laughed. "No—you can't, of course." Quickly, pausing occasionally to choose her words—alternate realities caused language problems—she explained.

"Are you sure?" Jay could not see the screen, but in those three words he recognized his father's voice. "Since the alternate Earths concept was publicized, there's been a rash of impostor games—some of them not very nice. Let's see the young man."

Jay stood and moved to face the screen. For a moment, seeing his father alive again—thin, serious face, dark hair, ears slightly too large—he did not hear the man's words. "—do have a name, don't you?"

"Jay DeLais originally—Jay Pearsall, now. You—on my Earth you let me use the name's influence to get into space training. Politics are pretty bad there."

He saw Harwood Pearsall frown, and waited; this was the

weakest part of the story. Then the man shook his head. "You're related, all right. Looks more like you, Glenna, than like Janine."

Jay held his breath, but Glenna said, "Well, so does Leonie—and on his Earth, Jay was born in her place."

"Yes." The older Pearsall nodded. "Well, Jay—I hope you'll be around for a while. I'm looking forward to talking with you."

Glenna said, "What time will you be home, Woody?"

"That's what I called about—I won't, today. Out here at the auxiliary port we've got supply problems, schedule problems, equipment problems—and half the force down sick from some bad food served yesterday. I'll be working most of the night, at best. Call you tomorrow, as soon as I have any idea when I'll be free. I'm sorry, Glenna; these things happen sometimes."

Jay saw her disappointment, but she smiled. "Of course, Woody. Don't run yourself short of sleep, now."

"If I do, I'll catch it up. All right then—that's all for the moment. It's good to have seen you, Jay. You and Glenna arrange how we can get together when I'm through with this mess here."

Jay nodded; Glenna said, "Good-bye, Woody," and the screen went dark.

Raelle said, "Is it—does your uncle look about the same, here?"

"Just about. Say—we forgot to introduce you."

"That's all right. Family first; there'll be time."

Now Glenna spoke. "Why—I hadn't thought of that. The differences, I mean. Am *I* the same here as on your Earth?"

No, thank God! You're alive. Shaken, Jay foundered over the lack of a correct tense in the language, and finally said, "Why don't I say it as though you *are* the same person and I haven't seen you for a while? Which I haven't, for two— almost three years. Training cruises, all that—and the last time I was in port, you and Uncle Woody were away vacationing." He hoped the improvisation sounded convincing. "Well, then." He looked at her. "You've lost weight—not a great deal, just about right but not really necessary. And your hair was long when I last saw you—and that's about all the difference I can see."

She nodded. "Your Earth must be closer—if that word means anything—to Woody's, than either is to this one." Her brows raised. "Oh—of course you don't know, do you?" And rather than admit he had snooped in the computer files, he let her tell him what he already knew, of *Hawk Flight* and the rest of it.

"And at first I couldn't accept him, Jay—because he wasn't *my* Woody, you see." She smiled. "And then I realized—I was making him unhappy, and myself as well, because of a creed that hadn't conceived of such a possibility, all the Earths, and the Drift between them. Oh, there was more to it than that—personal things. But finally I decided that a structure of beliefs is like a scientific theory—if it doesn't allow for *all* the facts, it must change."

Jay looked at this woman who had not borne him. She had been tested, he saw now, in ways his own mother had been spared—and from it, precarious balance or no, she had grown. He said, "That's a good thought to keep in mind. Thank you—Aunt Glenna."

She patted his hand. "Well, I hope I've learned a few things in life. Now then—how are Janine and Cimber?"

He had thought ahead, for this question. "I'm afraid you'll have seen them, if things were the same here, as recently as I have. I didn't go to Second Chance at all, you see. The time was so short, before my prespace training began." His eyes widened; he raised his brows. "The fact is, I stayed *here*, with you—this house, on my Earth—during that time. And I guess I've been thinking that you remember that, when of course you couldn't." And now he had set another leg to support his structure of kindly lies, explaining if he seemed too familiar with the place and his parents. He did not miss Raelle's approving nod.

"And on your world," Glenna said, "Woody and I weren't separated and reunited? Did we—?"

Before she could ask a more detailed question, he interrupted. "No—nothing like that. There, you see, he didn't ride *Hawk Flight*—Miro Frantiszek went instead. And of course when the problem became known..." His parents were dead by that time, but Glenna took the meaning he intended her to see.

"That's good." Then, "Oh—you know the Frantiszeks—of course! Why, you'll have lots of friends—their alternates, I mean—to see while you're here. And I'd almost forgotten you're in Couriers; how soon must you leave again?"

Miro and Ludmilla—certainly he must see them! How

could he be so singleminded? Raelle said, "We have at least two weeks here, to avoid cumulative memory blur. About our next assignment—well, no one's said anything yet."

"Good," said Glenna. "That will give us time to get acquainted." She stood. "Now you *are* staying for dinner, aren't you? When you called—expecting Woody, too, I set food preparing for four. Really—you can't expect me to eat it all by myself."

She laughed and they agreed. The rest of the visit, including mealtime, Jay found pleasant. As much as possible he steered the talk to his childhood years, but discussing others, not himself. Raelle and Glenna compared notes on mutual acquaintances and found several, though none especially close. When the two bade Glenna goodnight, Jay was satisfied with the first test of his camouflage.

But from all his life's experience he knew that Harwood Pearsall's mind was more inquisitive, less accepting, than Glenna's.

Their interview with Admiral Forgues came next morning; a young blonde receptionist showed them into his office. Jay liked her smile but something about her puzzled him; finally he noticed that her left eye did not track precisely with its mate. He decided that the defect titillated rather than disfigured.

The admiral greeted them; the young woman left and they sat. Forgues leafed through a report; Jay recognized his own folder. The older man looked up. "So. You both know me, I gather—elsewhere, that is. Here I know *you*, Raelle—just finished training, almost ready to ship out. Off on leave for a few days. You, though—Jay Pearsall—any relation to the commander?"

"Yes, sir. His nephew."

"Didn't know he had any."

"Not on this timeline, no." Time to switch subjects, before he had to use the name-change story. "But you, sir—it's hard to believe"—He shook his head. "I've known you all my life—you administered our Courier training—and you've never seen me before."

Forgues stared at him. "Takes some getting used to, doesn't it? You do look familiar—family resemblance, I suppose."

Jay was grateful when Raelle spoke. "We knew—you told us, yourself—we'd have to expect strange situations, Drifting the worlds this way. But your time's too valuable to waste, soothing novices; there's business, also, isn't there?"

Forgues nodded. "Thought you'd like to know about your next mission—if you go out again. Have you decided, about that?"

Jay hesitated; Raelle said, "We haven't talked it over yet. How soon do you need to know?"

"The one you're posted for—it leaves in fifteen days, gives you some safety factor for memory conservation. We've assigned backup personnel, of course. I'd appreciate a decision at least five days before takeoff."

Jay looked at Raelle, then said, "Certainly; that's reasonable. And the mission itself?"

"Down to cases; right. You've heard of the colony called Nobody Home?"

After a moment Jay nodded. "Yes, sir. Established fairly recently—and wasn't there some controversy about it?"

"Too right, there was. Funds short, for colonizing. A big fuss between Nobody Home's backers and a faction greedy for the exotic minerals in the traveling seas of Sluicebox. Plus the usual fence straddlers who think you can stretch your money by shorting your colonies' reserves; they always lose but they keep trying. Well, Nobody Home got first nod and Sluicebox got the ten-year delay—which may be more than that, the way things go."

"So our run," said Raelle, "would be to Nobody Home?"

"Yes. The first resupply ship got back and reported a minor cargo error. Except that to the colonists it's not so minor. Some small but vital equipment components were mislaid, not shipped. A Courier Can will carry enough to last until the next regular ship can get there. The schedule's tight, in a sense—but not tight enough to short you on your stay time here." Brows raised, he looked at them.

Raelle was silent; Jay said, "If we go again—you realize, this is our first return and we haven't quite digested the jolts yet—well, the assignment itself sounds fine." Raelle nodded.

"Good, good." The admiral sorted through papers, found one. "Something else—since you won't get the regular briefings, likely. For the big ships, we think we've eliminated Drift."

Raelle said, "An improvement in the Skip Drive? Could it apply to Couriers?"

"No—to both questions. We've gathered date, that's all.

Below Skip Factor twelve hundred there's been only one case of Drift—and on a long haul, that one—below one thousand, none at all. Whereas at two thousand only one ship on a brief practice mission, did *not* Drift. In between—well, the Labs are working up tables on it, for the few cases we have as yet. Eventually we can assign Skip rate for any given distance—with a safety factor, of course. For now—well, it slows things down, but we're redlining at ten-third and that's that." His brows lowered. "Of course this makes the Courier program all the more essential, for a time."

Jay grinned. "Sure—to let the colonies know there'll be delays, and fill in with crucial items that can't wait."

"You see it; good. Young man, if you don't go out again, I have work for you here, on the administrative end." He sighed. "You can't imagine some of the people I have to work with; they don't *think* in Skip terms. Even the math doesn't get it across to them."

Forgues stood and shook hands; the interview was over. "Let me know, then?" They affirmed their agreement and left.

Outside, "Raelle? Do we go again, or stay?"

"I don't know yet. I thought maybe you did."

"No."

"Then we leave it open, for now."

And back in their quarters, it seemed to Jay that they strove together more for reassurance than for love or pleasure.

The knock surprised them. Jay donned a robe; Raelle pulled up the bedcovers. Opening the door Jay faced a short, heavyset woman; she smiled but said nothing. He looked at her—not only heavy but downright fat—with green eyes in a pale face, and a huge mass of frizzy black hair. He liked the smile; he said, "Help you?"

"Messenger's receipt—brought me letter—this address for return. Raelle Tremona—she here?"

The sheet drawn around her, Raelle sat up. "I'm Raelle Tremona."

The woman came forward. Jay moved aside and she went to Raelle, and hugged her. "Honey—what you did—you'll never know." The covers slipped; Raelle pawed for them and the woman laughed. "No need for to be modest. You don't have the fats, like me." But she stepped back.

With neither haste nor deliberation Raelle left the bed,

walked nude to the chair on which her roomcoat lay, and covered herself. She said, "I've sent only one letter, here. Would you tell us your name?"

The woman nodded; her every move showed vigor. "Alisha Kazintogas, wife of Reyez Turco and Mordecai Destarn and—and one no ship brings home again, I think. Now—take coat off a while, can I? Have drinks, maybe?"

Jay stepped to the sideboard. "Yes, of course." He filled three small glasses, spirits over ice plus a dash of water. "Drink hearty."

"I always do—but not too heavy." With the coat laid aside, Jay saw that the woman's bulk was firm, not flabby. The thick arm reaching for the glass—its flesh rippled but did not sag from the strong bones. Alisha Kazintogas sipped, swallowed, raised the glass and said, "Here's it to you. Reyez comes home, any one of him, I'm welcome waiting. No letter, I'd be gone and never his again. Too mixup for explaining. Just my thanks, all you need—but them you got. All right?"

For a time they drank and talked; Jay was not sure of all of Alisha's meanings. At one point he thought she was offering—urging upon him—her sexual favors. But if so—and if his cautious statement had been understood, of why he must decline—Alisha took everything in good part. "Sure, Jay—everybody do what they got to. Come see us sometimes. Reyez pour *you* some drinks, much as you can stand up with. Maybe more; you come see."

And when the woman had gone, Raelle said, "Jay? I see why Turco was desperate about losing that woman. Do you?"

"Yes. Something about her—the spirit, the vitality she has. If you ever came to love Alisha, she could be *all* your life."

When Jay called the Frantiszeks, Ludmilla answered. He explained that he was a Courier, a relative of the Pearsalls in his own timeline, who had known Miro and Ludmilla in his childhood. The small, dark woman smiled—the same smile Jay remembered. Her long heavy braid swayed with her nod. "Of course you must visit us; Glenna told me of you, and of your wife. Could you both join us here at dinner this evening?"

For himself, Jay accepted. Raelle had gone out—"I have my own quest, remember? I'll call you as soon as I have anything to tell—leave the phone set to record when you're away, will you?" Her secrecy worried him, but she smiled and kissed him as she left.

"I am sorry she cannot be with us also," said Ludmilla. "Perhaps another time, before you go out again?"

"I hope so." The call ended, and Jay sat thinking—again he must keep clear in his mind the difference between his own memories and those of his hosts.

Two years and Drift had not changed Miro Frantiszek; the tall man, grinning, pumped Jay's arm in handshake. "Skip Drive has a lot to answer for, but when it brings new friends I can't complain." Jay followed him inside, where Ludmilla rose in greeting. "Milla tried to tell me just who you are in your own timeline, but I admit I didn't get it all straight."

"I am not *quite* certain, myself," his wife said. And when Jay retold his story, she said, "But—you mean there is no Leonie now? That dear girl! I—"

Jay waved a hand. "That's in *my* timeline, the one I left. In this one she went to Second Chance with the rest of the family, so—"

"No." Ludmilla shook her head. "She has probably Drifted, like so many—and is gone, and all your family with her. You do not bring good news, I fear. Though of course it is not your fault—had I thought, I would have realized."

"Hold it a minute, Milla." Miro held a bottle of wine; he gestured with it. Jay nodded, and the man poured three glasses. "Remember—Cimber and Janine and the girls, they emigrated *before* we had the Krieger power units—at low Skip, comparatively. So they're bound to be on our timeline, still. There hasn't been time for a message to reach us yet; that's all."

Ludmilla flushed. "Ah—so much turmoil, confusion, since we learned of Drift. I lose track sometimes. I am sorry."

"No," said Jay. "I don't blame you. Even when you're trained for it, keeping things straight isn't easy." And suddenly his camouflage burdened him.

He had to change the subject. "Would you tell me about my family as you remember them? You know—as a child I stayed with you sometimes. Did Leonie?" He knew she had; occasionally the Frantiszeks had taken the four cousins to a lake cabin, weekends. And Ludmilla told of these events, some almost the same as he remembered—except that here he had not been present, here he had not been born.

But by the time dinner and the evening were done, he felt as though he were a part of what she told.

* * *

Back at quarters he thumbed for recorded messages. The screen lit to show Raelle, smiling. She spoke quietly. "Jay—I've found it, what I was looking for. Time's short for me, though. I hope you won't mind too much, but I'll be away a few more days—four, I think, or maybe five. And then—I don't *know*, Jay, I just don't know. As soon as I do, I'll call you. And"—She shook her head. "No—for now, that's all. But I do love you."

The screen dimmed. Staring at its blank face, Jay sat unmoving. What had Raelle found—or whom?

Now I know how Turco felt . . .

The thought of losing her was intolerable—so he faced it squarely. No matter how total his own commitment, if she chose to go he could not hold her. And what then?

He stood and paced. Monogamism did not demand that a widowed or deserted spouse remain single. So someday—no matter that the prospect repelled him now—he would muster interest to seek another. Here, might it be? Or elsewhere? Go Courier again and hope to find her counterpart?

No. He shook his head. Whatever took his own Raelle would always lurk—if only in his mind—to strike again.

Someone else, then—but on this Earth, or not? He could not decide, and now his other concerns in this timeline, nagging at the back of consciousness, came to the forefront. He had not yet met his father's counterpart; that meeting would come tomorrow. But what of Glenna? Now he sat, recalling and visualizing her, trying to sort through his mixed feelings.

All right. He liked and admired her, felt a certain affection. But it was his mother he mourned and loved, and by the simple blameless fact of her miscarriage, this Glenna had not shared the experiences that built his love. The relationship was wholly in his own mind, not in hers. Even if he told her, she could not make the lost years real. Her motherhood would be an artificial thing at best—and then if he went out again, a cruel and unnecessary loss.

His decision made itself. He would meet Harwood Pearsall—and with some trepidation—but he would not reveal himself. So that whatever happened, he could stay or go without giving hurt.

Somehow the tension, his worry about Raelle, had eased.

Now, in relative calm he could endure the waiting. He shrugged and flexed his arms, stretching tightened muscles. "Pearsall," he said aloud, "you need a drink. Or more. But not too many." He showered, dressed in casual garb and set out for the nearest restaurant on the base. The bar there, the version on his own timeline, was quiet and catered to a friendly crowd.

The walk was long enough to feel like good exercise.

At a small corner table he looked around the place he knew and yet did not. Same lighting fixtures but a new color scheme; he favored the warm orange here over the pastel blue he remembered. Sipping a cold daiquiri he looked with approval at the carafe, sitting before him in a bowl of ice, from which he had poured it. No, he thought—not enough booze to turn his head over. Just the right amount...

To his left, past an empty table, a group of young people were slightly boisterous in laughter and loudness. From the few phrases he caught, Jay knew them for Courier trainees at their final preassignment party. He had the urge to join them—but pitting his experience against their anticipations would be unfair. He sipped the last from his glass and poured it half full again.

The girl sat across from him before he recognized her. She said, "I know you, don't I? You're—oh, let me see—"

He saw she was not drunk, merely allowing herself the exhilaration a little alcohol brings to those who drink seldom. And again he decided that her offtrack blue eye was an asset, not a detriment.

"Sure," she said. "The Courier—came in just the other day. From Harper's Touchdown?" He nodded. "On—what was it? *Seeker?*"

"*Search,*" he said. "You were close."

Smooth blonde hair hardly moved when she threw her head back, laughing. Then, "I'm not really drunk. But don't let me sample whatever you're having for—oh, at least twenty minutes."

"All right. Do you remember my name?" Her pale green dress was quite sheer—and her slim upper torso did not suffer by the exposure.

"Not exactly. I do remember—you're related to someone."

He grinned; this was fun. "Isn't everyone, nearly?"

"Oh, you know what I mean." Briefly, she frowned. "Now it comes—I'd forgotten—Commander Pearsall! Am I right?"

"Bullseye. I'm Jay Pearsall—his nephew, where I come from, but not here." He drank more than a sip. "And your name? I don't think I've heard it."

"Course not. You come in, I ask yours, punch you up on the desk screen. Depending on what it says, I let you in to see Forgy or I don't. Zip-zip. Big waste of time, you see, for me to introduce *me*."

He waited, until she said, "I'm Saela Blumquist. Shake hands?"

She stood, so he did also. Her dress was sheer not only at its top; all down the length of her he saw pale, smooth skin. As they sat again he felt urgency.

He shook his head. "How long have you worked at the base?"

"Four years—I'm older than I look. But not *terribly* older."

"Do you like your job?"

"Yes—lots. I'm where everyone comes through, you see, who's *doing* things. I'm only on the edges but at least I'm *in* it; that's something." She leaned forward. "Can you converge on that?"

Her hand was extended; he gave it a brief pat. "You want to go out yourself, do you, Saela?"

Her mouth made an ugly grimace; she shrugged. "Someday, maybe—if it's not too late for me." She looked at him. "Don't misunderstand—I do love my mother, and I'm not absolutely sure I want to leave Earth. But I can't even talk it over—every time I mentioned the idea, back when I was too young for training, even, she'd start to have one of her heart attacks. I *think* they're fake, you see, but still . . ."

Jay nodded. "Blackmail, it's called."

"Probably." Saela shook her head, hard enough to ruffle her short, fair hair. "That's enough about me, for now. And I think I *can* use a drink."

The bowl held extra glasses; Jay poured. She took a sip and said, "Where's your partner?"

Before he thought, he said, "I don't know." Then he heard the sound of it. "I didn't mean—it isn't—"

She was squeezing his hand. "The hell it isn't. Troubles; right?" She took her hand away and toyed with her glass. "You want to say it?"

He shook his head. "Too complicated."

"Nothing is, if you're ready." She smiled. "So you're not; that's all right." She drank a little. "Only one more question, on the topic. Would you like to come home with me—or me with you?"

A rush of warmth almost drowned him; he had trouble breathing. This girl—why was he so vulnerable? With one deep breath he braced himself. "Saela, how can I tell you how much I appreciate you—what you've said?"

Her hand gestured. "Easy enough—just say where we're going."

"But that's it, you see. I can't." Haltingly he explained his reasons—then, in a rush, he told her of Raelle's call.

When he was done, she said, "Really caught in the Drift, aren't you? And not much I can do for you, though I'm a good pillow, more ways than one. And not indiscriminate, by the way—I mean, give yourself some credit. But if you can't, you can't—I don't agree with your ideas but I do respect them." She smiled, and for a moment both eyes seemed to focus on him. "I'll tell you what. If you do lose out, look me up— whatever else, we can talk. Don't you think so?"

"Yes, and thanks. Now—let's discuss something else, shall we?"

When all the drinks were finished, the evening ended in compromise. Saela came to Jay's quarters and they slept in the same bed, warm together. But no matter what his urges— and Jay refused to think of hers—they did not share each other. And next morning, after breakfast, she left for work.

Harwood Pearsall, that afternoon, opened the door to his visiting "nephew." Shaking hands, Jay appraised the older man—tall, the hair still dark above his thin face—all the lines and contours familiar. No—over the left eyebrow, a scar his father had incurred before Jay's birth—it was missing. *Remember—he is NOT the same!*

Jay found himself under inspection also. "Come on in, son." *What?* No—only a colloquialism; Jay relaxed. "Don't mind if I gawk a little—trying to relate you to this timeline, that's all. I imagine you've already learned that these things aren't easy."

"Yes, I have." Entering the house this second time, Jay could pay heed to things he had not noticed before. But only briefly—Harwood Pearsall still watched him, and Jay marshaled his alertness. "You and Aunt Glenna—you seem enough the same as I knew you, it helps ease the Drift jolt." Did that sound right? Jay felt his armpits heat and moisten. "I suppose experience helps, for Couriers."

"Possibly. I'm not well acquainted with any; they're never here long enough."

"No, of course not." A new thought—*all* a Courier's friendships must be transistory. Except one...

They entered the living room. "Glenna's not home yet. She's working with her theater group again—directing now, though, more than acting. So I have dinner on—and I'd better go look at it. I warn you, I'm a plain cook—nothing fancy." And over his shoulder as he left the room, "In your lifeline, is Glenna into theater work?"

His mother had never acted; he was sure of that. He raised his voice to reach the kitchen. "Not that I know of. When I was little, maybe, but not in recent years."

Pearsall brought a pitcher and glasses. "Glenna said you and—what's her name again?—that you both like daiquiris, so here we are."

"Thank you. Her name? Raelle—Raelle Tremona." But he did not want to speak of her, not now. "I'm told you've Drifted once, yourself. I—" He broke off, realizing the matter might be sensitive.

But the older man smiled. "That was a rough time. I thought I might be going Courier myself, but it worked out all right." He leaned forward. "Reminds me—if you don't mind talking about it, why did *you* join the corps?"

To his own ears the story sounded thin—but if he kept it consistent, Jay knew, there was no way to prove it false. "Politics, I guess, as much as anything. I mentioned how we had to finagle to get me into space training at all? That was because I didn't have the usual bribe money." Jay knew of an earlier bribery scandal, but the situation was long since corrected. Harwood Pearsall said as much—for his own timeline.

"Well, on ours," said Jay, "it got worse, instead. Do you have the All Peoples' Benefits Party here? Everyone but the newstoadies calls it the Santa Claus Party, or Bread 'n' Circuses." The Party existed in both worlds; Jay was merely expanding its role.

Woody laughed, then sobered. "Those cretins? But if they ever got on top—I agree, they'd be no joke. And in your world, I gather, they did?"

"Yes. Unfortunately, the one thing they do well is hang

onto power. Their majority's usually slim but they always get it." He shrugged. "The corruption and abuse kept getting worse. I thought space would be a way out—but even on the base, in training, there were pressures. So when the Courier program began, with all its possibilities, I entered it."

"No reluctance—no misgivings?"

"Well—my parents and sisters were gone to Second Chance. I'd been close to you and Aunt Glenna, and to the Frantiszeks—until training took all my time, or most of it. When you know space is going to be your life, anyway..." He grinned. "And then I met Raelle, and she was going out—so I had to." The grin stopped; he remembered Raelle's call.

Woody nodded. "Not much to anchor you, then, and good reasons for leaving. And you're from spacing stock, at that—Cimber's parents, you'll recall, survived the first Tau Ceti expedition."

"I know. *Before* Skip Drive—crowding light and paying for it, returning decades out of their own time." He shook his head. "In a way, that makes Drift dislocation look like moving across the street, doesn't it?"

Pearsall chuckled, and left to check the kitchen again. Returning, he said, "You've got good perspective, Jay. I—" The front door opened.

"Hello! I'm not late, am I?" Glenna came in, kissed her husband and patted Jay's shoulder. She sat and accepted a drink. "I think I'm getting it right," she said. "The play, I mean. The trouble was, you see—" And she began to describe the evolution of a dramatic production—and her concurrent education as a novice director.

Jay was soon lost in unfamiliar terminology—and, glad to be out of the limelight, relaxed gratefully. Woody, judging by his comments, followed his wife's story well enough.

Then, soon, came dinner. After the first few bites Jay said, "Call yourself a plain cook if you like, Uncle Woody—but next time I won't believe you." He knew the meat was almost certainly culture-grown, but in flavor it equalled what he'd tasted from the herds on Harper's Touchdown. He said so.

Woody Pearsall smiled. "Well, thank you. I did learn a few tricks aboard *Hawk Flight*—our chief cook could make you smack your lips over broiled plastic."

Jay affected surprise. "On a ship that size, you had to put up with Couriers' rations?"

Glenna laughed. "It never fails—spacemen swapping whoppers. Oh, go ahead—I enjoy it."

After a time, though, the talk became more general. Occasionally Jay noticed Woody's gaze intent on him, but the searching questions he dreaded did not come. And when the evening ended, he returned to quarters in a pleasant mood.

That feeling lasted until he checked the phone. He found no messages.

Next day, leaving a recording in case Raelle should call, he went to a vacation resort that catered largely to space personnel. There he swam, hiked, sunned himself, gambled sparingly, drank to the brink of excess but no further, and sampled some approved hallucinogens his own Earth had not developed. After three days he could no longer convince himself that he was having a good time, so he checked out and returned to the port.

Still, Raelle had not called. For an uncomfortable part of that night, Jay did not sleep.

When she did call, he was out. Returning from breakfast he viewed the recording. Raelle smiled as she said, "Sorry I missed you, Jay, but I'll be back this evening—rather late, I expect." For a moment, laughing, she looked aside to someone outside his view, then back to him. "Jay—I'm so happy—it's every bit as wonderful as I'd dared to hope. And tonight you'll meet someone—a Courier, like us, who's leaving tomorrow." She paused, then said, "We'll see you tonight."

The screen darkened; after a time Jay looked away from it. Within him, thought battled feeling. *Who*, that Raelle had been with—was still with—would he meet tonight? She'd never told him who or what she sought. A lost love, a recapturing of the past?

But she'd said she was happy, *and* that the person was leaving. A brief fling, a completion of some sort? Or—would Raelle depart with the other?

He shook his head—*one thing at a time*. There was no proof that she had betrayed their vows. If she had, and still wanted to return to him—what would he do?

The answer hit like a hammer—*of course* he'd take her back. The hurt—to him and to their closeness—it could be bad, perhaps permanent. Even his mother's strict brand of Monogamism, though, allowed the right to forgive...

But what if she chose to leave him, to go with the unknown other? Suddenly he could not face a day of loneliness—but who did he know?

He thought, then turned to the phone and punched code for the admiral's office. As he had hoped, Saela Blumquist answered.

"Headquarters, Admiral Forgues—oh, hello, Jay. Well! I've thought of you lately—did your problem work out?" Her off-track gaze narrowed to a squint. "From your looks, I guess it hasn't."

"No. Saela, I'd like to see you again. Could we meet for lunch? Where we had drinks the other evening?"

"Let me check." She looked down; he could see the movement of her upper arm and judged she was turning pages of an engagement pad. "Yes," she said. "Sure—and I'll tell my relief that it may be a long lunch." She set the time; he nodded. "Then I'll be there, Jay." She smiled and cut the circuit.

What good it might do, he didn't know—but he had to talk with her. His motives? He shook his head—if Raelle left him, certainly Saela Blumquist could never fill her place; her attitudes and his could never match. But still his instinct drew him to her.

Finally he shrugged—Saela had warmth and compassion, and she already knew his problem. Comfort and understanding, he decided, were all he sought—and he would make sure to invite nothing more.

Jay arrived early; when Saela joined him he had obtained a table. She hung her light wrap over an empty chair and sat. She wore a blue-green dress, cut perfectly to her slim form.

"I told Forgy we'd probably be having daiquiris. He says that for lunch, two's my limit." Then, her expression serious, "What's happened, Jay?"

When their drinks were served and menus lay open before them, he told her. "So I don't really know anything—whether it's all right, whether I can *make* it all right, or nearly—or whether it's all shot to hell."

She touched his hand. "Poor Jay—your beliefs don't make life easy for you, do they? Too bad you weren't raised to be a little more liberal." He felt his face stiffen; she gestured and said, "Oh, nothing extreme—the Pansexualists seem to have just as much trouble with their own ideas." She shrugged.

"The more moderate ways—they're more comfortable to live with, that's all."

"Maybe." He shook his head, drank from his glass. "Most kids, I guess, do the rebellion part for a while and come out of it with whatever modification suits them, of their upbringing. I never got around to that; maybe if my folks hadn't uh, gone to Second Chance."

The waiter came; they ordered. When he had gone, Saela said, "Why me, Jay?" Before he could answer, "Sure, you know I like you—and you've already given me the background—so I'm the perfect listener. But are you sure you know why you asked me here?"

"You just said it. What else could there be?"

"Let's look at it." She raised one finger. "If all's well, then you're right—a little listening and support, that's all you need." A second finger. "Or if she leaves you—same again, because as a replacement I wouldn't suit you and you know that, too." Now a third finger. "But if things are broken a little—or maybe a lot, but not all the way—then I think you want something more, whether you know it or not."

Jay frowned. "I don't follow you."

"You will in a minute. Look—here you are—you've already forgiven what you probably think is her misspent past, and now maybe it's all to do over again. It won't be easy—"

"I know that—but I'd have to, anyway."

"Interrupting's bad manners. I was saying, it won't be easy to do it *right*—without resentment or being more-righteous-than-thou." Under the blonde bangs, brushed to smoothness, her divergent gaze held on him. "Your setup's out of balance, Jay—you have to do all the forgiving, and *she* has all the burden of accepting it."

Still he did not understand. With a brief pout, she said, "It'd be lots easier on both of you, if you had a little matching guilt to offer." She held thumb and forefinger a centimeter apart. "Just a little, you see." She smiled. "It wouldn't be at all difficult, Jay—I told you I was set for a long lunch break."

He stared at her. "But I don't even *know*, yet. And—" He shook his head. "I couldn't, anyway." Now their food arrived; again they paused until the servitor left. Then he said, "Why, it would be like retaliation—tit for tat, getting even."

"Not unless that was your motive—and I don't think you're the sort. Now about *my* motive—" She grinned. "That's simple. I like you and you attract me—and in my moderate way of thinking, there's no place for guilt. Especially if it turns out I'm helping do you both a favor."

While he thought about it, they ate. Then he put down his laden fork and said, "I can't share that view; I appreciate your intent, though. Thank you, Saela."

One side of her mouth smiled. "I can't help you, can I? All right—for now. But if the dice come up that way, think again, will you?"

From politeness he agreed, then changed the subject, asking Saela her impressions of the Courier service as an effective tool. But all the while he listened, he wondered: was she right?

He walked her to the Admin Building, then returned to his quarters. In the corridor approaching them he met Harwood Pearsall.

"Well—Uncle Woody!"

The other smiled briefly. "I couldn't reach you. Left a note on your door. All right if I stay and visit a while?"

"Of course; glad you came." At the door, Pearsall reclaimed his note and crumpled it into a pocket. Jay opened the door. "Come in, Uncle Woody."

Not until they were inside, the door closed, did the older man answer. "Let's be rid of Uncle Woody, shall we? You see, son—I know who you are."

Jay's thoughts would not focus. "How?—I don't understand."

"Neither do I, fully. Some, but not all of it. Let's sit down." Then he said, "How do I know? Well, not from the computer, of course. There's no point in taking extensive personal data on visiting Couriers—and you skimped some on what they do request. No—first it was just a hunch. Wishful thinking, I told myself. Then I began to notice. It's feasible you could resemble Glenna more than Janine—and in some ways, neither. But the other side of your genetic mix didn't come from Cimber Tanneha—it came from *me*." He paused. "Another me, obviously. Jay—you have my hands."

"Hands? But—"

"Fingerprint patterns. Not identical, of course. But the types of patterns, and their distribution—those can be inherited the same as eye color. Cimber's aren't too different from Glenna's or Janine's, except in detail; mine are. And yours and mine are so similar that—well, smudged a bit, it would take an expert to tell them apart." He grinned. "Does that convince you—son?"

Lowvoiced, Jay spoke. "*I* snooped the computer files. And here, I was never born; I miscarried. Mother—Glenna, I mean—never adjusted completely. I was afraid—the shock—and if I go out again soon—"

His not-father nodded. "I thought that might be why—and maybe you're right. Glenna walks a tightrope, Jay. She lost me once, you know—and even now, when Forgues says we can beat the risk of Drift, she's not willing for me to go to space again."

"And before I was born, she lost *me*."

"Yes. So I haven't told her about you—and I'm not sure that I should." The older man cleared his throat. "Now then—something I need to know. Why *did* you go Courier?" He waved Jay to silence. "A little thinking, and your story won't wash."

"But in *my* world—"

"No. I ran a computer simul; the odds against Bread 'n' Circuses gaining power are too long. But I don't need odds; one fact does it."

"I don't see—"

"With that outfit in charge there wouldn't *be* Couriers, and you know it. They'd ground our ships as soon as they returned, and leave the colonies to die on the vine. They don't look outward."

Jay grinned. "You've got me—but it was the best I could think of, on short notice."

"And not bad, if other things hadn't set me suspicious. But desk work gives me too much time to think—and I did." Before he could continue, a knock interrupted him. Jay went to the door and opened it—to Glenna.

She spoke first. "Why didn't you *tell* me you're the son I never had?"

She kissed him, they embraced, Woody hugged them both—*why, we're all three crying.* When he had breath again, Jay said, "Anyone want coffee, besides me?" *I need time to think!*

He made and poured it; they all sat, looking at each other but silent. Then Woody spoke. "Is it all right, Glenna?"

She pushed rumpled hair back from her forehead and turned to Jay. "I'd forgotten—suppressed the memory—what we'd planned to name you. And I wouldn't have remembered, probably. But tomorrow's Leonie's birthday, you see. And if it's yours, also, I thought—well, a party, of course. So I called the port and asked the girl in the admiral's office, if she could find out for me. And it was recorded."

Woody frowned. "Different worlds, Glenna..."

She shook her head. "Not so different. Jay's birthday can't be Leonie's; it's the wrong time of the wrong year. But it's within the *week* of when *I* was expecting. You see? And then I remembered."

She looked at Jay until he had to answer, to explain why he had chosen to conceal himself. When he was done, she nodded; a loose curl brushed her eyebrow. Fear for her gripped Jay as he waited, but she said, "Protecting me, were you? Both of you? Well, I appreciate it, how you must have felt—I didn't handle things too smoothly, did I, for a few years?"

Now she leaned forward, slowly thumping the edge of one hand against the other's palm. "I'll admit," she said, "my first reaction wasn't very good. But then I looked deeper." She smiled. "And do you know what I found?"

"What, Glenna?" said Woody. Jay merely shook his head.

"The miscarriage cost me my every chance of motherhood. But you, Jay—in this world it cost you your very life! Now by *any* standard, which loss is the greater?"

Tears trickled past the corners of her smiling mouth; Harwood Pearsall went to his wife and held her. She kissed his cheek, then said, "Seeing you *alive*, Jay, and knowing—it's taken away the load of all these years." He started to speak but she shook her head. "No, I don't expect you to stay and be my son. Do you know why it wouldn't work?" She told him; her reasoning was the same as his own. "And besides, you wouldn't be a Courier if you weren't looking for something. Can you tell us what it is?"

"Just before you got here," said Woody, "I was asking the same thing."

The time's so short—I have to be honest. Jay explained.

Glenna paled, then her color returned. "Dead, both of us? And you only sixteen. It's a real tribute to our counterparts, that you came searching. I hope Woody and I, here, could have—that you'd have—"

"I'm sure you would; it's just that—"

Harwood Pearsall shook his head. "That it didn't happen.

By our own brand of bad luck we're not your parents and can't be. So you have to go looking for a better matchup." He squeezed Glenna's shoulder. "We understand, don't we?" She nodded.

Pearsall grinned. "But somehow, Drift or no Drift—you and any other Jays who may come here, you're our sons. And next time, if ever, no hankypanky—I'll level with your alternate, first thing."

Thinking about it, Jay swallowed. "And on other Earths, if things are the same, so will I."

Glenna stood. "Then we'll all have gained, won't we?" She looked at her watch. "I'm late for rehearsal. But that's all right—I expected to be. Jay—you'll come see us again before you leave?"

"Of course. And—I'm glad you caught me out, both of you!"

"Me too—son," said Woody Pearsall. The three embraced and said good-byes.

Jay looked at the closed door, then turned away. "I could almost stay here. *Almost...*"

He spent the rest of the afternoon at the staging area, inspecting the maintenance work and loading of *Search*. He ate at the nearest cafeteria—the food was passable but he had no urge to refill his plate—and started back toward his quarters. Rain spattered from the darkened sky; gusty wind chilled him. He passed a small, noisy bar, then turned and entered it to wait out a sudden squall. After one drink, taken slowly, the loudness drove him out again. He bought a small bottle to take along.

Back at quarters he sipped the spirits, over ice, while he watched an entertainment channel. Soon bored, and fatigued from his restless night when he had last slept, he showered and went to bed.

"...rather late," Raelle had said. Without rest he'd be in no condition to cope with whatever he had to face. He dozed.

A metallic sound first roused him; then a knock brought him fully awake. *Raelle!*—had he, from habit, thrown the bolt? Probably... He fumbled at the bedside lamp and by its dim light got up, blinking, his eyes unwilling to focus.

He reached the door, opened it. Sudden glare from the corridor made him close his eyes but first he glimpsed

Raelle's smile—and saw that she was wearing unfamiliar garb, some kind of orange smock. No matter—blindly he caught and held her, kissed her, felt her hair brush his hand against her back...

Long hair? A wig? He stepped back, squinting against sudden illumination from the overhead light. Raelle, yes— and the hair was her own, no wig. She looked behind her and said, "This is your Monogamist? You didn't tell me he was a nudist, too."

Jay looked past her—to another Raelle, shorthaired and wearing ship's clothing, the familiar green. This one laughed. "Surprised, Jay?"

He shook his head, hard. "I'd better put on a robe." As he began to turn away, the Raelle he knew came to him and kissed him thoroughly.

Then, "Get dressed if you want to. Rae won't mind, either way."

He robed himself anyway and sat on the bed, greenclad Raelle beside him and the other in a chair, facing. Neither spoke; after a moment he said, "Would anyone like to *tell* me anything?"

Beside him the woman nodded. "Rae—that's her nickname— she's the me of *this* Earth. And to find her—that's why I came through Drift."

"Yourself? And she's who you've been with?"

Rae spoke. "That's right. I told her she should let you know. I hope you haven't worried too much—Jay, is it?" She chuckled. "You greeted me nicely, but we still haven't been introduced."

He ignored the social ploy. "I worried, yes. I'm still worried."

Raelle touched his shoulder. "What about, Jay?"

He couldn't answer yet; he knew too little. He looked at Rae. "And why are *you* going Courier?"

"Same reason. Raelle beat me to it, is all."

Narcissism? It didn't fit. "I don't understand."

"Let me tell it," said Rae. "I don't have the personal involvement with you, to maybe embarrass me—and we're both the same."

She breathed deeply. "I have no family—you know that—I grew up in a Child Care Center. Nice people—no complaints— but no closeness, either. All that time, my best friends were two girls my own age. Have you ever known identical twins, really well?"

"No—hardly at all."

"Then you can't know how it feels—your very best friends, always so much closer to each other than to you. Not even needing to talk, half the time, to know what the other was thinking.

"Oh, they tried to include me, they really did—but they were such a part of each other, all I could have was their leavings. It was this rapport they had, you see. That I'd never known—and never could!"

"And I *wanted* it so," said Raelle. "So badly, for so long, that when I understood what the Courier program meant I dumped a reasonably good life, just to seek what *they* had. Because there couldn't be anyone else, Jay—it had to be me, myself—or no one."

"My only difference," said Rae, "is that it took me longer, to decide."

He felt his face go blank, taut. "And you both found what you wanted." From his shoulders, aching muscles pulled at his neck. "All right. I can't ask you to give up something you needed that badly—so I won't." He shook his head. "I suppose you'll ship out together?" The calm evenness of his voice amazed him; he wanted to scream, wail, sob, shout, smash something...

"Oh, *Jay!*" Raelle turned to hug him. Well, gratitude was better than nothing. She said, "You thought—?" She shook her head. "What I—we—needed was the closeness, the instant knowing of each other, that came because we're the same. And—"

"And I'm not. Yes, I know. I—"

"But that's it, you see. Jay—we've had that; we'll never lose it. But you're *not* me—so to know you, I'll need you with me all my life!"

Rae smiled at them. Before Jay could speak, she said, "That ache's gone—even if we never meet other selves again, and we might, at that. Because now, you see, we *know*."

Jay went to her. "This time I'm kissing you on purpose."

When he stopped, she said, "But that's all, isn't it? Raelle told me."

"Yes. But right now I wish *I* were twins."

She laughed. "You're not, though. Well, on another Earth, maybe..." She looked at her watch. "Tomorrow it's up early,

for boarding. Raelle's told me why I need a haircut first." She
squeezed Jay's hand. "My Can's named *Quest*—maybe I
should rename it but I don't think I will; there's always
something more to look for, isn't there?"

The two women embraced. Above their smiles, tears welled
but did not flow.

"Jay? You really thought I could leave you?"

"I didn't *know*—" He told her what he had thought, what
he and Saela had said. Thinking that Saela deserved to know
the outcome; tomorrow he'd call her . . . Raelle hugged him.
Then he told of his meeting with Harwood and Glenna
Pearsall.

"Why, Jay—that's wonderful! And we *will* see them, won't
we?"

"Sure. It'll be lots better, everything out in the open. And
you'll like Woody."

"I expect to." She paused, her dark gaze meeting his. "It's
tomorrow, the admiral wants our yes or no?" He nodded.
"And it's yes, Jay, isn't it?"

"Well, we can't keep those small but vital components
waiting. Nobody Home, here we come!"

Now he could shrug his tensions loose. "Come to think of
it, I could use a yes, myself."

He got it.

PART THREE:

Ξ

NOBODY HOME

Up and out from Earth, hour after hour, Raelle lifted the Courier Can. Her second Earth—and how many would there be? Beside her, Jay grinned as the Can *Search* reached one tenth of c; he activated the Skip unit. "Now," he said, "let's see how close we can come to a least-fuel run."

Glancing at her husband's thin face, ears protruding below the reddish stubble of his scalp, she smiled. "If you want to. Though I doubt there's much to be gained over simply running at redline." Jay shrugged and adjusted the Skip Factor, bringing time dilation down to less than one percent.

Normal drive—the thrusters that moved them—still paid tribute to Einstein, to Lorentz and Fitzgerald. The Skip unit did also, in a way—but instead of c its theoretical limit was the product of c and Skip Factor. And no ship, whether full-sized vessel or two-person Courier Can, ever pushed Limit—redline was ten percent time dilation. The adjustment— the balance between Skip, dilation and absolute velocity— determined fuel economy. Well, if Jay wanted to hone his skills and in the honing save a minuscule amount—why not?

She eased normal drive up to recommended max and locked the control. "That should do for a time. Getting hungry?"

He shook his head. "Not yet. When I'm done with this part." She patted his shoulder and left her control seat to open a ration packet. When she had eaten she opened out her half of the sleeping couch and lay down.

She dozed; his touch woke her. Against the light she squinted at him. "I went to sleep. How long?"

"An hour, maybe. Took me that long to get Skip up to ten-third and plot the least-fuel curve into the computer. Now I don't have to bother for a while."

"You eat yet?" He nodded. "You want to talk about anything?" Another nod. "Can it wait a little?"

Now he grinned. "Sure. I expect we want the whole couch out, though."

What Jay wanted to discuss was Drift. Not the mechanics of it—the way high Skip suppresses most of your normal appearances in the quantized Universe and lets you cross into parallel timelines. They knew all that. No—what he needed to speak of were the consequences, past and future. And Raelle thought, *I knew he wasn't done with it* . . . Leaving their own Earth in search of his dead parents—as she had left to seek her own alternate self—finding, instead, parental counterparts who had never known *him*. He had taken the jolt well, she thought—but now, as with seismic quakes, was he having aftershocks?

He spoke slowly, cautiously. Watching the frown come and go between his brows, she listened more than she replied. They lay together, now touching only with hand and foot caresses, sharing a glass of wine. Jay sipped from it and said, "So it didn't get to me until we'd lifted. But now I wonder— should we have stayed? Would you have been willing?" She smiled and touched his face. "You would have, then—I wasn't sure. Well, what bothers me—it's the odds. Our own Earth, then the one we've just left. *Next* time, what do we expect?" He shook his head. "That's why I stayed on the controls—to think. I don't care about that little bit of fuel. I needed to stay busy, was all."

"Jay—we have to make this run. We promised."

"I know. But was that promise a mistake?" She had the glass now; she took a swallow and handed it back. He shrugged. "We'll find out, I guess, when we get back from Nobody Home. And then—"

"Then we'll see what we find—and decide from there."

"Right. I won't bother you with this again, honey. From now on we concentrate on getting the missing equipment components, whatever they are, to the colonists."

"Yes. Only a week, a little over, to get there. And two more aground, at least." Yes—for memory conservation, after high Skip. "And then—back to Earth. It's not so long, Jay."

"It wouldn't be, if we knew what kind of Earth to expect." And she knew he was thinking of Harper's Touchdown, of the ship's captain tortured by learning that he'd lost his own Earth—and by knowing that months must pass before he'd discover the extent of that loss.

"Jay? Remember what Admiral Forgues said? About reaching two Earths in a row, less favorable than the ones you'd left?"

"Give up and settle for what you have—yes." He gulped the last drops of wine, then turned and stood. "Oh, I'll do it all right, if it comes to that. Now—I'm just dithering. Hindsight needling me, I guess. Don't worry, Raelle—I'll be all right."

"Of course you will."

From the "settled" reaches of the Galactic arm they emerged into clear space; between them and their reentry point lay a long, vast spiral. As *Search* edged up toward Skip ten-sixth and toward the redlined forty-two percent of Limit, Jay showed no more signs of preoccupation outside their own relationship and mission. Alone at the controls he looked over his shoulder and called off the numbers. "We're crowding four hundred thousand lights, Raelle! You know what comes next. Want to get in place for it?"

Already the ionization, the roving potential fields, could be felt. Quickly Raelle sat at the other control position, prepared to minimize shocks and sparking by making every touch to the console—engaging or disengaging—quick and firm.

Skip passed ten-sixth—in the crackling blue haze she felt her hair stand straight out. Reflection from an unlit screen showed her that it had grown to about six centimeters since the initial cropping, when high-Skip ionization had surprised them so thoroughly. Now she shrugged. Unless she leaned far forward or to one side there was nothing the hair could spark against—for the time, then, she could ignore it.

Jay set Skip Factor constant; at his nod she adjusted drive power to maintain steady velocity. She checked course; he confirmed it. Then, until their "day" shift ended and they could reduce Skip below ten-sixth, the two were somewhat restricted by the ionization.

For the most part they remained in the control seats and exchanged occasional remarks. The distractions of high ionization, thought Raelle, didn't encourage light conversation or deep thought. She was glad when the shift was done—not even food attracted her when it sparked blue. And she was hungry.

*   *   *

On the eighth "day," probing back into the Galactic arm with Skip reduced to maneuverable level, they saw a yellow dot grow to be a tiny disc. "On the nose, I think," said Jay.

"Close enough, anyway." *So few days, but so tiring.* "My turn for a landing?"

He spread his hands away from the controls and nodded. "I'll tune for the beacon. All right?"

"I'd hope so. Wouldn't care to chase the planet down by visual." His brows raised—she remembered that Nobody Home's outsized moon made it unique in the planetary system. She shrugged and concentrated on balancing Skip against thrustor deceleration for least fuel expenditure. When she had it as closely as possible—and the muted hum of the "hell box," behind, confirmed the meters' story—she checked her screen. The beacon blip did not appear.

She turned to Jay. He shrugged. "Something's out of whack—either the beacon or our receptors. While I'm checking, use the computer coordinates." On screen the pulsed indications began. All right—for now, she'd follow them. She made a minor correction.

Minutes built an hour before Jay said, "Our circuits test normal—there's simply no signal."

Preoccupied with her decel pattern Raelle said, "Next step then—right?"

"Sure—I'm on it now." One side of his screen showed a terrain map; the other swung outside view back and forth near the approaching star. The searching beam fixed on two dots of light and zoomed them to higher magnification. "There's the planet—the big satellite pegs it solidly. Revised data coming up."

She needed to make less change than she expected. Satisfied, she said, "Nice spotting. The map, now—what altitude do we see it from?" Refreshing her memory she looked at it—to its right, a river fed a wide bay. At left two smaller rivers joined to make the large one. Between junction and river mouth the bed cut deeply through a range of hills. The location, she knew, was close to equatorial.

"The tape's not calibrated," he said. "But the main settlement, where the rivers join, is about twenty kilos from the sea."

She nodded. "Shouldn't be hard to find. The terrain's distinctive—and signal or no signal, the beacon tower will shine out."

"If they're having power failure—on nightside we might not spot it."

Raelle laughed. "That's where your fuel saving will help. We don't have to be in a hurry to set down." As *Search* continued to approach the planet, they said no more.

On dayside nothing resembled the map; on nightside no lights showed. Coasting in orbit they waited for the planet to turn their goal sunward—and finally it did so.

"There!" said Jay. "See it?" At Raelle's nod he sat back, waiting while she put them into a one-orbit descent pattern. When her attention was free, he said, "I couldn't make out any construction. I guess we were too high for that."

"Maybe." She glanced at the screened map. The scale was not so different from what they had seen below—and the picture clearly showed dots of buildings, and the blankness of a landing area.

The bay was there, and the hills and rivers—nothing more. Jay shook his head. "What could have happened? Did they move somewhere else?"

"To find out, we'll have to land. Can't waste fuel just hunting around, without clues." She brought *Search* down to a flattish clearing surrounded by low, brush-covered knolls. Once grounded, they checked through shutdown procedures without comment.

Then they looked at each other. "I'm tired," said Jay. "And you must be, too—you've been doing most of the work. But I don't think I could sleep until we check this out."

"Right." But first they ate—Jay had put rations heating when their final descent began. They dressed for the cool, brisk morning the outside sensors indicated. Knowing the air to be safe and drinkable water within walking distance, they descended from *Search* carrying only instruments and recording equipment.

Outside, breathing clear air that bore faint scents of vegetation, Raelle looked around her. She consulted a sketch map, then pointed to her left. "The beacon tower should have been over that way. Let's go see what's left of it." She began walking; Jay stayed beside her.

After a few minutes he said, "We have to look, I suppose—but we won't find anything." Raelle's gaze met his. "The landing area, you see—we're walking on it, where it should be. But this place, this slightly rolling ground—it's never been leveled. The brush shows that—it's certainly not new growth."

Raelle stopped. "I know. But as you say, we have to look."

As they expected, they found nothing—no sign that humans had ever visited this place. They quartered the area around the site mapped for the tower. They walked to a low hill that overlooked the river junction, and saw no signs of docks or abandoned boats. As they turned back toward *Search*, one of them—Raelle was not sure which—stumbled against the other. Then they were holding together, embracing, kissing fiercely.

"It's too cold out here!"

"I don't care."

"I know—neither do I."

"—in the way. There—that's better."

Back inside *Search*, relief of passion sustaining them while hot drink eased their chill, they sat, quiet. Finally Jay said, "You know what it is, don't you?"

She nodded. "Drift—what else? The admiral told us—on colonizing Nobody Home, the decision was close. We've Drifted to a line in which—what was the name of the other place?"

After a pause, frowning, Jay nodded. "I remember now—Sluicebox. Yes—here, Sluicebox got the go-ahead and Nobody Home got the ten-year wait."

"Or maybe more, Forgues said. And do you recall *when* that ten years would have started?"

"Let's see—on both our own Earth and the one we just left, Nobody Home's about a year old as a colony. So—"

Nine years, at best, the answer was—nine years to be marooned on this planet, alone. Unless another survey ship came—and was that likely? Neither knew enough to guess. And—the *reason* they were trapped—neither had the knowledge to start with native ores and *Search*'s meager complement of tools, and build a fuel synthesizer.

Having accepted that fact, they went to sleep.

Colonization On Short Notice—or, Light Planetkeeping Made Easy. Raelle smiled at her written heading, then sobered—fun was fun, but she wanted to set down the best possible outline, before showing it to Jay for criticism. Feedback between them—that was what they needed...

By now, Jay would be well into the hills—expecting to reach the bay, the sea, by midafternoon. They needed to know whether any ship had ever reached this version of Nobody Home—and not for the first time the irony of the name made her shake her head. But if a ship had come here—*if* it had—in the Earths they knew, the river's mouth had been the first landing site. And ships leave debris—castoffs, things no longer needed. Perhaps, Jay had said, he might find something useful.

"Too heavy to carry, probably—anything that's much good to us. But we've got *some* spare fuel—we could manage a hop over to the bay and back. It's worth the hike, though, to find out if we want to burn fuel that way or save it all to keep the Can's systems operational longer." So he had laden himself with food, sleeping gear and instruments, and left not long after sunup—planning to stay overnight and return the next day.

Now Raelle continued with her outline. First—things they knew and probably could take for granted, but still should examine. Air—ideal. Water—safe and abundant, with little seasonal variation, so near the equator, to disturb the supply. Temperatures within comfortable range, considering their available clothing—but when the garments at hand wore out? The fabrics were durable, but she made a note anyway. Reports stated that some of the local animals were furred—the matter could become important.

Food—the Can's stores would not last long. But this planet's basic proteins, animal and vegetable, matched human requirements almost perfectly—and somewhere in their cargo, Raelle remembered, was a hefty carton of mineral trace supplements. Food, then—animals of land and water, roots, leaves, fruits, flowers, seeds, berries, tubers, fungi (Must Be Boiled Thoroughly, she wrote), the riverbank moss—this planet's pickings could sustain them indefinitely. But without hunting weapons of any sort, she and Jay had best look to the skills of trap and snare...

Shelter. *Search* was the easy answer—while its fuel lasted and for another forty days or so, on batteries. Then, because of its total dependence on sophisticated energies, the Can would become an awkward, cheerless cave of metal and plastic. Native Hut, Native Heat, she wrote. *We must con-*

serve what we have here—later, if no one comes, we could need it badly. Standby maintenance functions used very little fuel—on the amount needed for a jaunt to the bay and back, *Search* could "live" for nearly a year.

Medicine. The standard kit aboard was quite comprehensive. Unfortunately it was designed for situations enduring no more than ten or fifteen days. Don't Get Sick!!!

Toothaches didn't count—if absolutely necessary, *anyone* could pull a tooth. Not that she liked the idea very much.

What else? Contraceptives—certainly they did not want to have children who, if no aid came, might someday be left alone on an abandoned world. Well. Her one-year implants were tailored specifically to her individual glandular balance, so it was cheaper and more convenient to obtain several in one order. She checked—four left, plus eight months remaining on the current one. After that? She shook her head. She was no surgeon, nor was Jay—there could be no question of sterilizing either of them.

She considered the alternatives—abstinence, complete dependence on noncoital methods, and the risk of conception—all of them repelled her. Suddenly she remembered reading of how the second Centauri expedition, years overdue because of breakdowns, had halted its population increase. She shuddered—as though Jay were present she said aloud, "You'll have to choose—it's your body." And thought that while the small urethral cut caused no loss of function, the permanent result was so damnably undignified!

She rose and made coffee, sat to drink it, rereading her list of necessities. If there were others she could not think of them now. Leaving the remainder of the sheet blank, she began another.

Beware Of. The briefing sheet listed known dangers from native life, but she made notes anyway. If It's Purple Don't Eat It—so much, then, for leafy plants and tubers. Animal dangers were more complex so she listed descriptions, only. Twenty kilos of river, she felt, should isolate them from the voracious "sea devils." The slow, shy, well-camouflaged little crawler with its spray of poisoned spines—only at dusk was it active aboveground. The chief diurnal carnivore shunned any prey larger than half a human's size—the predominant nocturnal meat eater fled from light. The furry hive-flyers, she read, never attack anything that remains still—and once past, they do not look back. The spitting amphibians—no, now she was past the real menaces and into the list of more common nuisances. All in all, she decided, this part of Nobody Home was less unfriendly than your average world.

Finished with her coffee she rinsed the cup, thinking, *there has to be more to it*. Well, she wouldn't find it indoors. She donned a jacket, put a notebook in one pocket and went to ground.

On first reconnaissance she and Jay had looked only for signs of human visitation. Now Raelle considered the terrain in its own right, seeking clues to what dangers might be here. *It looks so peaceful*—she saw nothing that might bring catastrophe. All right—what if this were Earth? *Think of Earthly menaces* . . .

Away from the sea, toward the morning's sunrise, the land climbed in a long undulating sweep. Broken by minor slanting ridges, it rose toward a distant irregular line of jumbled, craggy mountains. Patches of snow crowned the highest peaks.

She looked more closely. The main body of land bore the same sparse tree growth rising from the tan grasslike ground cover that here brushed her calves—the latter did not grow thickly enough to impede walking, nor did the bushlike trees, the size of large lilacs. In the distance she saw occasional blackened streaks, but none very large. Fire, then, was probably only a minor peril. Still it wouldn't hurt to clear the "grass" around *Search*—and later around whatever shelter they might build.

Fire and—yes. She walked the shortest path between brushy knolls to the riverbank and looked closely, moving slowly from water's edge to higher ground. The farthest high water mark was less than twenty meters from the present shoreline. So—floods, highly unlikely.

Storms? Perhaps—but so near the equator she expected they would be occasional, random rather than seasonal. Thunderstorms, she supposed—for what but lightning had fired the grass? No real danger, though, she decided. She entered her conclusions in the notebook, then strolled further.

The planet's sun—its light somewhat more yellow and a bit softer than Sol's—neared zenith. Abruptly she felt hunger and returned to *Search*.

* * *

She spent early afternoon taking detailed inventory of *Search*'s contents, beginning with the cargo manifest. When finished she headed the first sheet "Checklist" and taped the lot to the storage compartment bulkhead. From now on, each item used would be marked off the list. And she wondered—on Jay's expedition, would he find anything to add?

Between chores she sat and fell to musing. The thought came that a year ago the thought of being stranded indefinitely with only one man would have seemed unduly restrictive, even boring. Her adoption of Jay's Monogamist views had not come easily—but under the circumstances she had to admit it wasn't a bad idea!

Feeling restless, she went out again. The sun, she estimated, was at least an hour or two from setting. She looked up, trying to compare this sky's blue to that of Earth's, and saw the faint pale edge of the planet's major satellite—larger in viewing, if not in fact, than Luna. She'd forgotten—how closely did it circle? Quite near, certainly. Which meant—she turned toward the sun and walked to the hill she and Jay had visited the day before. Looking down to the river junction, she saw her guess was right.

Today the water stood higher. She walked down to it—a few minutes' stroll—and looked carefully. Yes—following that moon, the tide still rose. *I wonder . . .* She stooped to cup water in her hand, and tasted it. Brackish—*all this way, the sea reaches. And how often?*

Twice each lunar "day," of course. And that day, relative to groundside—how long was it? Longer than a solar day, since the satellite moved with, not retrograde to the planet's rotation. If the briefing sheet did not include the information, they could establish it by observation.

The matter could be important. Raelle had not, in her outline, considered the sea itself—not at such distance. Now she must. First because edible sea life—more abundant than the freshwater creatures—might come with the tide. And second, because in pursuit would surely come the sea devils, the planet's most dangerous life form. The sea devil, according to the briefing sheet, was not entirely restricted to water—it could make extended forays on land.

Stay Away From High Tide!

* * *

Early the next afternoon, surprising Raelle, Jay returned. She was outside, clearing grass from around *Search*, when she saw him. The huge pack he bore looked much too heavy to carry.

"Jay!" She ran to him. By the way he put the pack down she saw it must be lighter than it seemed. First greetings were largely nonverbal—then she said, "What did you find? Tell me about it."

"Sure—once we get inside, and I have some coffee and a bite to eat. I'm halfway starved!"

"What?—"

Walking as he answered, he dragged the pack by one hand. There'd been a ship landed, all right. "—as if you couldn't guess, from this stuff I've brought." He had bundled up most of the lighter materials that might be useful—then, at the far side of the beach, under shelter of some craggy rocks in case rainclouds fulfilled their promise, had built a cooking fire.

". . . and I'd taken about three bites when down at the shore the water erupted with what pass for fish here, flopping on the sand. And right behind them, the sea devils, eating them alive! Then one of the devils looked up and headed my way, and three more followed it. Earth's bounty, Raelle—you should have seen! They—"

As he described the creatures she nodded—the briefing sheet had been accurate. Huge fanged jaws, snakelike head and lean body, propelled at surprising speed by the undulating lower fin curtains that ran the length of that body. "The top spines and tail spike are poisonous, I think—I didn't wait to find out!" Into the maw of the leader he had thrust a burning stick—then scrambled up the rocks to safety. "They turn on their own wounded—the other three tore the hampered one apart. Then for dessert they had *my* dinner—it was scattered all over the map—and the rest of my food supplies. They nosed at the pack here but didn't smell anything they liked, I guess—there's nothing edible in it. Then they went back to the water." After a time he had climbed down for his sleeping gear—but he slept above the rocks, out of sea devil reach, and began his return inland at first daylight.

They entered *Search*; Jay sprawled in a seat. Raelle first gave him coffee—then, as soon as it was ready, food. "And what did you bring, Jay? Is there more—anything worth going after with *Search*?"

He shook his head. "About moving *Search*, I'm not sure—

we'll have to talk that over. What I brought—the bulk of it is light sheet plastic, discarded wrappings. Should come in handy. There's some miscellaneous metal—frame components, odd parts and fittings, that sort of thing. Aluminum alloys, mostly—not heavy. And a few equipment modules that may have components we can salvage. Most of the portable stuff worth taking, I think I got—maybe a closer look would find more."

Raelle sipped her own coffee. "Portable? Is there something more, then, that's important?"

"Except for a big coil of wire, too heavy to carry except in sections, I don't know yet." Frowning, he explained his other discovery.

The visiting ship, of course, had had its own fuel synthesizer. And once, at least, that device had malfunctioned. What Jay had found—nearly two cubic yards of piled debris—was a spoiled batch, jettisoned. "I sampled the tailings, washed downhill from the main pile—and then got away fast. It's part stable fuel, part raw ore, and a lot of intermediate products. Hot as hell—at night you can see it glow."

"Radioactive and lethal." She nodded. "So, what use is it?"

His fist thumped the table. "Scattered in that mass there's enough fuel—I'm certain—to get us home. All we have to do is extract it—without killing ourselves in the process." Without humor he grinned. "*I* don't know. Maybe between the two of us . . ."

She thought. The way to separate a mixture is to exploit the differences in the properties of its components. She asked questions.

"Sure, Raelle—I found their diggings, not far ahead. I've got a shielded box with about a quarter-kilo of the richest ore, for comparison testing. I expect we can spare a few grams of fuel to experiment with. But the problem is—*then* how do we handle that pile of death?"

There could be no quick or easy solution—they did not expect one. A synthesizer works with high energies, at low efficiency—first primed with existing fuel, its operation consumes a considerable fraction of its product. But Jay and Raelle had access to no such energies. They were limited to the use of gravity, hydraulics, some low-powered electrical devices—and only what could be arranged by the muscle power of two human beings, to operate at a safe distance by remote control. Their tests of the samples showed what was needed . . .

One afternoon he pushed a stack of sketches across to her. "Check me on this latest version? I can't see doing it with anything less."

She looked, nodding as she leafed through. River power was the key, they had decided—muscles and materials were the limits. First the dragline, to move the pile of mixture—a little at a time, without ever having to approach it. Then the pump and the sluice ditch. She looked at Jay's alternative, a centrifugal separator, and shook her head—it looked too prone to failure, and near that much radiation there could be no repairs, only the building of a complete new unit at a new, uncontaminated site.

The bucket chain for recycling, yes—and the remote recovery tongs and container. The magnets—and the waterpowered generator to energize them. Neither densities nor magnetic properties alone differed enough to give much separation in a reasonable number of recyclings. But working on both together? She made a rough calculation; the result was better than she had hoped.

She saw him waiting for her answer, and smiled. "It's good, Jay—except for the centrifuge." She explained her objection.

He shrugged. "So we lose it. If it works for a reasonable time it'll pay for itself. The design's simple—quick to build."

"How quick, Jay? For *all* of it, I mean. Can you make an estimate?"

He looked down at his clasped hands. "If we could live there, work on the fuel recovery and nothing else—six months, not much more. Two, maybe, to get into production, and another four for the rest of it. But—"

"Jay, we could move *Search*. I—"

"No. Not down there. I saw signs—the *ship* that was there, weapons and all, had trouble with the sea devils. Same as the one that reported this planet to the Earth we just left—four or five days after landing on the beach they noticed the sea devils gathering, and from then on it was practically constant siege and attack. I don't know how long it would take them to lose interest and disperse, once you leave. But I think we'd better figure to work there only two or three days at a time—and that's well back from the beach itself—doing as much prefab work as possible up here first." He sighed. "And on that basis, and with the *survival* work we need to do—"

"Yes? How long?"

"I don't see us off this place in less than two years."

He looked beaten—she said, "So soon? I think we can manage very well, for that long." She watched his expression change—he grinned at her and reached to squeeze her hand.

After a moment she said, "You mentioned survival work; I've made some notes." She handed him the outline she had prepared, of needs and precautions for living on the planet. "Here—see if you can think of anything I've missed."

When he was done with her lists he looked up and nodded. "It reads fine to me. And first of all we'd better get set up, here—if you like, we can start on the hut tomorrow."

The bushy trees provided no real timber, only sticks and poles. So Jay and Raelle experimented and settled on a woven structure—withes caulked with riverbank clay, and a sod roof over the framework. Door and two windows were plastic sheeting—three thicknesses—over metal frames. Raelle improvised hinges—metal studs, top and bottom, pivoting on holes in the thickest available wood. After Jay finished digging a perimeter drainage ditch he welded fittings to make a simple but secure lock. Inside, with the ground cleared of grass, hard-packed clay dried to make a firm floor. More clay cemented stones together to form the central fireplace. Above it, capped by a tee-joint to discourage rain, conduit pilfered from *Search* became a chimney.

Construction, plus clearing the grass from around both *Search* and hut, was completed in nine days. Then for the first time they slept in their new home.

Next they tackled the problem of an ongoing dependable food supply. Including storage—there was no reason to expect interruption of the area's bounty, but "Just in case . . ." Fruits and meat could be dried—tubers would store well in cool darkness. Some other foods could only be eaten fresh, not stored.

From a childhood summer on a Canadian prairie farm—a dozen of the girls at the Care Center had gone there to work—Raelle remembered and described the root cellars. "We could dig one, Jay." When they had done so, with special attention to a solid roof and secure door, they began stocking it.

Next came hunting. By practice Raelle attained skill with a

sling—and found she had the patience to stalk her prey.
Filching a coil of monofilament line from *Search*'s cargo, Jay
experimented with snares until his designs began to succeed.
Small animals, seldom weighing more than five kilos, made
up most of their catch.

Drying the meat presented problems—when they hung it
high enough to frustrate roving scavengers, it attracted the
hive-flyers. As a compromise they moved the drying racks
well away from the living area and draped them with some of
Jay's salvaged plastic sheeting—arranging it so that air could
circulate but the small flyers, baffled, bumped the plastic for
a time and went away.

In their fifth week Jay and Raelle went across the hills,
only a few kilometers from the sea, before they found a way
down to that reach of the river—and a suitable place for their
next project. Two days of digging made a ditch that allowed
high tide to flood a shallow basin. They damned it off again,
then—in a few more weeks they could return and collect salt
from the dry pan. Salt meat would be a welcome complement
to their dried stocks—and under the circumstances, no more
difficult to prepare.

They devoted their evenings to design and fabrication of
their "mining" equipment. Jay's first proposals had been in
the rough—putting numbers to them took longer, and actual
construction sometimes turned up flaws. The big waterwheel—
light metal frames covered by the salvaged plastic sheeting—
was one of the few devices that worked properly on first
testing. Jay brought it back—disassembled and folded—from
the nearer river, and said, "If we have at least half the current
downstream as we have here, I've got the torque we'll need."

He had to scrap the pump entirely, and begin anew. "The
design—well, it's standard, but not with the materials on
hand. It works but I wouldn't bet on it to hold up long
enough." Raelle sat with him, matching scribbles—did this
design or that use fewer moving parts under stress? Which was
least prone to failure? Later she did not recall which of them
suggested the simple device, rotating as a whole—Archimedes'
Screw. But she helped him shape the aluminum helix, held it
steady while he set the supports, one for each two-thirds of a
turn, that held it solidly to the central shaft, and cursed along
with him at the perversity of simple plastic as they shaped it
into water-lifting spiral and then sealed around it the outer

cylinder. At the river it did not leak—and in use it would be very lightly stressed.

Of the generator and magnets he could build only the frameworks. "Until we bring up a load of that wire, from the beach."

But at least, she thought, it was all moving now!

One afternoon when they were nearly two months aground, Jay came running toward the hut. Raelle, packing berries into nests of dry grass for storage, looked up at him. "Something's wrong?"

Out of breath, he took a moment before answering. "Not sure. Sea devils—first hill above the river junction; one of them's almost to the top."

Shaking her head, she stood. "Do we know how long they can breathe air—how far from water they can go?"

"Not really—all the reports are from seaside, like mine." He wiped sweat from face and forehead. "I thought, now's a good time to find out a few things—but I had nothing to work with. I was fishing—they were behind me before I saw them. Tried to use fishline as a noose but the damned beast was too strong—almost tore my fingers off when it pulled free. Then it charged me and I ran for daylight!" Now his breathing slowed to normal. He grinned. "The fire's going?"

"Sure. But?— Oh, of course—at the beach you used a burning branch to fight one off." She frowned. "You think we can keep sticks alight, that far?"

He laughed—for the first time in weeks she glimpsed the spirit that drudgery had dimmed. "In a bucket of coals—I carry it—you steady the upper ends." He looked around. "Rocks, too—the biggest you can sling. And I'll fix a noose, a snare—but with a handle I can *hold*."

Once they'd decided, she thought, the preparations hadn't taken long. She jogged alongside Jay, one hand holding the lengths of wood that nuzzled the coals in his bucket. The bag of rocks for her sling thumped against her back and side.

And atop the hill overlooking the river junction they saw four sea devils. Shifting, weaving on the undulating, curtainlike fins, the creatures milled. One, then another turned to face their approach. She and Jay paused on sloping ground, about level with the hilltop, and stared across the intervening dip. The animals were dark gray above—slightly tinged with green—and a pale, muddy yellow underneath. Their skins, smooth and rippling with their movements, looked moist. "How big are they, Jay? There's nothing near them for comparison."

"Two meters long, a little more. They stand not quite a meter high, but they can reach those jaws up nearly as far again."

Single file the sea devils came toward them—slowly at first, then gaining speed. Jay set down the bucket, added dry grass for tinder—soon his improvised spears took flame. "Let's separate a little, so we can come at them from two angles."

"Yes." Raelle took two of the burning limbs, along with her sling and the rock bag, and moved five meters to her left. "And by waiting here, we make them attack from below."

"Right. If we can't stop them—well, we're fresh for an uphill run, and they're not."

Fascinated, she watched the leading attacker. Mouth agape— long jaws like a crocodile's, but behind them a bulging forehead and widely mounted eyes. At the sides of the neck—were those gills? But in the chill air of late afternoon, steam came from the mouth. No matter, she thought—the creature's biology wasn't of prime importance just now. The crucial item was: could these things *learn*? Were they a hunting pack, or merely a herd?

Her pulse rate climbed, her palms sweat. Deliberately she slowed and deepened her breathing—yet she felt nothing. Except for pallor, Jay's face showed no sign of fear. Now the leading sea devil—undulating, darting its head from side to side—charged him. He thrust flame into the toothed maw and pivoted away. The creature shook its head, hard—jaws closed on the stick and snapped it, leaving Jay holding the remnant. Mouth opening and clashing shut in effort to rid itself of the smoldering wood, the animal wheeled toward Raelle.

The sling! Her first stone caught the forehead squarely where it joined the muzzle, but the creature barely faltered. Another stone into the sling's pocket—a larger one—but instead of throwing she held it, swinging from her hand as she aimed her own burning stick.

She missed—jaws closed and her thrust glanced away. She jumped to her right and—still holding both thongs—swung the sling against the side of that fearsome head. The blow saved her, knocking the muzzle aside as the charge passed. The sea devil turned to face her. She lunged and swung the stone again—this time at the undulating fin curtain, raking half its length. And the strange organ of propulsion folded— the supporting spines crumpled. At the front, the creature's left side slumped to ground. Now, watching its lopsided slither, she saw her earlier strike had crushed an eye. She lofted the sling, aiming for the spine behind the cranial bulge—and Jay shouted.

"Behind you!"

She spun, pulling her blow off target—no time to correct it. She leaped high, tripped on a lashing tail as she landed, rolled and then scuttled downhill before she dared turn and stand. Respite—for the moment, the first beast had the second by the neck. Not a pack, then—no teamwork.

She turned to Jay. He had partially hobbled one of the devils—a branch pierced both fin curtains—its movements were slowed and awkward. Jay's snare, handle gone, hung from its mouth. But the fourth animal had paused and was circling to their right, putting Jay between it and the hampered one. And now for weapon Jay had but one piece of smoking wood.

She looked back uphill. Her remaining spear was there, beside the sea beast that had now broken loose to finish off the cripple. And her rocks, save for the one still in her sling—they were there also. Too far—there wasn't time!

Abruptly she chose her course. While Jay warded against the last comer, she went toward the hobbled one and sidestepped its lunge. Again her swung stone damaged a fin curtain—and twice more, until the creature toppled. Then she tried for the spine behind the head. Whether she killed or not, the sea devil curled up and convulsed. Its struggles weakened—she reached and tugged Jay's spear loose from the remaining fin.

She looked to see him thrusting and swinging the stub of a branch—the rest was gripped crosswise in the fourth devil's jaws. Then the creature dropped it—with short steps Jay moved back, away, and looked at her. "Here!" She nodded and tossed the spear—he caught it, shouting, "Flank it!"

As the sea devil hesitated they approached it—one on either side, waving their weapons to distract. It turned to her—Jay jumped and attacked a fin. Snarling—the rasping noise surprised Raelle—it whirled toward Jay. She moved and swung the stone—breaking fin spines once, and then another time and another. When the animal crumpled toward her, Jay thrust the shorter stick at its left eye and threw all his weight on it.

Before the thing could die Raelle heard sound behind and turned. The second beast from above! Free of its crippled cohort and bleeding from neck wounds, it rushed down upon them. Raelle screamed a paean of wrath and outrage—she sprang to meet the beast. She could not face it squarely—she had no time to look to Jay's protection—she dodged aside and with all her might spun the slung stone into the sea beast's jaws. Staggering, brushed aside by the harsh edge of the undulating fin, she saw fangs shatter and the stone lodge firmly in the jaw hinge. She fell, turned and came up weaponless.

Jay! Down, thigh running blood, he rolled to sit up. In desperation she looked for some weapon—there was none—and the sea devil, jaws wedged apart by the stone, spun to attack again.

There has to be something! Her will, her volition, disengaged—she *watched* herself pick up the only human artifact, the bucket, and catch the gaping fanged snout. The beast's rush knocked her down—she scrambled up and stood watching. The creature bucked and writhed, rolling over and over. Only when its efforts lessened to a slow jerking of the neck did she realize she had thrown the burning coals down its throat.

"They're as near dead as doesn't matter." Jay's voice was flat, controlled. "Getting back to *Search*, I may have a problem." She looked. He was bleeding badly—she swallowed fear.

It was his injury, his decision. She tried to match him, to keep her own voice calm. "Which is best? Me to run get the emergency kit, or both of us to go together?"

Now his pallor was not from fear. "Together—if I wait, this will stiffen. Better to do the walking now."

What he said made sense. "All right. I've got to bind that wound, though—you'd lose too much blood."

"Sure. You mind using your jacket? I can't spare any clothes just now—I'd be risking chill on top of shock."

"I know, Jay." Quickly she folded part of her jacket to serve

as pressure pad and tied the sleeves tightly around his leg.
He still bled, but less profusely.

The walk back, she knew, could not be lasting as long as it
seemed. Blood seeped down Jay's lower leg—after a time, at
each step a small amount pumped out of his shoe. "Are you
all right?"

"I think so—I'll make it. Shoot me full of blood neutral
concentrate, first chance—that's all."

"Of course—and we'll go to *Search*, where the couch can
be set to warm you. Not to the hut, tonight."

"Good—we're thinking alike." Frowning, he shook his head.
"One thing—you know how to skin a carcass?"

"I dress out my own hunting catches—you know that.
Why?"

"We need a boat—the trail to the sea, such as it is, takes
too long. And we may run short of plastic sheeting. I want
those sea devil hides—and any bones big enough to help with
the framing. The hides, now—they'll have to be cut carefully."

"Don't worry, Jay—topology was one of my best subjects."

For a time the leg was bad, but eventually it healed. Raelle
skinned the sea devils before they stank, then dragged the
carcasses down and left them in the river to be eaten clean so
the bones could be salvaged. Jay knew how to cure the hides,
and did so. Once he said, "I suspect our remote ancestors
started out something like this."

Raelle grinned. "I hope they had a little easier time getting
their raw materials."

One day the boat was complete. Framed of wood and
bone, covered for the most part with sea devil skins and
the seams caulked with pitch, the narrow oval craft was
heavier than it looked. But as they carried it to the nearer
river, well above the junction, Jay no longer limped.

As they pushed off he knelt in the bow, Raelle in the
stern—though the two ends were identical, interchangeable.
At first they handled the paddles awkwardly, making the boat
yaw when one or the other lost the rhythm of their mutual
effort. But with practice they caught the knack and kept a
straight, smooth course. Only after several days of short
expeditions upstream and back, however, were they ready to
put their skills to real use. Early one afternoon as they pulled

the boat safely clear of the river, Raelle said, "If we bring everything down here today—except the food, of course—loading won't take long tomorrow. We can get an early start."

"Yes. Fuel supply, here we come!"

Launched and tethered, then weighted with cargo, the boat sat low in the water. "Pretty big load this time," said Jay, "but we saw from above, the river's smooth all the way. And besides the equipment, we do need to start a reserve food cache there."

They clambered aboard—Jay shook the line loose from its stake and pulled it in. Paddling, they turned the boat and pointed it downstream. Now, loaded, the craft was more sluggish, less touchy to control. In a few minutes Raelle had the hang of it, and compensated almost automatically for any imbalance in Jay's more powerful strokes.

They reached the hills. Between higher and higher banks the river bed became a shadowed cut. Current remained slow and steady—only occasionally at the sides, where material had fallen to obstruct the flow, did she see eddies. Hypnotized by the monotonous action and quiet sounds of the current, she fell into reverie. Where the river curved, it did so gradually. When one such curve brought sunlight fully across the water, she realized they were nearly through the hills.

She had no idea how long the trip had lasted. Then Jay pointed to their right, to a pocket of sloping beach. They nosed the boat into it. When she stood, and felt the protest of her cramped knees, she knew they had paddled for longer than it seemed. Wading, Jay held the boat as she hobbled ashore—then, on soft sand that would not damage the hide covering, they dragged it as far out of water as they could manage, before unloading. And then they moved it well above high tide mark.

Now Raelle paused to look around her. Less than a kilometer away, beyond a cut through one last craggy ridge, lay the sea. Here, above the narrow beach the land rose, split by a small gully, to meet the valley floor between the seaward ridge and the one behind them. Up the slope zigzagged a trail of sorts—brows raised, she pointed to it.

"The people on the ship, I suppose," said Jay. "I saw signs of them further inland, too, but only for two or three kilometers."

She nodded. "Their camp is above here, in this valley?"

"Remains of a work camp, only. The ship was on the ocean beach—if they ever moved it except to leave the planet, we'll probably never find out. But above here was their synthesizer operation—that's where our fuel is, if we can separate it out."

"That trail, though—the gully looks like easier walking."

Jay grinned. "If you're immune to radiation, it is. Where do you think the synthesizer's tailings washed down when it rained?"

"Oh, sure." Shrugging, she put on her personal pack; Jay did likewise. Each also carried food for the cache they planned to start. They climbed up the trail into the lateral valley—the land here, and its vegetation, were much like those at their own base. Then they turned left and ascended the seaward ridge, not stopping until they were among the rocky crags that topped it. There, out of sea devil range, they could eat and sleep safely. And first they ate.

From their site, near the end of the crag wall, they could see beach and ocean, the river and the terrain across it, the valley behind and the next landward ridge. Jay pointed to a hillock near the gully—similar to a number of others except that this one was bare of vegetation. "That's our contaminated fuel pile. I didn't spot it in daylight—only when I saw it glow. Should have, though—nothing grows on it, and the grass around is stunted and sickly."

Raelle looked at it, and estimated its distance from the beach. "Jay—it's too far. We'll never move that down to water—not when we don't dare get close. Your dragline—I had no idea!"

He shook his head. "I know. Oh, it'd work all right—but if we tie up that much of our monofilament line, we're in trouble. Especially as it might end up too hot to salvage."

"Then how?—"

"Basic idea's still good—the remote control bucket—open it, drag it across the pile, close it, get it down to the edge above the sluice ditch and dump it. Right? We just handle it a little differently, is all." He grinned. "You and I move down past the pile, one on each side and well clear of danger—with a line strung between us and the bucket in the middle. We guide it down the gully and stockpile where we'd planned."

"And from that point we could use a *short* dragline." Now they considered other changes in their plans—trying to simplify, to hasten, to minimize effort. Then after gathering firewood for evening they returned to the river beach, and there Raelle saw a way—by moving the pump site to make use of existing contours—to reduce the digging needed for their sluice ditch. "And if we set up the pump *first,* Jay—the water will wash some of it out for us."

So they cut slim branches for supports, drove them deep in the ground, measured angles and distances, notched other branches and tied them in place, and lubricated the notches—to serve as bearings—with crushed, oily leaves left from the cutting. At last they could mount the pump—Archimedes' Screw—and assemble the huge vaned water wheel to drive it.

The sun was low and Raelle felt hunger when they lowered the paddles into water and secured the shaft. Quickly Jay strung belts around his pulleys—for trial purposes he omitted the remote control lines and merely hung a rock in a bag attached to the idler pulley, to keep the pump engaged. Now they waited, and were rewarded—even such slow current, pushing against so much area, produced rotation. Jay's pulley ratio gave the pump a faster turning—river water began to climb the screw.

Glancing toward sunset, Jay said, "We'd better watch this from above—I don't want us climbing that trail in the dark." So up they went, and light remained long enough for them to see water emerge at the top and spill into the natural channel they had improved. Then in sudden dark they climbed to their crag, barely silhouetted against sky. When the fire came alive to her kindling Raelle was glad—and more so when Jay served their hot meal.

Their sleepshelter was warm and comfortable. If Raelle dreamed, she did not remember it.

The following day they began a new project. Flow from the pump lacked vigor for real sluicing action—the solution was a catch basin with a spillgate and its necessary control lines. After disengaging the pump, letting the waterwheel run idle, Jay drove stakes to guide their work. Raelle was relieved that his plan involved more damming than digging. A plastic sheet weighed down with rocks rendered the loose fill more or less waterproof, and when the pump was tried again, leakage at the improvised spillgate was minor.

While the basin filled—they guessed it would hold nearly three thousand liters—Jay chose a control site, above and behind their new reservoir, and anchored his lines to a stump. "We can get fancier later." After a time he opened the spillgate—water washed down the ditch with a satisfactory rush. "Controlled batches," he said. "Maybe it's a good thing. We'll have a better idea how it's working as we go along." He reclosed the gate.

That day's job was done; they walked up the trail. Fatigued, Raelle was glad to go to bed early.

Next morning they descended the seaward side of the ridge. Near the bottom they paused to look carefully at the littered beach. No sign of sea devils—they continued.

Around the blackened depression where the ship had sat lay its discards, scattered haphazardly. Jay showed the coil of wire he'd found—the torus was nearly a meter in diameter and more than a tenth of that in thickness. Raelle saw why it had been left—along one side something had slashed through perhaps an eighth of the turns. On a ship, wire in such quantities was handled by a mechanical dispenser—the coil would be worthless. She said so, and added, "But here it's priceless, instead."

"Yes." They undid the ties that held the coil and carefully removed the cut pieces and laid them to one side. "Might come in handy later, for something." Now, using a metal bar to pry the heavy layers apart, they divided the coil into two, cut the strand between them and tied them separately. Jay tipped up the smaller portion and lifted it briefly. "This is enough to carry—and only over to the river, at that. We'll bring the boat down for it."

He looked around and picked up a two-meter piece of thick metal pipe. Then with the coil slung on it, one end on his shoulder and the other on Raelle's, they made their slow way to the river. Where ridge, beach and river joined, they set it down.

"Whoosh!" Raelle laughed. "That's *work*."

"I agree. The original coil—I'd guess that at close to two hundred kilos."

They rested a few moments, then returned to the landing site. She looked here and there, briefly inspecting one pile of litter and then another. "I don't see anything useful enough to take along. Not this time, anyway."

"Me too." So they climbed the ridge again and ate lunch. It was still morning, but Raelle had good appetite.

After arranging their food cache and a supply of firewood

for future use of the campsite, they went down to the river. The pump worked perfectly—over the dam came a steady flow that had begun to wash their adapted channel clear. Jay did some digging to improve that action. Then they pulled the boat into the water, grounded only enough to hold it against the current, loaded their gear and prepared to leave.

"Tide's out and just turning," said Jay. "We'll want the harpoons handy." Raelle nodded—the lengths of aluminum rod, tipped with great jagged barbs, were Jay's innovation for fighting sea devils. Once jammed into a carnivorous maw the weapons could not be removed, short of dissection. Raelle put three into the loops near Jay's station and three more for herself.

"All ready."

Pushing off, they paddled downriver past the ridge, to where the coil of wire lay. They placed that weight carefully over the central intersection of major frame members—and now the upstream journey began. Incoming tide further slowed the gentle current against them—they made fair progress but Raelle soon realized they could not travel upstream without occasional rests. She said, "Our salt pan—is it too soon to check it?"

"Might as well. It's not much farther." A few minutes later they sighted the place and went ashore, to find more dried salt than Raelle had expected. She collected it, saying, "Don't worry about the sand, Jay. Salt dissolves, sand doesn't." He laughed.

They reflooded the pan, closed the access ditch again and were ready to leave. As they got into the boat, Jay pointed. "Sea devils—coming upstream. They're moving faster than we can."

Raelle knew what he meant—the harpoons were for emergency, not for any deliberate challenge to the beasts. "Yes— and if we wait here and let them pass they'll be ahead of us, maybe coming back and meeting us before we get there." She sighed. "I guess the wire has to wait. Let's drag the boat up to safety and take what we can carry on foot."

"I suppose so." He frowned. "Let's wait a while, though— up above, where we can still see what happens down here."

"Why—"

"The hides—the boat. Will the sea devils go for the scent, or did the curing process change it enough?"

Raelle shuddered. "I'm glad you didn't mention that idea before!"

When the boat was secured, Jay again untied the coil of wire and separated it into two parts. The smaller, now tied separately, he slung over his shoulder. After checking to see that they left nothing they would need, they hiked to the top of the river's cut. Turning, they watched the sea devils—six of them—breast the slow current.

The creatures did not turn toward the boat—without pause they continued on their way.

"So much for that," said Jay. "Let's go."

"Yes. It's a long walk."

Passing the junction they stayed well away from it, and circled to approach *Search* and the hut. They saw nothing move—but paths of flattened grass ended at their clearing, and the root cellar's door bore scratches. "Tooth marks?" said Raelle.

"Probably. And the grass—those long curtained fins—"

"They couldn't have got here so soon!"

He looked at her. "Others could, while we were gone. We'll have to—" He stared at the hut and the space around it, then shook his head. "I don't know. Let's eat—and then go to *Search* before dark, and spend the night there."

Raelle's fists clenched. "I *won't* give up what we've built."

"Neither will I. The only thing is, we need to look over our resources and see what's best to do."

Next morning, after considerable discussion, they began to do it. Some sort of electric fence seemed the best solution—the details did not come so easily. The source was simple enough—the Skip exciter used high voltage pulses. Jay disconnected that output from the exciter itself and brought the lead outside the unit. "Now," he said, "how do we use it?"

"The wire you brought—is there enough?"

"And more. But that insulation's tough—and melting point nearly as high as the metal itself. It'd take us a month to strip enough for the perimeter we need—but we may have to do just that."

"May I have some—to experiment with?"

"Sure. And I'll be running the alarm and control circuitry—no matter how we work the rest of it, we'll need that." He cut off a few turns for her, got out a tool kit and left the Can.

Raelle studied the wire—almost three millimeters in diameter, including the thin, tough insulation. Obviously it could carry many times the current they'd be using. She adjusted a stripping tool to the proper size and slowly, with difficulty, stripped a short length of wire. Jay was right, she thought—*at least* a month's work. She set the tool aside, stood and poured herself a cup of coffee, then settled down alongside the "junk box" of miscellaneous tools and parts that didn't quite fit any standard storage classification. Sitting on the deck she picked up, looked at, tentatively experimented with one item after another.

The insulation was crushproof—it still held when the wire flattened. A scraper, with all the weight she could bring to bear, slid along and barely left a mark. And this tool—and that—nothing worked. Idly she squeezed the handles of a three-jawed device used for applying crimp-on taps, then neatly recoiled the power cord that heated the jaws for faster penetration. Now if only they had two or three thousand crimp-on taps...

She was pouring her second cup of coffee when the idea came. Cold and forgotten, that cup still sat full when Raelle finished her first hundred meters of wire.

"Well, it struck me we didn't need the insulation *off*, Jay—just breached at close intervals. So I cut one of the taps into thirds and brazed those to the jaws—and went whomp-whomp-whomp every ten centimeters or so." She flexed her right hand. "It gets tiring."

Wiping sweat from his forehead, Jay smeared dirt. "So at every whomp the hot tap punched—what is it?—ten or fifteen holes through the insulation and made melt spots on the wire itself. How'd you ever happen to think to try it?"

The question had no answer—Raelle shrugged. "Want anything more to eat? More coffee? And tell me what you've been up to?"

"I'll get it—thanks." Sitting again, then, he said, "It's easier to show you than explain it, but..." What he had done was to build a circle of stone cairns around the area containing *Search*, the hut and the root cellar. "And I'll tell you, that's a lot of rocks."

"To carry the wire, for our fence? But how?"

He moved his shoulders, the way he did to relieve tension, and grinned. "The laser drill won't light dry grass at fifty centimeters, but it'll punch through stone for nearly twenty. I just drilled holes in the top rocks—we'll thread the wire right through, all around."

Then he told the rest of it. The wire loop itself would detect intruders by body capacity, operating the high voltage pulser. In the inactive mode, current drain was minimal. "One of the spare sensor modules, with a few changes, will make the switch-on unit. Then I need to rig three items, duplicated here and at the hut—an alarm when the thing triggers, an activating switch and a red light to *show* it's activated, so we don't forget and go out and fry ourselves by mistake."

"This thing's definitely lethal, Jay?"

"If it isn't, our Skip exciter's in big trouble."

That afternoon they finished processing the wire—perforating the insulation to unleash the high voltage pulses—more than enough for the simple perimeter Jay had staked out. Next day they completed the installation. Jay built two more cairns and they strung a second line of defense across the section that faced the river. Then at Raelle's suggestion he drilled more stones in every cairn—so she could lace each one together, with monofilament line, into a solid unit rather than a loose pile. And finally they arranged three floodlights so that either from *Search* or from the hut, the entire area could be lighted.

Lunch came late that day, but the sense of accomplishment gave it an added tang. Afterward Jay checked his traplines and returned with a catch of three, strangled in his snares. He tied a line to one furry leg, crossed the defense perimeter and signaled Raelle to activate the unit—then he dragged the creature toward the innocent-looking wire. Before it touched, the wire *hummed*—near it, wisps of grass jerked and flattened—then a raging blue maze of lightning reached out to the small carcass. When Raelle turned the system off and Jay pulled the remains to him, he found a charred rigid mass.

He showed it to her—she shuddered and said, "I think we're safe here, now, from sea devils."

Now they concentrated on gathering food and building more components of the fuel recovery system. Raelle's first attempt at salting meat went bad—the second and later batches were successful. Then it was time for another sea-ward trip. With shelter and food provided at their cache among the crags, they burdened themselves only with items for the fuel project.

Still, it was a long hike to the boat. They found it undisturbed. Before boarding, Raelle gathered the new accumulation of salt—on the return trip they might not wish to stop. And again they flooded for the next batch.

The rest of the journey went quickly. Finally, rounding a bend, Jay shouted, "The wheel's still turning!" and in a moment Raelle saw it also. Soon they beached the boat and inspected their handiwork. "Looks fine so far," said Jay. "We might as well unload this stuff and lay it out for assembly." He paused. "On the other hand, you're probably as hungry as I am. I can do this by myself about as soon as you can have something cooked up. All right?"

"Fine," and Raelle started up the trail. Besides a waterbag she carried only the remote control bucket with its attached lines coiled inside it. Up in the valley, where her path most nearly approached the bare, deadly hillock, she set it down. Then, almost unladen, she climbed to their base.

It too was undisturbed—the sleepshelter, food cache and stack of firewood. She built fire and selected food for cooking. When it simmered with a soft, bubbling murmur she turned away and moved to look down on the ocean beach.

A movement caught her attention. Out from the shadow of the rocks below, where Jay's tracks and hers emerged onto the sand, moved a sea devil. Its undulant course took it toward the water, crossing and recrossing the path they had taken to inspect the ship's leavings. When the animal reached the strewn debris it nosed at one item and then others, circling among the littered piles. Smelling? Raelle didn't know—she kept watching.

Finally it reached a heap of light materials—scraps of plastic, disposable wrappings and other miscellany. After nosing at the mass it put its head down and slowly burrowed in until it was completely hidden.

Then, although Raelle looked carefully, she saw no further move.

When Jay arrived, she told him. He pointed. "You mean it's still under there, right now?"

"Unless it can dig like a mole, it is."

He started to frown, then looked more closely and matched her smile. "You think it smelled our tracks—and has brains enough to lie in ambush? But why wait so long? It's days since we were last here."

She thought. "Maybe it comes every day—it or another—and sniffs at our path just to see if we've used it again."

"One thing," he said. "We'll make sure that here—and at the river beach, and up home—there's no haystacks to hide in."

While they ate—and later, as long as they stayed to watch—the hidden sea devil gave no sign.

The bucket was a success. From safe distances to either side, each pulling on a line, Jay and Raelle dragged it to and over the pile. The leading edge dug in and stuck—they moved downhill to get a better force vector, and eventually the bucket followed. It came over the crest of the pile nearly filled—jerking on the auxiliary line, Jay closed it. Then, merely a matter of herding the weight down the gully—moving ahead, pulling until it rolled free, snubbing the lines tight at the end of each move. Through the perforated surface, at every turn useless dirt dribbled. Finally, far enough up the gully to leave the beach safe, Jay reopened the bucket and they dumped it.

"Safe for now, that is," he said. "Once we start working the stuff down there, it's all off limits and we do everything by remote. Let's bring a couple more loads down and then go set up the stuff we brought."

They did so, ate and spent the night amid the crags. Next day, shortly after midmorning, Raelle said, "One more bucketload, and let's go. We can beat the tide enough to be past the hills before any sea devils could catch up to us."

They saw none of the creatures. This time they returned the boat all the way to home beach.

The next trip they equipped the sluice ditch—framework and tilting baffles, the electromagnets, the handbuilt generator with its own waterwheel to drive it. And for all these things the control lines—some electrical, others mechanical—operated from a safe distance above. "Once we start processing," said Jay, "we don't want to go in there for *anything*."

"Even a brief exposure?"

He smiled and squeezed her shoulder. "Yes—I'd take that chance, if need be. But we have to *plan* it the way I said."

"Sure." Raelle shrugged. "Well, we can check everything out each time we come here, before we start a real fuel run."

And when they next returned it was to place still a third waterwheel, driving a monopole generator. "Low voltage," said Jay, "but in this water, considerable current." Constant potential across the ditch, near the lower end of the controlled section, would help sideline two of the more dangerous radioactive contaminants into a branch of the exhaust channel. A small advantage, but worth the effort.

Jay's pet project, the centrifuge, died on the drawing board. "With the current we have, and available materials, I just can't get enough angular momentum. Except maybe a tiny unit, for pea-sized batches—and we have no means of handling anything so small, from a distance."

Between trips they worked at finishing the rest of their "mining" equipment, gathered more food, built a second root cellar and another hut—windowless—for storage of nonperishables, and continued normal maintenance routines on *Search*. Now and then they checked the communication bands for signal, but neither really expected any contact. Not here—not on Nobody Home.

One day Raelle, bringing in a harvest of berries and tubers, heard sounds behind the hut. Dropping her bag she pulled the harpoon from her belt and shook loose its attached coil of line, looping its end around her other palm for a solid grip. She looked to either side of the hut—nothing moved. She stepped back a few paces—to circle at greater distance, with more room to maneuver. As she sidled to her right—slowly, watching for the thing she feared—a sea devil came around the far side of the hut. For a moment it did not appear to notice her—then its head swung toward her and it charged.

Turning to face it she stumbled to one knee. Before she could rise the creature closed with her. Two-handed she thrust the harpoon into its gaping mouth—the jerk of its neck pulled her off balance. She fell to one side and the jagged fins writhed across her legs. Rolling, she came to her feet—harpoon jutting from its maw the sea devil wheeled toward her.

She still gripped the line. Now holding it with both hands she ran to one side—but the beast turned also, balking her attempt to snub it to a halt.

The circling brought her near a tree—she angled to and

then around it, pulling the line taut. The sea devil tried to follow but she was faster—she lapped it, threw a bight of line around the harpoon and tied a quick knot. Panting, she jumped back.

Lunging against the barbs in its throat the beast screamed—again and again—never before had she heard one make that sound. Legs shaking, she got a knife from the hut and cut the creature's throat.

As soon as it ceased to move she skinned it, heedless of the blood that drenched her. This time she excised the great neck muscles and those that drove the propelling fins, and cut the flesh into strips. She was hanging these in the drying rack when Jay returned.

He ran to her. "What happened?"

The question hardly needed answer. When they were done kissing, he was as gorestained as she. "I don't know if the things are fit to eat," she said, "but we'll find out. The harpoons work, anyway—especially if there's a tree handy, to snub the line on." She drew a shaky breath. "Will you help me drag the rest of it down to the river?"

"Sure. Get yourself another harpoon first, though."

To avoid leaving a blood trail they dragged the carcass on its own hide. At the river each washed while the other guarded. Later they tried sea devil steaks. Not good, was the verdict—but edible.

That night the alarm woke them. Jay turned on the floodlights—they looked outside. Just beyond the guarding wire, sea devils milled. "How many, Jay? Can you see?" She blinked, trying to adjust to the sudden brightness.

He shook his head. "Six, at least. Blood or no blood, they backtracked that carcass. I—*look!*"

One moved forward, hesitated and then came on. As the great snout moved above the wire there came a highpitched hum, then a forking blaze of blue fire—the floodlights dimmed. When they brightened again, smoke rose from a charred, still lump. The other sea devils were gone.

"One problem," said Jay. "I knew it but couldn't see any way to beat it. While that beast is there, as long as the unit's turned on it's going to draw more power than I like."

"The others won't be back right away, I'd think."

"No. All right—I'll go out, with a harpoon for luck. When I signal, cut the circuit—I'll move the carcass as fast as I can.

Anything comes at me I'll run for home—and soon as I'm inside, hit the juice again. All right?"

"Yes." There was no point in asking him to be careful.

And no need—the sea devils did not attack, nor did they return that night.

When the fuel recovery installation was completed—somewhat reduced and simplified from Jay's original plans—the weather was beginning to change. Gradually it became warmer, and wetter.

"We're practically on the equator," said Raelle. "How much change can we expect—and why?"

Jay frowned. "Nobody said anything about our orbit's eccentricity. But it looks as if there's enough to matter." Now, with the changes, they began to record temperature and precipitation. But as yet they lacked enough data to extrapolate.

Once more they took the boat downriver. This time the load was mostly food for the cache. With Jay at the controls and Raelle studying the operation carefully, they gave the recovery plant a trial run and confirmed that reasonably pure fuel could be extracted—though at a heartbreakingly slow pace.

Now they ran batch after batch—bucket, dragline, sluicing by use of gravity and also electric and magnetic vectors—for three full days. At the end of it—using normal safety gear, for even pure fuel was slightly "hot"—Jay measured the result.

He turned to Raelle and shook his head. "It's going to be slower than I thought. At this rate, it's six months of *workdays*, rather than the four I'd guessed. And we've been nearly that long already, just getting started."

Raelle thought. "Can we take a few more days here this time—whatever it takes to finish with the bucket and have the whole pile within dragline range?" He waited, so she said, "That way, either of us could operate here alone while the other handles things up at base. We'd have to figure a schedule—how to make as much progress as we can, here, without being apart too long at a time."

Another idea came. "This is the longest we've ever stayed down here, and the sea devils haven't even begun to get interested. I don't know if you've noticed, but along here they give this bank of the river a wide berth."

He frowned, then snapped his fingers. "Sure—our wastes

are poisonous as hell and probably smell like it. For now, this area's out of bounds for sea devils!"

Briefly she thought of using a shielded container to salt the beach below their home base with the deadly mixture. But— no, on a longterm basis it would harm too much other aquatic life. Here, with the large volume of water, dilution would render the contamination harmless fairly soon. She shook her head—at home they were relatively safe so long as they stayed alert.

He had not answered her first question. She said, "But what *about* a split work schedule, to speed things up?"

"Getting the pile moved, so one of us could work it alone—yes. But any system that separates us much of the time—I'm not in that big a hurry to get off the planet."

She smiled and went to him. When they released each other, caressing through workstained clothing, she said, "Come to think of it, Jay, neither am I."

One more day and part of another saw the deadly mix, all but spillings not worth gathering, heaped above the valley's edge. They processed what they could before the tide turned; Jay tonged out the meager harvest and disconnected the pump. On their way upriver they collected the latest salt deposits and refilled the pan. Arriving at the river junction not long before dark, they reconnoitered as they approached their base—but found no threat.

Jay adapted a power tool to pulverize the fuel nuggets. Before and after adding the powder to the shielded bin he marked down the indicator readings. "We've more than tri- pled our supply," he said. "If we want to, we could lift and check the coastlines for signs of other landings—and still have left the maintenance power we had before."

"And our way home? How much of that do we have?"

His mouth made a sour grimace. "Not quite ten percent. More like eight, in fact."

Increasing rains changed their minds about need for a more intensive "mining" schedule. "I don't know how much worse it gets," said Jay, "but just to be on the safe side..."

The plan involved more separate than joint travel, so they pulled the boat well above high water mark. Then Jay left, on foot, for the recovery plant. Two days later Raelle joined him, and after another two they returned to base together. This time the fuel indicator registered nearly fourteen percent.

Two days between moves: Raelle operated the plant alone, Jay joined her, she returned to base, he followed. Then the cycle began again.

To Raelle's thinking the schedule was not ideal either for fuel production or personal inclinations—but it was a fair compromise.

When increasingly muddy footing made hiking more difficult they changed to three-day intervals. The river began to rise, but not enough to endanger their operation—Jay raised the waterwheel mounts to compensate and the work continued. The wetter climate did affect food gathering—fruits, leafy vegetables and berries could not be stored without first drying the surface dampness. Such produce, spread on a plastic sheet under a heat lamp, filled one corner of the hut. And at the river's edge a pile of rotting vegetation bore witness to the need for the procedure.

Twice, once at night and once in daylight, sea devils made forays and fell prey to the perimeter defense. Now though—with the leakage over wet stones and through moist air, the creatures did not die. They suffered burns and writhing convulsions, but each time the injured beast managed to crawl away—slowly following its companions that fled at the first eruption of blue flame. Raelle, alone on both occasions, wondered if nonlethal pyrotechnics might not be equally effective. She held no brief for the voracious carnivores—but she was always curious.

If their observations were accurate, and correctly fed into *Search*'s computer, Nobody Home was nearing perihelion. Once past it, Jay said, the rains should diminish. Raelle hoped he was right—the matter was outside her own fields of expertise.

Suddenly, fuel yield made a dramatic increase—the dragline had reached a part of the pile that was rich in finished product. "To bad we couldn't pick that first," Jay said, "but working by remote, we have to take what we get." Two days before estimated perihelion, when he left for the working site, the bin indicator showed nearly three-fourths of the fuel they needed. But when she set out to join him, only a few kilos from base she met him returning.

He moved as though fatigued—she closed the distance

faster than he. Only after they kissed and embraced, rain-wet lips slippery and cold, did she see that he was crying.

"It flooded out, Raelle! Most of our work—washed away. And for rebuilding—*I don't think we have the stuff to do it!*"

Lightly laden, she said, "Here—let me carry some of that." He transferred part of his burden. "Now let's get back. You can tell me on the move—how bad it is—or wait until we're home and warm."

He told her. That morning when he went to the river, it had overflowed into their workings. He'd fought the rising water for the last bit of salvageable reclaimed fuel, then tried to rescue as much machinery as he could. "I saved the dragline, of course, and most of the control apparatus. The generators—too heavy to move, in that current, even if I could have got them off the mountings. Well, maybe they're too heavy for the river to take, too. Or too well anchored, with luck. We might be able to salvage them—but don't count on it."

"No." Carefully she kept her voice calm. "And the rest?"

"Pump, pulleys, driving wheels—the things made from materials we can't replace—they *went*, Raelle!"

She had no answer. Now the path narrowed—leading the way she slogged ahead. When there was room again for them to go abreast she paused. "Jay? Is there any place we can get to—any colony—with what we have?"

After a moment's silence he said, "I don't know—we'll have to check. I'm not sure if we have that data aboard *Search*."

"All right. When we get back—*after* we're fed and warmed—let's see. Shall we?"

After a hot meal, eaten silently, Jay looked more cheerful. He got up to pour coffee and sat again. "I've been thinking. If we have to, we can do it—start over again when the rains let up."

"You've figured it out? Tell me."

"Rebuild the catch basin—it hadn't washed out when I left, but I expect it will. Haul water up by hand—not climbing up and down, but buckets and lines. We can't rely on either generator being there—but if they are I can try a wood-framed wheel, covered with hides. Tear up the boat, if need be."

As he talked she saw his assurance resurge. "Make the

sluice ditch longer—cleat the bottom all the way and run small batches with lots of washings. What we get—it'll still be hotter than I'd like. But if we have to, we can do it." He swallowed coffee. "The bad part, Raelle—figure most of a year for the job."

He was looking closely at her; she smiled and said, "If that's what it takes, that's what we'll do." She pushed her hair back—it had grown long enough to fall across her face but still too short to tie back. "Shall we go to *Search* now, and see what we can find out about alternate destinations?"

He reached for her hand. "Would a little later be all right?"

The computer had coordinates for several colonies—but no approved routes between them. All routing data was to and from Earth. At Can or even Krieger speeds, courses were prescribed to avoid "settled" stellar regions. The fullsized ships merely arced above the denser part of the Galactic arm—Cans generally went outside it entirely and reentered on a charted path in "clear space." Given enough fuel, Jay and Raelle could have reached any of three colony planets— by reversing their incoming course out to clear space and then computing a helix to the entry points of colony-Earth routes.

"But for us," said Jay, "those are angled wrong. Backtracking— really wasteful. Might as well try for Earth in the first place."

They discussed possibilities. Slower speeds? Cut to Krieger limits on reentry and rely on the Can's sensors to map their own path? The parameters interacted...

First, though, cut the odds. Discontinue all but absolutely essential drains on ship's power. Dump all mass—including cargo—not needed for the survival of Can and crew. Add the mass of their accumulated, stored food. Computer readout indicated five percent gain.

Now the trick was to find the best tradeoff between the various ways the ship ate fuel. Nonpropellant functions made a constant load—though larger in space than aground. Thrustor—"normal drive"—consumption varied directly with mass and effective acceleration. Sublight operation followed Newton's First Law but Skip Drive introduced an analogue of friction—thrust was needed to hold redline, and at that point mass was up ten percent...

Skip unit's fuel hunger went up logarithmically with Skip

Factor. At ten-sixth it consumed about half as much as normal drive.

Time—would a faster or slower course use less fuel? And what about food supply, and the need to reenter the arm more slowly? Jay jotted figures; Raelle punched them into the computer, trying simulations at both fast and slow extremes. Neither was feasible. By cut and try they edged into the spectrum from either end, finding only moderate improvement. Twice the curve dipped, but neither time decisively. Jay shook his head.

"It's close, I think—but we can't bet our lives on it."

"I know. Hogan's Goat—easy range if we didn't have to go around that dust cloud. But—" It wasn't worth the try. The cloud's size was listed as being only approximate, only partly mapped. She pulled at a strand of hair that brushed her cheek. "Wait a minute—you figured all this at redline?" He nodded. "What if?—"

For the longer, slower reentry section she punched in Limit at ten percent of Skip-times-c, not forty-two, and adjusted the difference with higher Skip Factor. She called the figures aloud and saw Jay shake his head—not quite good enough.

Then, silently, she tried one more idea and read the result. Turning to him, she tried to smile. "I had a hunch, Jay—and for a minute, I thought it worked."

He waited, and she said, "We could make it on a Krieger course, at slow Krieger speeds—if only *one* of us had to eat!"

She showed him—*Search* could store whole-bulk foods, without spoilage, for only slightly more than half the projected voyage. Finally he said, "All right—for now, we're stumped. But while we wait to start up in the fuel business again, I'll be knocking heads with this problem." He paused. "Otherwise, how does it read?"

She studied the readout. "To Waterfall with nearly three percent fuel reserve—or to Mossback with half of that but less chance we'd need to use it. Mossback's on a clear space corridor."

Jay nodded. "We'll tackle it on that basis, then."

"Sure. But, Jay—we can't convert enough space to controlled environment for food storage. The power drain, for that length of time—we wouldn't get there."

* * *

Almost constantly, now, the rain fell. For the time, they gathered no more food. One last time Jay slogged around his trapline—and left the snares unset. "I don't want to catch anything I can't go collect."

Raelle felt a nagging unease. Her mind was so fully occupied by their predicament that several days passed before she realized the last of her contraceptive implant was triggering her body's signal. She checked the Can's calendar—no, she was not too late. Relieved, she implanted the new capsule high in her right thigh—then limped for a day or two until the soreness eased.

For the most part they stayed inside the hut, making only the necessary routine checks aboard *Search* and getting food from a cellar as needed. Once the hut's drainage ditch clogged—they had to clear it in darkness, digging frantically as the floodlights flickered but gave no real illumination. For two days they wore the mud collected in that effort—in view of the necessary return trip, going to *Search* to bathe was fruitless.

Finally, gradually, the rains diminished and the ground drained. Counting back, Raelle found they had gone more than fifty days without glimpse of sun or sky. Outside one day, on a bush she saw among mildewed buds a flower that had opened. It would be the first of many—she picked it and took it into the hut. "See, Jay? Soon we can *live* in this place again!"

Even when the mud dried to decent footing the river still ran high. Another ten days passed before Jay and Raelle took the boat downriver. They carried six days' food—if the cache had flooded and spoiled, they would need to renew it.

Still higher than normal, the water treated the boat roughly. Safe handling required constant care and attention—when they reached the saltpan they welcomed the excuse to pull in to shore. The lowering river level had isolated the pan once more but it still held water; no harvest was possible. They reembarked and continued downstream.

Jay first spotted the fuel recovery site; he pointed. "See? The shielding ridge didn't wash away—the basic ditch should be there." And once ashore, with the boat pulled up to safety, they assessed the damage. For one thing, the generators were gone . . .

The worst, though, was that some of the pile itself had

washed down the gully, into the ditch. Raelle shook her head. "It's all hot now, down there—all the ditch from the gully seaward. Jay—how can we work with *that?*"

They stood well away from the contaminated area, upstream beside the catch basin's remnants. Jay shook his head. "I'm not sure—I hadn't expected this. Should have, I suppose . . ." He peered down at the sluice ditch as though he could analyze its contents by eye. "I wonder—how much of the hot stuff washed right on through, and away? I left the radiation counter stashed up above. Getting to the trail, now—I suppose the steep part of the gully is pretty well scoured by runoff. It should be safe to cross—but let's move fast."

They did, and soon climbed to the crags. The food cache, their stored tools and equipment, the tumbled stack of firewood—all were safe. Jay built a fire; they ate a hot meal. Sipping coffee without hurry, Raelle looked down to the ocean beach.

"Storms took a lot of the ship's leavings."

He nodded. "I suppose that was to be expected."

Suddenly she realized—"No, Jay! You see what it means?" His brows rose, he gestured incomprehension. She said, "Before the rains, all the debris lay on *top* of the sand—now a lot of it's half buried. Jay—in this timeline, that ship left within the past year—*since* the last rains."

Now, she saw, he understood. "Then if that was the discovery ship—help is more like fifty years away, than nine." For a moment his face mirrored the death of hope. Then he shrugged. "What the hell—we weren't planning to wait for rescue, anyway!"

From the bank Jay checked radiation levels in the ditch below—pointing his detector at various points and correcting for distance. Finally he switched the device off. "The gully's washed clean enough. The ditch itself is too hot to work in, but not much. A lot of washing—and I mean a *lot*—can fix it."

She looked at him. "What do we do first?"

"Rebuild the catch basin—we can finish that by tomorrow. Then I haul water up to it by main sweat and keep flushing the ditch until contamination's down to safe levels." He frowned. "The bucket we used to move the pile—it's the best size. I can line it with sheet plastic, to hold water."

"And what shall I be doing?"

"Well—once we've fixed the basin, two can't do much more than one here, for a while—except use the food up twice as fast. So maybe you should return to base day after tomorrow, overland. And in about a week, come back with more food. By then the ditch should be in shape for refitting, and when we've done that, we can both go up for a rest—take the boat, maybe get some more salt on the way."

She saw the logic of it and agreed. They set to work, the rest of that day and the next, restoring the catch basin. And the day following, she trekked back to *Search* and the hut. The routines on *Search* were a day overdue, but as usual she found that all was well with its self-maintaining mechanisms.

Bored, she spent the next two days at food gathering, processing and storage—and activated part of Jay's trapline. At twilight the second day she saw a sea devil near the defense perimeter—and was shocked to find that she actually welcomed the threat. But she tried something new—after energizing the barrier wire she brought from *Search* a narrow-beam signal lamp. She walked to safety's edge inside the wire, pointed the lamp and flashed pulsed bursts of blue-green light at the questing beast.

The sea devil whirled, snapped at its own flank and raced away. Watching it descend the hillside, Raelle began to laugh. A time later, sitting on the ground and flashing light at nothing in particular, she wondered why that laughter was so hard to stop.

Brushing damp soil from her clothing, she stood. Aloud she said, "I can't afford to let the place *get* me this way!"

On the damp fur of the small, trapped animal, sunlight glistened. Raelle hated the creature—for its gullibility, now she had to kill it. Slaying sea devils was different—this little beast was helpless. It looked *cuddly*, like a friendly pet.

Staring into its roundeyed unwinking gaze, Raelle cursed. When she had exhausted her repertoire of blasphemies, obscenities and scatological oaths she cut the small throat, drained the blood, and skinned and gutted the animal. Hide and carcass went into separate pouches at her belt.

The sound came, and at first she did not recognize it. The tears she still blinked from her eyes blurred her view of the thing that passed overhead. Then, somewhere beyond the ridge that rose between the two rivers, it made thunderous descent.

*   *   *

A ship! All her purposes deadlocked—she could not move.
Then she slapped the bloody knife flat against her other
palm. The blow stung—she shook her head and started
walking, briskly, toward *Search*. She thought, *Jay must have
heard it—seen it—too. He'll come here—I don't have to go
tell him.* She walked faster.

Aboard *Search* she monitored the communication bands—
no one was calling, and her own calls brought no answer.
Well, perhaps the ship hadn't seen the Can—hadn't been
looking for so small an artifact. Maybe she'd better go meet
Jay, after all—to cross either tributary, let alone both, they
would need the boat.

Not now, though—this day was too near its end. Anxious,
stimulated, Raelle finished her chores and went to a restless
night's sleep.

Next morning, nervous with anticipation, she rose early.
She forced herself to eat a normal breakfast and, aboard
Search, to perform her routines without hurry. The ship, she
reminded herself, might or might not change their plans—
what if it lifted before they could reach it? As though the ship
did not exist, then, she packed food for the trek and was
ready to leave.

She shouldered her pack; in the measured pace she could
continue indefinitely, she began walking. She was partway
around the first hill, still in sight of the hut and the far ridge,
when she heard the new sound.

She turned to look. Down the ridge and then across the
river, throwing sheets of spray, came a ground-effect vehicle.
For a moment she felt panic—then she shrugged and began to
retrace her steps.

Leaving the river, the car climbed the slope and neared the
hut. Raelle broke into a run and waved for it to stop.
Whether or not she and her signal were seen, the vehicle
set down short of the fenced perimeter, leaving it unbroken.
Now she slowed. When she reached the wire from the other
side, her breathing rate was down to normal.

The car—she was familiar with the model—had seats for
four but now held only a driver. As she approached he got
down and walked toward her—a short, chunky man with a
rolling gait, wearing bulky jacket and trousers; a visored cap

shaded his eyes. As she stepped over the outer perimeter wire, only a few meters from him, he took off the cap and she could see him plainly—the dark, chubby face and the head nearly bald on top. He smiled; three front teeth were missing.

"Hello there!" His voice was husky, almost harsh. "Serro Gama at your service—off the ship *Star Flame*." He gestured toward *Search*. "What kind of toy ship is that? You come here all alone in it?"

First instinct was caution—then the thought came: *there's no harm in this man*. She stepped forward and shook his extended hand. "I'm Raelle Tremona. *Search*, there—it's a Courier Can. Carries two. My partner, Jay Pearsall, should be here soon."

"Partner, eh? Spouses, or just companions?"

"Spouses. Now then, Mr. Gama—can I give you some coffee while we wait, or a bite to eat?" Briefly she thought of their going in the car to meet Jay. Then she visualized the route—passages the vehicle could not manage—and shook her head.

He looked at her but she said nothing. "Coffee's fine—I thank you." As they reached the hut she stood aside and let him enter first. At her gesture he sat on a stool while she made coffee.

"What's your ship doing here, Mr. Gama?" Why must she sound so casual, yet formal, in asking what she needed to know?

"*Star Flame*? Figured to refuel at the colony here, maybe get some repairs, too—but there *ain't* any colony! Dol sent me over here to take a look, see what happened. Didn't expect to find *you* here—missed your Can on the screens, coming in." He squinted at her. "The colony—you know anything about it?"

Figured to refuel—then the ship was little better off than they. "I—maybe. Tell me—is *Star Flame* Krieger-powered?"

"Sure is—one of the first! And set out on the longest trip ever assigned. Up to then, I mean—maybe longer ones by now."

"Then I do know what happened. It's—" She paused. "It's rather complicated. Do you mind if we wait until Jay gets here, and we can go explain to your captain—and all of you—at the same time?"

He grunted. "Hope we don't have too long to wait. Dol's gonna be unhappy if I don't report right away, finding *people*."

"Doll?" Now Raelle poured coffee. "She's your captain?"

"She?" Gama laughed. "Oh, I see—but it's Dol, short for Dolman." Yes—the sound was nearer to "dawl" than "doll." "Dolman Crait. He's—uh, *acting* captain."

"First Officer? Your captain's ill, perhaps?"

Gama looked puzzled. "Like you said, it's sort of complicated. I better let Dol tell you, himself."

She had to leave it at that. To break the awkward pause she asked Gama about his own space career.

The man grinned. "It's a long one. Nearly a hundred and fifty years ago, I was born. Believe that? Well, it's true. But more than ninety of those I never lived through—I'm that far out of my time."

"What? Oh—sublight travel!"

"Sure. We went out on *Far Shot* to—it's got no name, just a number—I forget now. Two planets the right size, but neither fit to live on. Couldn't go offship without a suit— repairs, smelting fuel, all of it." He sighed. "Got back—no family left, of course—we knew that ahead of time. But here they'd gone and invented Skip Drive for us. So I stayed with space—it's not a bad life, mostly."

She looked at the man whose memories reached back six times as far as hers. "Where do you come from, originally, Mr. Gama?"

"Call me Serro. Well—born in the Amazon Valley. Father was Indian—*his* father caught fish with a spear. And my grandmother—I remember seeing the tattoos on her scalp, that the old women put there when she was a little girl." He shook his head. "Real primitives. All the civilization came by way of my mother—half black, half Portygee. Dad was a man grown when he came out of the jungle and started school . . ."

"Then this isn't your native language, Serro?"

"Might's well be, by now—it's what's spoken in space, and I first shipped out when I was nineteen."

Again she tried to learn more of the current situation, but he put her off. "That's Dol's department—if he wanted me to speak for him he'd have said so." Raelle shrugged—Dolman Crait sounded a bit authoritarian.

To fill the time she told him some of her own background. After a few minutes she realized she was censoring—she'd said nothing of Drift, of alternate Earths or of *Search*'s extremely high Skip Factor. She had not, in fact, mentioned that *Search* needed fuel. Briefly, she considered—then decid-

ed that if she were riding a hunch she might as well stay with
it.

The wait seemed endless. Occasionally she rose and looked
out along the trail, but Jay did not appear. She made more
coffee and offered Gama some dried berries. After sampling a
few he smiled and nodded. "Some good things on this world,
then."

"Yes." Again she looked outside—and there, just topping
the nearest ridge, came Jay. "He's here!" Gama started to rise
but she said, "No, no—stay comfortable. I'll run out and
meet him—we'll be back before you know it."

She put on a jacket and literally ran the first hundred
meters or so before slowing to a fast walk. At the foot of the
ridge she and Jay met—after their greeting embrace she said,
"You saw the ship too?"

"Heard it—was pretty sure it landed somewhere up here."
He pointed to the ground-effect car. "They're here already?"

"One man, only." Quickly, as they walked, she described
the morning's experience. "And that's all I know, so far.
Anything else, Serro says it's up to Dolman Crait to tell us."

"The man who's here—what's your impression of him?"

"A person out of his time, committed to space, loyal to his
chief. There's a friendly feel about him."

Ahead, Gama came to the door and waved. Jay said,
"Looks harmless enough." And when they reached the hut
and Raelle made introductions, he smiled and shook hands.

Indoors then, Jay poured himself coffee and sat. "Now
then, Mr. Gama—Serro? All right. What comes next?"

"All go back to *Star Flame*, I was hoping. Dol's gonna want
to talk with you—put together what you know with what we
know—help each other out, you see? Might be, figure to stay
over a day or two, bring whatever you'd need for that."

Raelle and Jay looked at each other. She said to Gama, "I'm
not sure our own work should wait that long. Couldn't we just
visit briefly this first time, and return here today?"

Gama fidgeted, looked down and then up to them again.
"I—"

"Or if Crait needs a longer conference right now," said Jay,
"he could come to us. You've got the mobility—we haven't.
We could move into *Search* and put him up here at the hut, if
he likes."

Raelle shook her head. "That's not fitting, Jay—asking a
commander to leave his ship. Let's compromise—go with

Serro now but come back today. We can work out later meetings when we have time to schedule things better."

Jay nodded, and Gamma looked relieved. Jay said, "I'll go to *Search* first—add the latest haul to the bin. It's hotter, Raelle, as we expected—I have it triplebagged for safety."

As he left, Gamma said, "What's he talking about?"

Without thinking she evaded the question. "Some samples."

Gamma smiled. "I've done a bit of that—just as helper, usually—starting with the two rocks *Far Shot* visited. Usually it's been fuel ore we're after."

"We—we've checked some of that, too, of course."

Then Jay was back. "All right—I guess we can be ready in about five minutes."

With a sure touch Gama lifted and moved the car. It bobbed and tipped very little, less than Raelle expected. He had the folding top up but kept two side windows open; the rush of air felt pleasant. Down to the river and across, he took them, spray sheeting beside and behind—up and over the ridge, then across the second, wider river they had never seen. Now up a long, rolling slope—at the top he let the car dip and then gave it max thrust to hop a low rock ledge—and there, in the valley below, stood the ship.

"*Star Flame*," said Gama. As he glided down the hill to a landing, Raelle saw no outside activity—all crew members were either in the ship or working elsewhere.

Following Gama aboard and upship they passed one man— an Oriental youth, hardly grown. Wide-eyed he nodded to them, but said nothing. "Rit don't talk much," Gama commented. Then, "The galley, I guess—you wait there. Have some coffee—or a real drink, if you'd rather."

The galley was empty, too. Gama gestured toward coffee-pot and cups, the small bar in one corner. "Help yourselves. I'll go tell Dol—he'll be here pretty quick." And he left.

Jay said, "I think I can use the real drink. How about you?" Raelle nodded. In a moment they sat holding glasses of iced spirits.

"It's awfully quiet," she said. "Where do you suppose everyone is?"

Jay shrugged. "Scouting expeditions, maybe? But you'd think that right after a landing there'd be a certain amount of checking and minor repairs going on. And you know as well as I do—that means a lot of coming and going in the galley. But there..."

They said no more. It was perhaps another twenty minutes before Gama returned. With him were three other men, including the young Oriental.

The tallest stepped forward. With one hand he brushed back a longish mass of curly blond hair—the other he extended to shake first Jay's hand, then Raelle's. "Dolman Crait, commanding. Serro's told me your names." He repeated these for the benefit of the other two. Then, "Arth Frenkel." A slim, redhaired man moved up to shake hands. "And Ritter Siu." The Oriental followed suit, touching hands briefly and stepping back. "Let's sit down."

Raelle guessed Crait's age, give or take a little, at thirty. He topped Jay's height and her own by several centimeters— over a broad chest and shoulders his jacket stretched tightly. He gestured to Gama. "Coffee, huh? *And* a drink." The older man moved to obey; the other two poured coffee for themselves. When all were seated, Crait looked from Jay to Raelle. "What ship brought you here? Serro told me about the pintsized bucket you have over there. Some kind of scout vessel for local use?" He grinned. "He had the idea you made real trips in it—didn't you, Serro?"

Raelle touched Jay's arm; he glanced briefly to her, then said, "We can tell you about that later. I understand your main problem is that you expected a colony here. Is that right?"

Crait leaned forward. So did Arth Frenkel, who said, "Do you know what's wrong? Is the listing mistaken—somebody ascribed a colony to the wrong system?"

"Not exactly," said Jay. "It's a little hard to explain, but we'll try." And between them, Jay and Raelle described the phenomena of parallel continua and of the Drift between them.

And Raelle said, "We expected a colony here, ourselves."

Crait looked at his crewmen, then back to her. "You mean, we get back to Earth, it won't be the same one we left? How much different?"

"No way of predicting," said Jay. "The longer your hops and the higher your Skip Factor, the more change you're apt to find."

Gama chuckled. "Not a patch on what *I* found, I bet—

coming back on *Far Shot* almost ninety years after we'd left. Don't worry, Dol—you'll manage." Then he sobered. "I forgot— there's still the other matter."

Crait glared at him, then said to Jay, "I think you'd better tell me about *your* transportation. Maybe there's some answers there."

Raelle cleared her throat. "Captain Crait—Acting Captain, I understand—we'd have a better chance of finding answers if you'd tell us your problem."

While Crait hesitated, Gama spoke. "Tell 'em, Dol—there's no hiding it." When Crait did not protest, the older man said, "Our Skip unit's busted to hell. We can make fuel, all right—got to, in fact. But when we have it, all we can do is crowd c—and eat time doing it, just like on *Far Shot*."

Raelle shook her head. "But surely you have spare components, and the technicians—" She looked around at the four men. "Wait a minute—your crew—are you shorthanded?"

Crait's finger pointed at her. "You're getting it. We four right here—out of the original two dozen, we're all that's left."

She gasped. "*Plague?*"

"Mutiny." After a moment, she realized that the soft voice was Ritter Siu's.

She stared at Crait—he nodded, and said, "Not that it changes this situation any, but we weren't the mutineers. If we had been, we'd still be on Kagan's Trap—chewing the pretty little chartreuse flowers that won't let you stop, and burning out under two-to-one neural acceleration."

Captains name the planets they discover. Stacy Kagan, commanding *Star Flame*, was not given to whimsy or imagination—when the habitable world was spotted—it was her first—she listed it simply as Kagan's Planet. It was the survivors, Crait said, who renamed it Kagan's Trap.

At the start all went well. They landed in a pleasant, scenic environment, at a latitude approaching summer. Plenty of work to do—exploring, taking samples, finding ore and synthesizing fuel, putting *Star Flame* in top shape for the return trip—and the crew made a good working team. Fifteen men and nine women, they had settled into flexible living patterns, clearing up initial frictions during the first few weeks.

Two ecologists, exploring above timberline in the nearby mountains, found and brought back the chartreuse flowers.

Crait did not know who first nibbled on a bloom. But within a week *Star Flame*'s crew had become two factions—those who had and those who had not. The flower was totally addictive.

And as Crait had intimated, the users' reflexes were nearly twice as fast as those of normal persons.

Star Flame had done its work, was refurbished and almost ready for the return voyage—but nearly half the crew refused to go. More than that, they would not allow the ship to leave. Two barricaded themselves into the drive room and put the thrustors on local manual control—other addicts passed food and flowers through the emergency port. *Star Flame* stood stalemated.

After three days of fruitless talk—onesided, for the mutineers ignored commands, arguments and outright pleas—Stacy Kagan armed herself and all nonaddicted personnel. She gave a few tactical suggestions but only one firm order: "Get this ship back!"

Eight hours later, *Star Flame* left the planet.

Raelle shook her head. "And only you four survived?"

"Six," said Crait. "On the ship, I mean—some of the petalheads got away. Eight, maybe—putting it together we accounted for only ten known dead. But no one of us saw all of it . . ."

Jay frowned. "Then what happened to the other two?"

They thought the fighting done with. Five—including mutineers—died before the drive room was secured. A simultaneous attack on the ship was beaten off. Leaving guards—one each at Control, the drive room and ship's entrance—Captain Kagan took her two remaining men offship to see if any of the fallen still lived.

One lay feigning injury, moving feebly. The captain bent down—before she could straighten again, she died. But no neural acceleration could free the killer from the grip of the man who fell upon her then. Crait took her aboard, *Star Flame*'s one prisoner.

"Neesha Gort," Crait said. "Beautiful woman—smart, kind, loving, sexy—all of it, until the petals. She was one of the two that first found them. But being dragged up the ramp—" He shook his head. "Not the same person any more. Her eyes— even Tony Vermont could see it, though he didn't want to."

Seeing their bewilderment he said, "Tony's the other who left Kagan's Trap with us. Poor Tony!"

Gama snorted. "Dumb sumbidge Tony you mean. Wasn't for him..."

Crait made a sharp gesture; Gama said no more. "You and I hadn't been in her sept much, Serro—Tony had. She influenced him a lot—though before the petals I don't think it was on purpose. After, she almost got him to try them—and at the last, maybe she did."

On *Star Flame* five men and one woman—and the woman, imprisoned, an implacable enemy. Yet she coaxed, she wheedled, she promised—during the next ten months she pried at the men's needs, their weaknesses. But Dolman Crait would not unlock the quarters that had become her cell.

It happened after the one-week-to-landing party. Vermont pleaded fatigue and retired early—the others drank and sang for hours more. How much later it came, the crashing shudder that threw Crait half out of his bunk, he did not know.

"I was still drunk, you see, and half hungover—I couldn't think. I headed for Control. Halfway there, just outside Neesha's empty cell, I found Tony—naked, and with his neck broken, it turned out. But at first I thought he might be breathing. And when I bent down to check—I think I smelled the petals. She had some hidden—we knew that—but it hadn't been worth the risk to go in and search."

His fists clenched. "In the drive room I was lucky—I slipped on oil and nearly fell—the steel bar missed me. Then her lunge brought her throat to my hand. And all the trickery, all the speed—she was accelerated, all right—none of it kept her alive. But then I saw what she'd done to our Skip unit."

He looked at Raelle. "Spare components, you said? Sure we have them—we just don't have the basic framework and circuitry to plug them into. And no data to build it from."

Jay spoke. "The crashing that woke you—that was *Star Flame* being kicked out of Skip?"

Crait nodded. Raelle said, "*Why* did she do it?"

"I have part of that—before I got her wind, she tried to argue. Of course I'm guessing a lot, just from a few words. Mainly she didn't want to stand trial—and without Skip we'd be so long getting to Earth, maybe she figured her crime wouldn't count by then. Especially if she seduced the lot of us first, the way she'd been trying—and by *damn* it was hard not to take her up on it. So Tony did, I expect—and then probably refused to be her accomplice, so she killed him."

He stared at his hands on the table, then looked up again. "So instead of getting here in a week, the way we'd celebrated for, it took us two years.

"All by ourselves—just the four of us."

Silence held, until Ritter Siu pushed back his chair. "Lunch—it's my turn." He went to the galley's rear and began preparing food.

"Too bad it isn't Gama's," said Crait. "He's the best of us."

"Had lots of practice, I did."

Arth Frenkel sat straight. "I'm tired of it." It was Crait he spoke to. "Just the four of us, you're always saying—and whose fault is it?"

"I did what I had to."

"Had to? I would have—"

"You'd have been dead, Arth. You can't fight, for little blue beans."

"I'd have *talked* to her. She'd done her worst, hadn't she? Why would she want to kill any more?"

"I don't know, but she sure tried."

"You say that. I think she's dead because you were afraid of her. Afraid she'd get to you, like she did with Tony."

This time silence lasted until Siu served the food and it was eaten.

Raelle did not sense, among the group, the tension that exchange should have produced. Finally she thought, *it's an old argument—they've said it all before*. Still she wondered—why did Dolman Crait, obviously in command, allow talk that was close to insubordination? *There is more here than we know. Watch!*

Crait pushed his tray back and turned to Gama, then waved a hand. "You're still eating, Serro—I'll get it myself." He brought the coffeepot, poured for himself and handed it along. Siu, the last in turn, took it back. Crait looked to Jay. "You've heard our troubles. Let's hears yours—beginning with that craft of yours, over there."

His voice held a demanding edge. Raelle thought, *well,*

we've got to tell him sooner or later. For the fact was, even if they could improvise a consistent lie there was no advantage to it. She said, "It's called a Courier Can. It carries two people, no more—that's the limits of the life support gear. And the food storage capacity—for two, it's only about fifteen days."

Crait's brows raised. "Then what the hell good is it? Where can you get to, in that time?"

"Earth," said Jay. As Crait began protest, he added. "What's your top Skip? Under two thousand?" Crait nodded. "Well, *Search* can beat ten-sixth—one million."

After a moment, Crait laughed. "Then there's no damned *problem,* once we get the fuel synthesized. We'll just put your Skip unit into *Star Flame* and all go home to Earth in style!" Sitting, he made a half-bow. "We can carry the rest of your crate as cargo. And you yourselves—why, be our honored guests!"

It was a shame, thought Raelle, that the idea would not work.

Carefully she explained, Jay filling in when Crait interrupted. The interruptions were many—naturally, the man did not *want* to believe what he heard.

But the facts would not change—Skip Factor was governed by fixed parameters. Given the power capability of any specific unit, the product of ship's mass, ship's volume and maximum Skip was a constant. Overload the unit and it would blow. Q.E.D.

Jay supplied the figures for *Search.* Crait left for Control, to put them—and those for *Star Flame*—through the computer. When he returned he was scowling. "You know what I got?"

"I think so." Jay spoke quietly.

"Skip Factor of *one*—a little less, even. Meaning, no Skip at all."

"That's about what I'd guessed."

"I'll recheck the figures you gave me—you know that."

"Sure. Believe me, Crait, I'd like to be wrong."

"I guess you would, at that. Meanwhile you're staying here, both of you. Serro, Arth—see to it. You can have the double quarters just below mine, for now. Later—well, we can discuss that after I get back from visiting your ship."

Ignoring the threatening implications of his words, Raelle

said, "You're making a mistake. You don't know *Search*—push the wrong button, you can kill yourself."

Jay stood facing Crait. From behind, Frenkel had a hand on his shoulder—Jay glanced back, shook the hand loose, stepped aside. Now no one was behind him. Crait said, "No. You don't want to get yourself hurt—and you could, easy. Listen first."

Jay moved again, circling toward Crait. "So far I don't like it. Let's hear you do better."

He mustn't! Jay's good, but no match for Crait—even without the rest. And I can't take out more than one of them. But before she could speak...

"We'd help you if we could, Crait—but we can't. And obviously you won't help *us*. So just let us go—pretend we don't exist. Is that too much to ask?"

Feet apart, hands out from his body and slightly extended, Crait rocked up on his toes and then back again. Before he spoke, Raelle knew his answer. "Yes, it is. What's your next best offer? Such as, what kind of help do you want?"

Quickly she said it. "None—none at all. Take us back to *Search*—you can check Jay's figures, there, and see that he told the truth. Then—Jay's right. Thanks for your hospitality but our problems are separate. Let's keep them that way."

Crait ceased bobbing and stood flatfooted. "Not quite—but I'll compromise. He stays here while you show me how to check out your little boat. After that, we'll see."

Her thoughts raced. "Who else comes along?"

"Serro? Is he all right with you?"

"No." It was Frenkel. "He's already seen this midget ship—I haven't." Crait scowled, and the redhaired man added, "You're not making any deals behind my back, Dol. *No* kind."

One deep breath, then Dolman Crait visibly relaxed. "It's been established that you can't threaten me."

"I don't have to. You drive a car like a turtle flies—that's my insurance."

Crait did not answer. Jay shook his head. "Raelle—I don't like this. If he chooses to go to *Search* and blow himself off the map, let him. We—"

She went to him. "Jay—" Close to his ear she spoke softly. "There's a pattern here. But I don't know what it is, yet—too many crosscurrents. It comes closest to clear in those two. If I go with them—it's not dangerous so long as the balance holds. And Gama and the boy, here—try to make friends with them?"

After a moment he nodded. She kissed him and turned to Dolman Crait. "All right—what are we waiting for?"

Crait sat in front beside Frenkel, with Raelle behind. Frenkel wasn't the driver Gama was, but he got them over the ridge and off the ledge well enough. As they approached the first river, Crait said, "When do you plan to leave?"

For a moment, she thought. "Not for another two months, maybe three."

"That's good. We'll be about that long, finding ores and synthesizing the fuel we'll need."

Now? Why not? "We can show you a good ore supply. In return for saving your time—well, if you make a little extra, we'd appreciate the chance to top off our own supply."

As though he heard the plea she had not made, he paused and looked at her. "So that's it! You're stuck here—no fuel. Interesting—I'll think about it."

"That's not true!" What to say? If he wished he could rob the fuel bin, strip them clean. "We—we plan to leave a cache. So that if another Can comes here, its people won't have to do the work we've done. It's not full yet—a small donation would save *our* time."

The river now, and Frenkel threw more spray than Gama had done. Entering and leaving the stretch of water, the car jounced heavily. Crait asked, "What size donation? How much fuel gets your Can to Earth?"

There seemed no reason to lie—she told him. After a brief silence, he laughed. "That'd just about get *Star Flame* aloft and up to Skip-twenty. If we had Skip." He looked at his spread palm as through reading answers from it. "Those figures—the time you quoted—all that. I'm going to check, of course, but I'm convinced you both told the truth."

Over the middle ridge to the second river. Now Arth Frenkel controlled less harshly—the car transferred to water with a smoother touch. Crait said, "Your husband. I hope he's not as possessive as he sounds."

All along, she realized, she had been trying to ignore the obvious. Pitching her voice to calmness despite the rush of fear, she spoke with care. "Jay's a generous person, certainly. But if you're referring to *me*, you may as well forget the idea.

We're Monogamists, you see—both of us, and vows sealed with death pledges." *If I have to lie, this is a good time for it.* And, *ARE there such things as death pledges?*

Leaving the second river the car bucked and swayed. Crait lurched in his seat, caught himself and stared back at her as they climbed the slope and passed between knolls, approaching *Search*. As they neared the wired perimeter, Frenkel showed no signs of slowing. Raelle shouted, "Stop *here!*" No response. "*Now*—you'll damage the car!" With a jar, he dropped the vehicle to ground.

Crait turned to her. "What was that all about?" He waved a hand. "Never mind—we'll get to it later. First—death pledges, you said. You mean, if one dies, the other suicides?" He shook his head, blond hair flying. "I can't believe that."

Try to sound reasonable! Hoping to salvage something from her impulsive statement, she said, "No, of course not. We're dedicated people, yes—but not fanatics."

"Then what *does* it mean?"

"Why—why, that so long as we're both alive we're together. Exclusively."

"Then maybe widows have some advantages over wives." Crait grinned. "I wonder if your husband's thought of that?"

Raelle gasped. Arth Frenkel said, "Space it, Dol! You've got your faults—don't I know it?—but you won't kill, in this matter. And *you* know it."

Face flushed, Crait reached and buffeted Frenkel's head. "Don't tell me what I'll do!" He turned to Raelle. "You can't know what it's like! Ten months, the five of us—and *her*, there locked up. Treacherous, we knew—but oh, God! I—"

"A great temptation?" *No—that was the wrong thing to say.*

He didn't appear to notice. "Then two years—just the four of us." His laugh was hideous. "Oh, we made do!"

"Some better than others, of course," said Arth Frenkel.

Crait turned on him. "It was all right for you—you were *raised* Pansexual—I never noticed you complaining. But me—I—"

Slowly, deliberately, Frenkel spoke. "What Dol wants you to know—what he has to be sure you understand—is that all through the whole trip he was never the one on the bottom. Not even once."

Crait half stood—in his face Raelle saw death—then he sat back. "Don't bait me again, Arth, for not being able to break my early conditioning. That's not a matter for pride or shame, either one. So leave it alone—or some time when I don't need you, to drive—"

Push it! Not quite lying, she said, "Don't give yourself ulcers, Crait. I can drive this thing."

Silent, both men stared at her. Frenkel shook his head; Crait said, "You almost—but that's not—oh, I see. Levels of meaning—I won't underestimate you again, Tremona."

She shrugged. "Then you'd better let me go in ahead of you, and deactivate some devices that can tell us apart." Without waiting for answer she got out, stepped over the wire and entered the hut—thinking, *I hit one of his buttons— but how?*

Inside, she touched the defense switch. Crait would lead the way, of course—and she and Jay could handle the others. But she could not do it—she took her hand from the lethal switch, stepped to the door and called. "It's safe now."

Dolman Crait, she soon realized, was no fool. She hid nothing from him, nor tried to—it was too late for that. He looked briefly at the hut and storage facilities, and nodded. "You've been here a while. Haven't wasted your time, either." Then he gestured toward *Search*, and she led the two men inside the Can.

Crait looked around. "I'd heard of this project—it was on the boards when we left. Looks like a good design, within its limits." He searched, not asking directions, until he located the fuel bin. Looking at the indicating meter, he said, "You lied, Tremona. You'd fill this first. There isn't any charity cache, is there?"

Hawklike, his face went taut. "This changes matters. I was looking for the easiest way to keep you here a while without getting tough—but I don't have to do a thing, do I? Because without us, you can't leave anyway."

What could she say? The truth—any lie she could think of—any of it, he could use against her. And no lie would stand up if Crait thought to quiz Jay in her absence.

She licked her lips. "Maybe—maybe not."

He looked more closely at the bin's instruments. "Hey— this stuff's hotter than it ought to be. Especially toward the top. This never came from Earth's supplies." His eyes narrowed. "And there's no way you could carry a synthesizer on here." His brows raised; he snapped his fingers. "Of course—a ship's been here, even if colonization didn't follow. You found its synthesizer slagpile—you've been mining the tailings." He scowled. "Damned if I see how. Hot products like that—"

When she did not answer, he shrugged. "Doesn't matter—you can't mine any more unless I let you." He gestured for Frenkel to go outside—then he stepped toward her.

Her throat tightened—her voice came shrill. "Crait—maybe you can take me by force. But I promise you—you won't enjoy it!"

He seemed genuinely puzzled. "But I wasn't—just hug you a little, maybe. See how it feels after so long. I—what hurt would that do?"

Did he mean it? "No harm—if we were friends, if I trusted you. But how can I trust someone who denies us freedom, Jay and me? How do I know what else you want to force on me?"

"You don't understand? I don't want you *that* way—against your will. I want you to tell me, all right, Dol—here I am for you."

Unexpectedly she wanted to laugh. She knew she must not—she fought it back. "I've told you why that's impossible. I'm sorry."

"Sorry we can't be lovers? But maybe—"

"No! I'm sorry you didn't find someone here who could." She could afford him no semblance of encouragement—she knew that much. "Now then—is there any more you want to learn, here?"

He wasn't ready to give it up, she knew. But he said, "Your log—let's have a look at it."

Well, why not? At the control console she punched the access codes. On the screen the entries appeared, rolling upward at a moderate reading speed. Until it was done, Crait was silent—then he said, "All that way—out and back and out again—in so little time!" He shook his head.

"We pay for it, Crait. Look what happened *this* time." She wanted to get back to Jay. She turned the controls again to standby and moved toward the exit. As she expected, he took a last look around and followed. Over her shoulder she said, "I'm beginning to get hungry. Whose turn is it to fix dinner?"

"Maybe yours."

"Fair enough. Someone will have to show me where things are."

"I think someone's going to have to show you *how* things

are." She looked at him, but until they were in the car he did not speak. Then he said, "Let's go, Arth." A moment later the car moved out.

This time Crait sat behind with Raelle. When he spoke it was softly, so that Frenkel could not hear. "I've been thinking. You're going to do what we want, all right—because it makes sense for everybody. The only question is how to change your mind."

She had to derail this line of thought. "Crait—only friends have any chance of persuading me of anything. And so long as you think as you do, you're my enemy."

Onto the river—over the sound of spray he spoke close to her ear. "Because I want you? And if I say I don't, I lose, too. Damned either way—is that it?"

She had had enough—as the car left water to climb the ridge, she said, "Yes, it is! I'm not available on *any* terms—get that through your head. Then we can be friends or not, as you choose. Before all this came up, I liked you well enough."

She started to touch his shoulder, then drew her hand back. "Dolman—you're a grown man, not a lovesick boy. And a *young* man—still young when you reach Earth, with many good years ahead. Why can't you wait for that—instead of trying to wreck the lives of people who've never harmed you?"

She spoke louder than she intended—Arth Frenkel glanced back and said, "Yeh, Dol—what makes *your* macho so important?"

Crait glared at the man's back. "You'd share willingly enough, if she agreed."

"Agreed, yes—coerced, no. If you do find a handle on these people, don't expect me to help you pump it."

Water again—Frenkel said something more but Raelle did not hear his words. Crait did, apparently—he shouted, "I don't care what *any* of you do or don't do. I was arguing for all of us—now I'll just work it out for *me*! And while I'm doing that, you'll take my orders."

Frenkel pulled the car up onto land and slowed, barely hovering. "Concerning the ship, I take orders. When it comes to personal problems I'm not your soldier. If you don't like that—well, one of us can jump out and walk the rest of the way, and I guess it's me."

Redfaced, Crait drummed clenched fists on his knees. "Say

it all the way, Arth. You refuse to act with me on this?"
Frenkel nodded. "But you won't act against me, either?"

The man hesitated. Then, "Not on the ship, I won't. That's
as far as I'll promise."

Crait laughed. "Then get us the hell back to *Star Flame*."

For the rest of the ride, the landing, and walking to the
ship, Raelle tried without success to think of a course of
action. Aboard, again they went to the galley. Serro Gama
was there, no one else.

She walked to face him. "Where's Jay?"

Smiling, Gama spread his hands. "Where Dol said—the
quarters. He's fine—we had a good talk."

"I want to see him." This to Crait.

"Later. Right now, *I'm* going to see him. You stay here."
Crait left—Raelle made to follow but Gama spoke.

"Dol said you stay. Don't—*I* don't want to have to stop
you." She looked at him—his expression showed concern.

Frenkel said, "Dol won't hurt your man. He'll *lean* a
lot—arguments, dickers, maybe threats. D'you think that'll
work?"

What kind of threats? To Jay's life, or hers? She shook her
head—there was no way of knowing—and said only, "No. It
won't."

Gama began preparing dinner—apparently Crait's suggestion that Raelle do so had been in jest. He said, "Dol leans
pretty good."

"So does Jay." *If only we could talk together!*

She went to the bar, made a drink and sat sipping it, deep
in thought. What were the *limits* of this situation—how far
would Crait go, or Jay—or she herself? She considered—in a
similar predicament, two planets ago, unhesitatingly she had
told Reyez Turco that he and she would both die at her hand
if he separated her from Jay. Today she had made no such
threats—why not?

The answer startled her—the threat would have been
empty. Separation by Drift she would *not* tolerate—but no
circumstance, no matter how hateful or humiliating, that left
her and Jay together afterward, was worth dying for. She
wondered what Jay would think of her conclusions . . .

Crait's return startled her. "Well there, dutiful wife—I've
just had a nice talk with Jay." He smiled. "It's all set—he says
you should cooperate."

What—? Blindly she shook her head. "I don't believe you! How—what did you do to him?"

"Nothing. He saw reason—that's all. So now—"

"No! Let me see him."

"Sure. All you want—afterward."

Glass and all, she threw her drink. He knocked it aside and wiped at the liquid on his face and jacket. "Damn!—" He started for her—she stepped back and to the side, putting the table between them. "What the hell—"

She wrenched a chair loose from its snap-in deck fastenings, swung it at him. He ducked back—she missed—on her backswing she threw it. His warding arm passed between the rungs—a leg caught him in the face. He staggered back and fell.

A quick look—Gama gestured but Arth Frenkel, shaking his head, held the older man. Raelle vaulted the table—as she came down, one foot caught the juncture of Crait's neck and shoulder. She stumbled, caught her balance on the deck, turned in time to kick a knife from his hand. She ran and picked up the weapon—now Frenkel freed Gama and both came toward her.

"No! I won't hurt him if he leaves me alone!" The two men stopped—as Crait came to his feet Raelle turned and ran.

The quarters below his, Crait had said—well, he'd be occupying the captain's cabin, surely. Down two levels she went, hearing Crait behind her. She turned a corner—and before the door she wanted stood Ritter Siu. Slowly he dropped into a fighting crouch.

She paused. "All I want is to talk with my husband. Don't get yourself cut up trying to stop me—it's not your argument. And I'm good with this thing." *I wish I were!*—but the young man straightened, gave a slight bow and moved aside.

She opened the door. *"Jay!"*

The door also bolted from inside. Once that was done she dropped the knife and went to him. Kissing, embracing, both mumbled words that meant little—and yet, a lot. Finally she pulled back. "You *didn't* say I should go to bed with Crait— did you?"

Someone—probably Dolman Crait—pounded on the door. Its thickness muffled his shouts, made them unintelligible. Jay looked at her. "No—it was the other way round—he said you already had." She shook her head; he continued, "Said he'd told you I wouldn't get fed unless you gave in, so you did. Asked me if I blamed you—and of course I couldn't. But—" He grinned. "The way you came in here—the knife and all, and somebody out there hammering the door pretty good—it strikes me he lied."

She nodded. "If he'd told me that, he would have won, Jay. What he did tell me—well, I said that already. And when I asked to see you—" She made a sour grimace. "—he said, *afterward*. Then I—I think I went a little crazy, Jay."

He squeezed her shoulders. "Sometimes that's the only thing that makes sense." The pounding had stopped, and the shouts; Jay looked to the door. "Sooner or later we have to talk to him. Is he armed?"

"I don't know. I didn't think he was, before, until he brought the knife out."

"That's *his* knife? Well—" Jay moved to pick it up. "You want it again?"

"No, Jay—you've had more training. A gun, now—but I don't suppose there's one handy."

"No. Well, here goes." He rapped on the door and shouted, "Parley?" When an answer came in kind, he threw the bolt and opened the door. Crait stood there, his men grouped beside him. Jay said, "This isn't a fight, now or ever, unless you insist. We'd rather go up with you and have something to eat. And talk."

"What's to talk about?" Explosively, Crait said it.

"You gave me plenty of time to think, in here. I didn't spend all of it worrying about our personal problems."

"What—" Receiving no answer, Crait moved aside. Jay and Raelle came out into the corridor. As one they turned and led the way toward the galley, their backs unprotected.

Ah, Jay! I knew you'd realize this is the way to do it.

Before dinner they had wine. For his guests Crait deigned to pour—the others served themselves. The big man fidgeted but seemed unwilling to open conversation—Jay, in contrast, was quiet and appeared calm. As they ate, Raelle wished she had thought to ask him, while she could, what his trump card was.

Finally Crait could hold back no longer. "All right—so you two made a fool of me—and I guess I helped, some. And three to one my crew votes I have to take it. I suppose I owe you the meal—but then I'd like nothing better than to send you back to your pocketsized ship and see the last of you. Still, though—you say you did some thinking, Pearsall? What about—that means anything to *me*?"

"Skip Drive." That was all—Jay waited.

"So? We don't have one—you know that."

"The four of you." Jay waved his wineglass from one to another, then sipped from it. "What are your individual skills here?"

"What difference?" said Crait. "Oh, well—I was navigator—doubled in drive tuning, Skip and normal. Serro here—he's done a little of everything, I think."

Gama chuckled. "Yeah—everything a little, nothing real good. Just enough to keep going on, that's me."

Frenkel was an apprentice pilot—he knew, also, how to maintain sensors and viewscreen indicators. And Siu dealt with telemetry and control circuits. "So what does that tell you, Pearsall?"

Jay smiled. "That between the four of you, with our help, you can have yourselves a working Skip unit."

Crait didn't convince easily. "There's a trick here."

"No trick." And as Jay told it, Raelle wondered why she hadn't seen the answer herself. Of the framework and circuitry Neesha Gort had battered and melted to destruction, nothing was *quantitatively* critical so long as it was heavy enough to carry the power load. *Star Flame*'s circuit diagrams were gone, also—but the Skip unit on *Search* was basically similar, though of course simplified. *Search* carried no diagrams—Jay would trace the paths and draw his own, setting load figures by transposing computer-derived values.

Crait had materials for framework, conduits, shielding—he had spare connectors as well as components. He simply didn't know what to do with them—Jay did, or soon would. And whereas Crait was short of wire for such extensive rebuilding, Jay and Raelle had left most of the large coil at the beach—it would suffice.

"Yeah—so what do you want in return? A ride home?"

"Yes—but on *Search*. We want fuel—now, first, before anything else. The way it is, you'll have to trust *us*."

Crait, Raelle saw, was thinking it over. Finally he nodded. "You'll stay until the unit checks out on test?"

"Of course," she said.

And Jay added, "We wouldn't leave right away, even if we

could. There's some work of our own that we have to do
first."

"Then it's a deal."

The next day, after Gama drove them back to base, Jay
brought up the other project he had in mind. "If we'd had a
way to store enough food without spoilage, we could have
taken the slow route to Waterfall or Mossback—right?"

"Sure, Jay. But we don't have that—and now we won't
need it."

He grinned. "Maybe we won't—but I want it anyway. Why
waste all we've harvested here? And as I told Crait, I had lots
of time to think—to keep my mind busy so I wouldn't worry
about you when I couldn't help."

Her eyes narrowed. "If you don't *tell* me—"

Again, the answer was simple. "If we can't afford power
refrigeration, what's wrong with *space* refrigeration?" *Star
Flame* could spare the necessary material to wall off and
insulate a sufficient volume, provide shelving and spacetight
doors—including a remotely controlled outside valve.

"Of course," he said, "we won't load our space locker from
the cellars, until we're ready to leave."

The repairs on *Star Flame* went well—until it came time to
interconnect Skip unit and thrusters. "It won't work!" Crait
shouted. "It can't—the leads don't match—your gadget's one
short."

Jay hadn't checked the ship's normal drive. Why should
he?—it was in good order. Raelle agreed—but Crait was
angry.

Now Jay studied both units, and said, "Crait—do you have
a good electronics junkbox? I need to build a phase-splitting
circuit."

Crait took him to a cabinet in the supply compartment,
opened it. "Will this do?" After a quick look, Jay nodded. "So
what's wrong?"

"Nothing much. On the Cans, handling less power, things
don't have to be so efficient. Your interface is three-phase—
ours is single. Don't worry about it."

"If you say so."

A few days later, *Star Flame*'s preparations needed no more
outside help. The rebuilt Skip unit tested perfectly—and

Search was primed for liftoff the next morning. Inside the hut—now almost empty—Raelle looked around, suddenly realizing she would miss this shelter they had built.

To her left the screen beeped—the one Crait had provided for fast communications. She turned it on and Gama grinned at her.

"Hey—the last night, this is! We like to have a party—you agree? We bring the food and stuff. I'm the cook. All right?"

"Why—" Jay was aboard *Search*, but she was sure he wouldn't mind—working together had gradually built trust. "Yes, of course—it's a fine idea. When we hear you come in—we'll have the floodlights on—we'll cut the perimeter alarm. Wait until one of us comes out and waves, before you cross the wire."

"Sure—same as always. Got you." The screen dimmed. She looked outside. Twilight was nearly done—she put the outside lights on, called Jay and confirmed his approval. Not long afterward he joined her, and after a short wait they heard the car approach and come to ground. Raelle opened the door and saw the four men getting out. Then she looked more closely.

Sea devils charging! Almost upon them—but there was time!

She shouted. "Three seconds! *Then* jump the wire. Do you hear?" She ran inside, cut the defense circuit, counted three more and reactivated it. Grabbing up a harpoon she ran out again—and heard Jay follow.

One man was down—humped over the wire and entangled with a sea devil, both charring in the blue lightning. Inside, one of the beasts savaged another man, tearing at a leg while the victim screamed. She ignored the other sea devil that had got in, and ran to help. She slashed at the attacker's eye—the beast opened its jaws and swung its head toward her—she jammed her harpoon into the gaping maw. No tree was handy—she ran to one side and jerked the line to turn the creature. She almost fell, but recovered and made to repeat the maneuver. Someone passed her and jumped—locking legs around the sea devil's neck, then reaching a knife to saw at the spine behind the domed skull. "Thanks!" she cried, and turned to see what else still menaced.

"I got the other one!" Jay's shout was cheerful, but then his voice came hoarse. "Somebody's dead on the wire!"

A bloody shape detached itself from the sea devil Raelle
had harpooned. "That's Rit. He tends to hesitate in a crisis—
he did it once too often." And now Raelle recognized Dolman
Crait—without volition she ran to him, kissed him, held him
until she stopped shuddering.

"What's this?" he said. "I thought—"

"You *fought* the thing with me, Dol!" She saw his expression start to change, and said quickly, "No—it can't make us
lovers. But *this* much—" She kissed him again, dug her
fingers into his taut muscles. "This, I really mean!"

His face relaxed again. "Yes, I know." Before, she would
have resented his caress—but not now. "And so do I. Well—
we'll see you on Earth."

...*on Earth*. As they watched Jay and Gama, frantically
tending Arth Frenkel's leg and finally assuring him he would
not lose it, she decided not to tell Dolman Crait how impossibly
wrong he was.

PART FOUR:

Ξ

NEVER SO LOST...

Two days out from the planet, Jay leveled *Search* off at a Skip Factor of ten-fourth. With "normal" drive—the thrustors—held down to a tenth of Limit, the small Courier Can was doing a thousand cees. He turned to Raelle—she checked the indicators and nodded.

"You guessed right," he said. "Our Krieger-range sensors handle this much speed, just fine—we can take the same kind of path the big ships use, but faster."

She pushed her brown hair back—a recent trimming left it just short of her shoulders. "I'm glad. Because it's a good idea—checking on Drift with another colony, on the way home. And going outside the Arm twice would be wasteful."

"Right." He flipped a switch. On an auxiliary screen a star map lit. "Mossback's easier. But Waterfall's longer settled—there's a safer chance it's colonized on this timeline. Still agreed?"

Again she nodded. Looking at his wife without really seeing her, Jay Pearsall thought about Drift—and how, with their Skip unit suppressing all but every ten-thousandth of their normal appearances in the quantized Universe—it moved them into parallel continua. It was to minimize that Drift—to shift from their own timeline as little as possible—that he and Raelle traveled merely at high Krieger speeds and not the Courier Can's potential of over Skip ten-sixth: one million.

Finding a supposed colony planet uninhabited—the months spent toiling for survival and salvaging bits of fuel from the lethal pile some unknown ship had left—finally winning free of the aptly named world, Nobody Home—these things had shaken the assurance with which they had first joined the Courier Service.

Now Jay said, "We haven't discussed this—when we get to Earth, do we settle for what we find and drop out of Couriers?"

Steadily she looked at him. "Whether your parents are

there, or not? Jay—I went looking for *me*, and found me. I'm
satisfied. You didn't find parents who knew you. What if you
don't?"

Jay needed a moment to phrase his thought. "On Earth-
one, where we started, I couldn't accept being orphaned at
sixteen. On Earth-two last year, Woody and Glenna were
alive but *I* hadn't been born." He smiled at her. "Somehow
that's a long time ago. I'm twenty now or maybe closer to
twenty-one—I've lost track—and *you're* my life. Sure, on
whatever Earth we hit I'd like to find Woody and Glenna.
But if not—well, just knowing they *are* alive on some of the
infinities of Earths—that's good enough."

She reached to touch his shoulder. "Just so you're sure,
Jay."

"I think I am."

Search's cabin, nearly a third of it now walled off for food
storage, looked odd. The "space locker" worked well; Jay had
relocated insulation from the hull, to shield it. Now their kills
and harvest from Nobody Home, gathered over the months,
lay preserved by cold and vacuum. Simple controls allowed
them to close the hull and open the locker; by agreement
they ate the planet's produce first, saving what remained of
their issued rations. As Raelle had said, "Once we land, the
locker's out of business—we can't open it or everything will
start to spoil."

In other ways as well, *Search* was supplied for a longer
time in space than Courier Cans were expected to need.
Their fuel bin was filled—the reclaimed tailings from Nobody
Home topped off with purer fuel synthesized by the fullsized
ship that had come there—but the ship *Star Flame* had also
provided and filled an auxiliary bin.

Jay wondered—*will those three survivors, out of two doz-
en, get that ship back to Earth? And to which Earth?*
Certainly, he and Raelle would never know.

More than two weeks to Waterfall—at usual Can speeds it
would have been perhaps four days, with most of that time
spent in leaving and reentering the Galactic arm. At any rate,
they were conserving fuel—though when some of the "wild"
batches went through the hellbox, Skip Factor jumped
erratically.

At last Waterfall's suns could be distinguished. The planet

circled—almost exactly, with very slight eccentricity—the smaller of two widely separated components. The larger was too young and too hot to support a habitable planet. When the Can's sensors reported the planet itself, Raelle said, "Cross your fingers—we don't *need* the colony this time, but I do hope it's there!"

And soon—squinting against the farther sun's diffuse glare as Skip Factor lessened and the universe slowed to its proper, imperceptible motion—Jay saw on Waterfall the signs of man's intrusion. He flashed a reference chart on the side screen, checked briefly and said, "It fits the map pretty well—we're not far from the Earth-two timeline."

"Good. You have all the controls?" At his nod, Raelle rose from her own seat and console, took a step and stretched. "I'll break out some food. Before we get there, we need a meal."

Instead of a computer-generated response, Jay's identification signals brought a human voice—but no picture—from below.

"Your ID category isn't registered here. Repeat, please." He did so. After a pause the voice resumed. "You're a new one on us—we have no two-person ships listed. That's all right—land according to the beacon signal and you can tell us about it later. Estimated time?"

Jay checked his indicators and gave the reading; the unseen speaker approved. Jay cut the circuit and turned to the beacon.

In leisurely fashion he and Raelle ate. "That's the last of the tubers," she said. "I've managed to jam most of what's not sealed into standard refrigeration. The rest of what's in the space locker we'll have to eat up fast, once down, or throw it out."

"Maybe we can invite some of the locals to sample what grows on Nobody Home."

She grinned. "There's a thought. And some of the berries—if we can get the seeds planted, maybe they'll grow here."

"Or on Earth, for that matter. So let's save some, shall we?"

Then it was time to match the planet's velocity and prepare to land. Jay had scanned the data on this colony—he knew it occupied a lowland strip at the west of the mountainous equatorial continent. But the maps and figures had not prepared him for the sheer mass of those mountains, or for the size and number of the rivers that plunged down them to the sea. "Now," he said, "I see why they named it Waterfall."

The beacon signaled them toward the northern end of the lowlands, about a fourth of the way from that tip and back only a short distance from the ocean. The shoreline was approximately at midmorning. When they were close enough that the planet became "down" to them, Jay pointed out the difference between mountain and lowland flora—the bluish tinge of mountain foliage shaded to a brighter green as the terrain flattened.

Raelle took the landing. "The port," she said, "seems to have a town of its own—not like Harper's Touchdown, where colony and port administration were all lumped together."

"This colony's been here a while and drawn fairly heavy immigration—it's spread out more. I think the capital's about halfway down the coast—or was, to begin with, at least."

"We'll see." The beacon's directional and altitude signals continued to guide and report—eventually Raelle brought *Search* down to rest overshadowed by two fullsized ships, the farther one with its hull opened for repairs. She gave them the usual safety margin, landing well away from the blackened circles around them.

She called on the ID channel. A voice—a new one, this time—acknowledged and said, "The Acting Port Commander will be out to see you in a few minutes." Raelle agreed and signed off.

"There's no biological hazard here," said Jay, "and we have no cargo to invoice. Shall we get outside and stretch our legs?"

Raelle shrugged. "Might as well. Want to crack the door and check temperature?"

"Sure." When Jay did so, there was a slight but noticeable outrush of air. He checked the pressure indicator. "Lighter atmosphere than Earth's—just like the book says—but not enough to matter." Leaning outside, he sniffed it. "Plenty of Oh-two, at any rate. And warm outside." He climbed down to the ground—Raelle followed. They walked around *Search* and looked toward the nearest major building.

"Gravity's a little light, too, I think," said Raelle. She looked up, one hand shielding her eyes from Waterfall's sun.

"Can we see the Companion from here? Coming down to land, I lost track of its orientation."

Also squinting aloft, Jay shook his head. "We should be able to spot it, I'd think. Must be turned away from it now."

He gazed toward a grove of trees edging the port, perhaps two hundred meters distant. Slim trunks—bare of branches, either by nature or pruning, for twice a man's height—topped with a rounded flattish mass of thick foliage. He wondered if they bore flower or fruit, and in what season.

Raelle nudged him. "Company's coming." From behind the building they faced came a small-wheeled open vehicle. The slow-moving cart approached and stopped, and the driver alighted—a woman, very tall, very thin, wearing a snug green coverall. Short black hair made a smooth cap above her high forehead. Eyes and complexion bespoke the Orient of Earth—high cheekbones and a long, narrow jaw dominated her strong features.

She stepped toward them and shook hands with both. "I'm Setra Tuang—currently in charge of North Port here." Jay must have shown his surprise, for she grinned. "Why do I do my own driving—no escort, all that? It's simple—ordinarily I don't. But half our people are down at South Port on some emergency repair work, and the fact is I couldn't afford to pull someone off the job, just for show."

He liked this woman, Jay decided. Now she looked past him and Raelle—standing hipshot, one thumb hooked into her belt, other thumb and forefinger rubbing her chin, an eyebrow cocked higher than its mate. "Now what's that, you've brought us here? It doesn't look big enough to go much of anywhere, but you first called from quite a distance out—and it's certain your toysized ship wasn't built on this world."

Frowning, Raelle turned to Jay. He said, "Ms. Tuang— first, maybe we'd better ask a question or two. Are you familiar with Krieger-powered ships?"

She nodded. "Why, yes. *Star Chaser* there—the nearest hull—it's the second Krieger vessel we've had." She gestured. "Fantastic! Skip Factor well over a thousand—close to twice that, if pushed. And we'd been used to sixty or eighty, of course. Why, *now*—"

Jay shook his head. "Wait a minute, please. The Krieger

ships that came here—in each case, was it their *first* trip from
Earth?" And as she looked at him, eyes suddenly wide, he
knew the answer.

Setra Tuang's quarters complex adjoined her office—as she
led them inside, Jay saw that for all her height and thinness
she moved with grace. Looking around then, as they walked,
he had the impression of more rooms beyond—but they
turned aside into a study decorated, with moderate luxury, in
a Chinese motif. Subtly different, though, from the usual
style of that mode of decor—and when Raelle commented on
the difference, Tuang laughed.

"I'm Mongolian, really—with an assist from some displaced
Tibetans a century or more back. Our preferences, traditions—
not quite the same as the old central Chinese provinces, you
see." She saw them seated, and prepared and poured tea.
"Now then—I can see that you have something to tell me
and that you don't like doing it. But please do—if something's
wrong it's my business to know it."

So they explained—all of it—the discovery of Drift and of
its cause, the timelines they themselves had experienced, and
their own place in humanity's struggle to cope with these
phenomena. When they had finished, the woman shook her
head. "How could we have known? How could *anyone* have
known? Well—you've done *me* a favor, at least—me and
mine."

"We have?" Raelle's mouth essayed a smile, abandoned it.

Tuang nodded. "One of my husbands must go to Earth, to
do a sales job on a crucial project that's short of funds. He
was going on *Star Chaser*—we were thrilled that his absence
would be so short. But now—"

Jay leaned forward. "He still can. It'll take a little longer
than you were told—but not much. One fact the Courier
Service is trying to pass to every colony, every ship—that
below a Skip Factor of one thousand, Drift never occurs."

Tuang frowned. "You're sure?" He explained that higher
Skip was safe on short runs but that ten-third as a limit gave
added assurance. Visibly the woman relaxed. "Good! Then
Farig can ride swiftly, after all." She rubbed an ear. "*Star
Chaser*, though . . ."

Jay spread his hands. "It's probably Drifted from its own
Earth, yes—but it will go to yours. And the return ship—it'll
be safely briefed, of course."

Tuang stood. Staring past them—apparently at nothing—slowly she rubbed her hands down her sides, past her hips to full armslength at her thighs, then back again. She shook her head. "Tea is well and good—but for this saving information I think we deserve something stronger."

The planet's prize domestic liquor reminded Jay of whiskey but had its own distinctive flavor. He liked it.

Farig Mellieur entered while Tuang was pouring seconds. The big man—not as tall as his wife but largeboned and heavily muscled—acknowledged introductions and made a drink for himself. He sat, smiling; large white teeth contrasted with his dark complexion. Except for a jog at the bridge of the nose his features were regular; curly black hair, worn a little long, bore gray flecks. "Well—visitors! Always welcome—and what's the news from Earth?"

Setra Tuang told him. Mellieur's face tightened. "Hard to believe, this." He waved a hand. "No, no—it's not your word I doubt—merely I find it hard to see the universe playing us such tricks." He shrugged. "But you say—keep *Star Chaser* to no more than Skip one thousand, and I can with certainty return here?"

Raelle nodded. "That's supposed to give ample safety factor."

"Then I'll trust it." He turned to Setra. "Word from Felipe—he and Jiddu won't be rejoining our household soon. They estimate another week at South Port—maybe more."

She spread one hand and closed it. "That's what I get for marrying key personnel. Well—you and Tom and I will have to keep the place going, by ourselves." She looked to Jay and Raelle. "Excuse us for intruding private matters. Now then—" And she asked them about news from Earth, their own travels and future plans. "—and how long will you be here, do you suppose?"

Raelle began the explanation, omitting personal complications. "And whichever Earth we reach, we'll probably stay there—or at least not risk Courier-level Drift again." And—at least a week, they would stay at Waterfall. Even with lower Skip on the latest hop, they did not care to risk memory damage.

Tuang and Mellieur grasped the new concepts readily, surprising Jay. The woman said, "At the university a few kilos south of here, we have some good theorists. Would you be willing to brief them—give them a chance to work with these ideas?"

"And you should go on the Tri-V net," said Mellieur. "—or at least provide a summary for one of the regular commentators. The public here—it should be informed. I'll prep my chief on the matter first, of course—but I'm sure he'll authorize the disclosures." He stood, and left the room.

Tuang looked after him. "Actually, Farig has enough status to act on his own. He's merely being tactful, as always." She smiled. "Are you getting hungry? I am."

First, though, she showed Jay and Raelle further into the Tuang quarters—they were, she stated, listed in her name—to a suite she offered for their use. They accepted, and Jay decided his earlier guess at the size of the complex was correct. "We can bring your duffel in later," Setra said, and Jay seconded Raelle's nod.

At lunch in a dining nook just off Tuang's office, they met the other husband currently in residence—Tom Dardeen, redhaired, average in height and build, with bushy brows and a great beak of nose. He spoke seldom, and then in a soft voice. When he was briefed on the problems of Drift he said only, "It'll be a time, won't it—before all ships are alerted and can be sure of where they're going?"

"Sure?" Jay's chuckle held no amusement. "At least they're a lot surer than we can ever be." A thought came to him—he looked to Tuang. "It hadn't occurred to me to ask, before—but in this timeline, do you know if Nobody Home is colonized?"

The tall woman shook her head. "I remember seeing it listed on the schedule, but I don't recall the timing. Since there'd be no direct contact anyway, it's not a matter we'd think to ask about. We can see if *Star Chaser* has any information—or perhaps the reports the other Krieger ship left."

Raelle grinned. "But neither ship, most likely, is from *this* line. And when we return to Earth, *we* won't be on it." She turned to Jay. "So what's the point?"

"An indicator, that's all—as to whether we've gone further from our Earth-two line, or maybe Drifted back closer to it."

Tom Dardeen nodded. "It's a strange way to have to think. I'd hate to need to learn how."

Thinking of their instructor Ginith Claare, back on Earth-one, Jay forced a grin. "Raelle and I—well, we can't say we weren't warned."

In the afternoon, with Farig Mellieur's help, Jay and Raelle moved their gear in from *Search*. Also they brought in the remaining unrefrigerated produce. Tuang was interested both in sampling the fruits and vegetables from Nobody Home and in the possibility of growing some of them on Waterfall.

Once again, ship time and planet time were out of joint. Jay found himself yawning and suspected Raelle was refraining by sheer power of will; they excused themselves. The bedroom was large, its dark paneled walls hung with tapestries showing unfamiliar animals. Real ones, he wondered? He'd ask later; now it was time to catch up with sleep.

When he woke, Raelle was bathing. He joined her; then they made love in a leisurely fashion he had almost forgotten—in space, under high Skip, sex tended to become a hurried thing. Afterward they lay quietly, communicating more by smiles and touch than speech.

They got up to find they had missed the regular dinner time and settled for a snack, refusing to put anyone to the trouble of making an extra meal. For the rest of the evening they studied summarized reports on the planet—Setra Tuang, before retiring, showed them the applicable computer access codes. They went to bed rather late but woke early in Waterfall's morning, now attuned to planetary time.

They arrived at breakfast as Farig and Tom were leaving. Setra, sipping Waterfall's version of coffee, stayed and talked. In answer to Jay's query she confirmed that the tapestried animals did exist. "I drew them from life, up in the fringes of the Central Mountains." She grinned. "That was a miserable day—I kept sneezing into my oxygen supplier." At their puzzled looks, she said, "The gravity here, the sheer height of those mountains, composition of the atmosphere—I'm no chemist so I can't tell you exactly why, but here a sea level dweller needs oxygen at a much lower altitude than on Earth. If you want to do some climbing—hiking—we'll fit you out with breathing rigs."

After the sedentary days aboard *Search*, Jay was in no mood for heavy climbing—moderate hikes struck him as more to the point—but Raelle nodded as though she liked the idea. Oh, well . . .

He asked about topping off their fuel supply. Tuang assured him it would be done immediately. He thanked her and fell silent—finding no way to introduce the question he really wanted to ask.

When next she spoke, it seemed she might have read his mind. "I suppose our family situation—Farig, Tom, Felipe, Jiddu and I—appears a little unusual to you." Before Jay could enter a disclaimer she continued. "It was a matter of serious imbalance—a shortage of females that still exists to some extent. Actually the five of us are only part of a larger household, now split by the needs of circumstance. My sister Sualna and—no, the other names would mean nothing to you—they're stationed at South Port the past two years and more." She sighed. "It was happier when we were all together. Some day, perhaps—"

Raelle cleared her throat. "Are there children?"

Tuang smiled. "Oh, yes! My four and Sualna's three—but they're always together, either here or there. Another eight tendays or so—our year begins when Companion reaches full opposition—and Sualna will ship them back to us again." She chuckled. "There's one good thing about it—when you live with children only half the time, you really enjoy them while they're on hand!"

Suddenly she looked apologetic. "Why I tell you all this—I don't know your ways, you see—there are so many ways now, on Earth, and even when I left there as a young girl." Tuang shrugged, thin shoulders moving with grace. "But you should know—the reason we don't invite you to share bed with us, it's not personal rejection, but because we adhere to strict polygamy among ourselves. Only when a new person is under consideration—and it's been years since Jiddu became one of us. Otherwise we're a closed group."

Jay hastened to explain that as Monogamists he and Raelle were even more exclusive. Nodding, Setra changed the subject. Jay was left to wonder, how did they decide on new admissions? Unanimous vote? He shook his head and listened while Setra Tuang, her fingers ruffling the short hair above one ear, made suggestions for the next few days' activity. When she was done he looked to Raelle and saw agreement. He said, "Sure—we'd like to see the mountains up close. And then, tomorrow's as good a time as any, to talk with the University people."

They saw *Search* fueled and its water supply replenished. Setra offered a supply of Waterfall's own native foods—to take along, when the time came, in the improvised space locker. Then she turned the agenda over to Tom Dardeen, for a flight to see the lower reaches of the Central Mountains.

The aircar combined features of jetcopter and fixed-airfoil craft. Seeing Jay's inspecting look, Dardeen smiled. "You won't have seen this before, Pearsall. Local design, for our uncommon atmospheric conditions."

Raelle's brows tilted. "What's the emphasis?"

Jay thought the question vague, but Dardeen answered, "Redundancy—for safety. So it's a fuel hog, of course—but we can afford that."

They boarded and strapped in, abreast across the foremost of three rows of seats. Dardeen moved the car along the ground, tilted its nose up and lifted it at a steep slant. Jay looked ahead, then back—below, the buildings dwindled to specks before forward motion left them behind. He said, "This one rises well."

"Yes. Now we're above good breathing." Jay felt no lack of oxygen—then, hearing the whir of a small motor he realized the cabin was pressurized. Tom Dardeen said, "Anything ever pops, oxygen's ready in your righthand armrest. Just pull up—it unfolds, all standard."

He said no more, but pointed ahead. Even still distant, the mountains towered high above the car's altitude. Below, the vegetation they passed changed slowly from bright green to a bluer tinge. Jay recalled the view from space—the ground beneath must be rising faster than it appeared to do. He looked straight ahead then—and seeing one of the mammoth falls of water caroming down a vast chasm, drew involuntary breath.

"They named this place rightly—that's certain."

Smiling, Dardeen nodded. "We did, that."

At half the height—a little more—of the initial range, the aircraft labored and would go no higher. There were other vehicles—short range spacebuggies, almost, not dependent on air for fuel or lift—those could penetrate the Central

Mountains. "We've explored, a little," Dardeen said. "It's all much the same up there. Nothing useful to us at this time—almost a whole continent we can't live on without carrying oxygen. Later, maybe—valleys full of hardwoods, and the minerals and all—but not now."

The car's utmost lift brought them level with a plateau, a huge meadow with only scattered growth of trees. "We'll land a bit, if you like." Raelle nodded; he coasted into the gently sloping incline, midway between two flanking ridges. They slid to a halt amid grasslike growth that rose almost high enough to block their surrounding view; Dardeen backed the car and turned it. "Up here, I like a downhill start."

Then in the stilled vehicle they sat without speaking. Jay turned to ask a question—Dardeen pointed to their right, and Jay saw animals emerge from high undergrowth to cross a shallow clearing.

From the tapestries he recognized their outlines. "Why—I thought she'd stylized them. But that's how they really are." Short-muzzled rounded heads sat neckless against the heavy shoulders. The reddish brown pelts, streaked with white, at first camouflaged the rest of body shape. Then he realized the strangeness—the lanky trunk was no thicker than the upper segment of any of the four limbs, though the lower portions tapered abruptly to skin over bone and tendons.

Jay shook his head. "There's not room enough for the *organs* to supply that much muscle."

Dardeen chuckled. "That's what we thought, too—until we dissected one."

"Oh?"

"Those heavy limb segments aren't all muscle. You realize, the organs don't rightly correspond as we'd expect—but roughly the torso pumps blood and digests food. Breathing apparatus in the upper forelimbs—kidneys and the like in the matching rear portions." The redhaired man grinned. "Not the most survivalprone design, maybe—as our biologists found when they tried to knock over a few for study without killing them." He shrugged. "But these creatures—mostly grazers but not above snaffling smaller animals or grubs or bugs—they've got no real enemies at the active adult level. So they do well enough."

Jay knew what he meant—predators that attacked only the young, sick or elderly had little adverse effect on a life form. He said as much, and Dardeen agreed.

* * *

On the way back to the lowlands they landed once more—to see inconclusive evidence that intelligence might once have begun to develop on the planet. As Dardeen watched, smiling, Jay and Raelle looked through an area that could have been ruins or fortuitous natural formations. Occasionally they picked up rock shards—weathered artifacts, or frost-riven accidents? After a time they rejoined their pilot.

Raelle frowned. "What's the general scientific opinion?"

"Divided, of course. But the theory Setra and I agree with—two or three million years ago, during a wet era that allowed very few remains to be fossilized, we think a life form came close to intelligence." He shrugged. "But not quite close enough to cope with a drastic climate change."

Jay frowned. "But it was an Ice Age that pushed man over the top."

"Granted. But man was already warmblooded. These creatures, so far as anyone can tell, weren't."

To that, Jay had no answer.

Swooping down the mountains, watching foothills and plain unfold and expand before him, Jay felt exhilaration. He reached to clasp Raelle's hand—her own grasp responded. Tom Dardeen said, "I always like it—the run back down to home."

"I can see why," said Raelle.

In Setra Tuang's office that evening the next day's appointments were arranged. A quick flight next morning, south to the university—key personnel from *Star Chaser* would go with them. And the crucial interviews, to inform Waterfall of Drift, would be recorded for later broadcast. "That way," said Tuang, "you won't have to sit through all the longwinded commentary—they can splice that in afterward."

"Good enough," said Jay. "We'll be ready in the morning."

Chav Baedig, captain of *Star Chaser*, carried his short stature with an air of confidence; the dark compact man smiled as he agreed with Tuang's arrangements. "I understand you have some rather startling information." As Jay started to answer, Baedig waved a hand. "There's no hurry, no need to go through it twice. I've heard the rumors—I can wait for the facts."

Shaida Laroux, his engineering officer, frowned. On her round, chocolate-hued face the expression looked childlike. Her fingers worried her closely cropped Afro haircut as she said, "Those rumors worry me—I'd as soon know the worst now."

The two followed Jay and Raelle into the aircar. Last came Setra Tuang, who seated herself at the controls with the captain beside her. In the row behind, Jay sat between Raelle and Shaida, and once aloft he began a brief, simplified explanation of Drift.

Baedig listened also, for at the end he turned and said, "Not as bad as I'd been guessing—I'm relieved."

Laroux touched his shoulder. "Not for you, maybe—you're not *quite* a loner, Chav, but nearly everyone you care much about is on *Star Chaser*." She paused. "And I guess that's almost true of me, too—not quite, but almost. The trouble is, though—how about the crew? A lot of them—they'll panic when they hear. It could be one hell of a trip, Chav."

His hand patted hers. "That's why we're not going to tell them, until we land on Earth." He faced toward Setra Tuang. "Can you keep a lid on this—not publicize it—for a few more days until we leave?"

After a moment the woman nodded. "It's your ship."

Baedig and Laroux could shed no light on *Search*'s Drift position—on their own Earth both Nobody Home and its "rival," Sluicebox, had been colonized. Jay shrugged. "Well, that doesn't tell us much about this timeline, let alone the one we'll reach on Earth—but thanks for the information."

The town was larger than the one by the port. At one edge sat the university—its uniform architecture, spires and ornament copying a style once popular on Earth, set it off distinctly from the rest of the settlement. Landing in an open area, Setra taxied slowly along graveled ways—giving the few pedestrians ample leeway—until she found the building she sought. In a marked area, less than a hundred meters away, she stopped. "This should be close enough. Let's go in."

Inside, high corridors were tiled in pastel shades. At one intersection Tuang asked directions, then led the group to a medium sized conference room. A heavy, graybearded man set his pipe on the table and rose to greet them.

"I'm Doctor Cleydron." Introductions, handshakes, then,

"I've called Doctor Rendova—she should be here soon." At his gestures they found chairs and sat. "My branches of physics probably come closest to bearing on your question, but for some of the more exotic maths I rely on Isabel."

Conversation had hardly begun when Cleydron said, "Here she is now," and another round of introductions occurred. A small, quick woman, Isabel Rendova moved like a young girl—and looked like one as well, until a closer look showed weathering and tiny wrinkles in the fair skin, and gray in the blonde hair coiled at her crown.

She sat beside Cleydron. "Well, Henrik—I don't suppose you ordered along any refreshment?" By his look, he had not. She smiled. "Don't worry—I took care of it. Now then—" to the others, "tell us about this thing—all you know and can suggest about the discovery that reality is multiple."

At the end of it, after many questions, she made half a smile. "Not much to go on, is there? Nothing quantitative at all—except for the empirical data used to set up your safety factors. Henrik—do you see any way to extrapolate some kind of dimensional analysis?"

Cleydron sucked on his unlit pipe. "It's all speculation, of course—doesn't mean a thing as yet—but yes, I can set up a model to think with. I'll try first one additional time dimension, then two—and see which gives the best picture for possible distribution of timelines." He turned to Jay. "They didn't tell you *anything* about the theoretical approaches taken on Earth?" Jay shook his head. "Then I'll probably duplicate most of their mistakes, too."

Rendova said, "There has to be a force—though dimensionally speaking that's not the proper term, of course—that tends to hold an object on its own timeline. The few cases we've been given—Skip Factors and travel times for ships that did and did not Drift—we can use those to assign some arbitrary constants." She grinned. "Then at least it will *look* as if we know what we're talking about."

The session broke for lunch. Doctor Cleydron suggested the building's own cafeteria but Setra Tuang, smiling, shook her head. "I did my graduate work here—remember? Students can eat anything, I suppose. But we—well, frankly, while we're here I'd hate to miss a chance to eat at the River Shore—and my expense account can handle the lot of us nicely."

As the group walked outside and to the aircar, Jay noticed that the two doctors' expressions seemed more pleased than protesting.

The River Shore restaurant occupied a low, rambling structure with massive, exposed wooden beams and hardly any walls that were not mostly windows. An entire side of the building extended out over the water that ran, uncovered, beside their table. Outside air did not enter—the outer wall dipped slightly below the water's surface. The group was offered the opportunity to fish in the slow current—"Catch your own lunch!"—but only Captain Baedig accepted an angling rod.

"I just want to try it," he said—and ordered from the menu with the rest. When just before the food was brought, he landed a writhing, goggle-eyed creature that snapped huge teeth together and waved handlike flippers, he freed it from the hook and dropped it back to swim away.

The meal—an assortment of aquatic creatures prepared in various ways—was very much to Jay's taste; as he pointed out, it beat institutional cooking several ways from Sunday! Over coffee Raelle brought out her Earth-status sheets from the two timelines she and Jay knew, plus comparable data provided by *Star Flame* on Nobody Home. Questioning Baedig and Laroux on key points regarding their own Earth-of-origin, and Tuang and the two doctors concerning theirs, she filled out two more outlines.

"They're all fairly close," she said when she was done. "But the two Earths Jay and I have known, and the three listed here that we haven't known, do form two definite groups, I think."

Rendova nodded. "That fits what you told us—the higher the Skip, the greater the Drift. Too bad there's no way to quantize the data."

Henrik Cleydron cleared his throat. "Maybe there is. Oh, nothing exact—it's all grossly approximate. But I think I can work up a fairly responsible-looking curve on it, something you can use for rough prediction."

"Prediction?" Raelle leaned forward. "You mean—given the trip parameters, we could know what kind of Earth to expect?"

"Oh, no." The doctor smiled and shook his head. "Nothing so concrete. Simply, judging from changes you and others have found, how much Skip you'll feel is wise to use on your way to Earth."

To Jay, the words sounded rather final. Not, he thought, that they had any great choice in the matter...

On the way back to the university Isabel Rendova said, "I think we have all the information you can give us, for now. If you come up with anything else, or if we have more questions, we can call each other. I know you're busy, Setra—so if you all want to make the Tri-V tape now and return to the port..."

After a moment's pause, Tuang said, "Yes. That's probably best." So when they returned to the university building Rendova led them to a recording studio and Cleydron found an assistant to operate the equipment.

They took seats along a table, facing the Tri-V camera—Jay and Raelle at the left, the two doctors in the middle, and Baedig and Laroux on the other end. Isabel Rendova introduced herself and the others, then asked questions from a scribbled list, drawing answers from Jay and Raelle in a logical, informative order. Jay felt strange repeating things his questioner already knew, and had to remind himself that they were performing for a larger audience. When it came to their individual experiences, he and Raelle told them impersonally, as though they had happened to others or as hypothetical possibilities. Then Baedig and Laroux discussed their own expectations. And it seemed a very long time before Rendova smiled and said, "That is all the facts—*and* speculations—we have for you at this time. I wish to thank our guests for their time and consideration." She waved a hand—the assistant turned off the camera and she said, now in a conversational tone, "If we repeated ourselves a little, they'll edit it for us. Frankly I think we all did very nicely!"

The two doctors came outside and accompanied the group to the aircar before saying good-byes. "When we have anything for you," Cleydron said, "*if* we do—we'll call. In any case—" this to Jay and Raelle, "do check with us, won't you, before you leave?"

They agreed, and Setra Tuang took the car aloft.

Departing from their previous direct route she followed the shoreline, staying low enough for good observation. The terrain varied—first, near the river, a stretch of level beach, then a rocky section that rose to form a craggy headland before dropping again, then gravel and hummocky sand dunes topped with sparse growth.

They saw very little animal life—only a few gray, smooth creatures floating half awash, heads on short necks dipping occasionally to the surface as though feeding. "You wouldn't believe how fast they can go," said Tuang, "with the little killerfish after them." Then she corrected herself. "Not fish, really—they defy classification by Earthly standards. Anyway, this isn't the season for them, here."

Near the port another beach started, but there they turned inland. In a few more minutes they had landed.

Free for the afternoon, Jay and Raelle ran the routine checks aboard *Search,* found all equipment performance well within limits, and adjourned to their quarters for a time of privacy. At dinner that evening the table seated seven—Chav Baedig and Shaida Laroux were the additions.

The captain seemed preoccupied, but not until after eating did he open his subject. Then he said, "I wish I'd taken notes today—about *Star Chaser* and what our chances are."

Sidelong, Tuang looked at him. "I thought the chances didn't worry you, Captain Baedig." Then she reached to put a hand on his wrist. "I'm sorry—I don't mean to tease. It's only—"

He grinned at her. "Sure—I know how it sounded. But it's not for me—it's the crew. Somehow they've heard. Nobody's fault, you understand—there wasn't any clamp on discussing the whole thing, and so far as you people knew, no reason for one. But I can't—as I'd planned—keep them all ignorant and happy until we reach Earth. I have to tell them something. And it seems best to tell the most accurate truth I can manage."

Raelle said, "Your own trip parameters again then, Captain Baedig?"

When he gave them, she nodded. "We don't have to count the time you spent below Skip ten-third. Basically you drove two and a half months at close to fifteen hundred, plus brief buildup and decay periods which hardly matter." She consulted the data Admiral Forgues had given them, back on their Earth-two, and paused.

Waiting, Baedig said, "Is it that bad?"

"Oh, no—I'm only trying to think how to say it, to give

your crew a realistic picture but not a needless fright." After a moment, she nodded. "You can tell them that in large—major items—their new Earth won't differ much. But individually, things that depend on chance or minor decisions—these may or may not be changed. And tell them they're not alone—that others have faced the cost of Drift and managed to adjust."

"Most of them," said Jay. He thought of what Woody—the Woody who was *not* his father—had told him, and continued, "This next—it's up to you, whether you want to tell your crew or not. But one thing that can happen—*has* happened—is two of the same ship landing on the same Earth." Seeing Baedig's startlement he added, "Yes—you could find yourself and your crew, or most of them, already there. Or arriving after you. And come to that, there's no rule that says there couldn't be *more* than two duplicates."

Baedig turned to Shaida Laroux. "What do you think—should we tell them *that*?"

The round, brown face looked solemn. "I don't think so, Chav. Give them the general statement, only—keep the specifics to ourselves." She smiled at Jay. "But it's good to know the chances—we can be braced to help, if they do happen."

The captain touched her hand. "Doesn't it bother you at all? I confess—it's the one thought that's jarred me personally. I mean, with two of me there—which one has the job and the assets, and which is out in the cold?"

"In the case I know of," said Jay, "the Space Service took care of its own, duplicates and all. Personal problems—well, it provided counseling, as best it could. But—there were some tragedies, I'm told."

Raelle spoke. "*I* met myself—in fact, it was for that chance that I went Courier. And it was wonderful! Captain—if it happens to you, *welcome* the opportunity."

Brows slanted, he looked at her. "There's one difference. I suspect that you're a nicer person than I am."

Laroux laughed. "You're not so bad, Chav."

Next morning aboard *Search* they found an intermittent malfunction in the telemetry backup equipment. The problem was more in Jay's specialty than Raelle's so she left him to locate it. He had never found intermittents easy to pin down and this one was no exception—more than an hour passed before he found and replaced the faulty component.

And still, on the test set the balky unit operated correctly eight or nine times out of ten! He came outside, saw an aircar landing nearby and walked toward it. The vehicle taxied in his direction—he was surprised to see Raelle at the controls, Tom Dardeen sitting alongside.

They stopped, and climbed down to greet him. Grinning, Raelle said, "Jay!—Tom's shown me how this thing handles; he says I'm checked out to fly it. So if we like, we can go exploring for a day or two. Do you want to?"

After a moment, Jay agreed. First they had lunch, then packed provisions and other supplies aboard the car. Jay was pleased to find that the last two rows of seats converted for sleeping and contained the necessary coverings. He said nothing when Dardeen brought portable oxygen supplies and instructed them in the use of the devices. But once Raelle had lifted the vehicle and pointed it toward the mountains, he said, "If it's up to me we won't be using those. We're out for a little exercise—exploration. There's no point in going where we're dependent on these gadgets."

She smiled at him. "I agree—but Tom thought he was doing us a favor, giving us a chance for a new experience. So—"

"Right—that's why I didn't say anything at the time. I can't see taking risks with unfamiliar gear just for fun, though. So let's leave the cabin unpressurized, and stay within our own limits."

Raelle nodded, and began to explain the aircar's controls— they were more numerous and complicated than Jay had expected. "Yes, but it's a hybrid vehicle," Raelle said. "Dardeen told us that—remember? And everything's handled separately. This now..."

Jay watched and listened—in case of need he wanted to know how to handle the car. Once he said, "The design could be improved. There's too much duplication—one lever could control those two functions, with circuitry to phase between them as the speed changes."

She adjusted the two controls he had cited. "Yes—much the way our various sensors on *Search* multiplex in to the same set of indicators. When we come back, shall we suggest this?"

He shrugged. "We might hint a little—and if they're

interested we can develop the ideas. But we don't want to sound patronizing. These people have done a lot with what's available."

They were barely into the rising slope of bluish vegetation when thinning air hastened their breathing. To stay as low as possible, Raelle turned to follow a broad, winding canyon. Soon they neared the end of its relatively level part—ahead it rose abruptly. "Hyperventilate a little," she said. "I want to pop up a way, for a quick look."

He grinned and obeyed—after all, oxygen was available in the armrests. She swooped up level with the canyon's banks, and higher. To the right lay a gentle upward slope. On the other side, past the ridge, Jay glimpsed a long valley—Raelle turned and dipped into it. Down into more breathable air again, she said, "Does this look like a good spot for a quick vacation?"

"Sure. How about that clearing beside the little lake, at the upper end?"

"Looks fine." She turned in that direction, brought the car to its best approximation of a shallow glide, and landed.

After that first afternoon they stayed one full day, another, and then one more—hiking, exploring, sunning in the lee of the ridge that stood against prevailing winds. The small lake was too cold for prolonged swimming—but not for brief plunges, with the sun's warmth for drying afterward. The freedom from schedules, pressures and people encouraged lovemaking.

Once, afterward at twilight, they lay together and watched a silent, stately parade of small furred creatures whose ears and tails were bobbing, extravagant plumes. And late each night they saw Companion rise—its cold glare almost half as bright as day.

The lake's water and several kinds of native berries—a manual in the aircraft pictured a number of edible species—stretched their provisions to make the third day possible with comfort. On their fourth morning Jay said, "I suppose we have to get back now." They arrived in time for lunch.

Setra Tuang and Farig Mellieur—Dardeen was not present—greeted them pleasantly and asked what they had done and seen. At one point Farig nodded. "You were lucky, to see the little paraders—they're a rare species. I've seen them only twice, myself—and I used to spend considerable time in the near uplands." He sighed. "Taking creatures, they are."

A little later, Setra commented, "It's as well you didn't camp in low-oxygen country. I know Tom was dead set you'd want to, and usually it's safe enough—but you both being new to it, I confess I've been a little worried while you were gone." She smiled. "You had no difficulty with the aircar, I expect?"

"None." Raelle shook her head. "Tom's a good teacher—I'll want to thank him."

After a moment's silence Mellieur said, "He's at South Port—should be back tomorrow or the next day. You won't be leaving before then?"

Raelle looked to Jay. He shrugged, and she said, "There's no real hurry. We'd thought, perhaps tomorrow—but another few days wouldn't matter."

"That's right," said Jay. Then, "Is anything wrong?"

Setra spread her palms, raised her brows. "That's the trouble. We're not sure yet—or whether there's any help for it." To further questions she shook her head. "Until we know more, there's no point in guessing."

Feeling somewhat excluded, Jay left the table as soon as politeness allowed, claiming *Search*'s maintenance checks as excuse. Raelle stayed, saying, "Then as soon as I've finished my coffee, I'll take first turn at a good hot soakout."

On *Search*, Jay gave close attention to the telemetry equipment that had recently given trouble, on the chance that some part of the supporting circuitry might have caused the module to fail. Eventually he satisfied himself, and in the maintenance log crossed off his question mark.

Coming outside he saw Shaida Laroux descending *Star Chaser*'s ramp. He waved to her; she waved back. Reaching the ground, she stood waiting—he walked to meet her. "How are things coming? Is *Chaser* close to departure?"

She nodded. "Another week, perhaps—everything's moving on sked. I wish I could say the same for *Thor's Thunder*." She inclined her head toward the further ship's opened hull. "Maybe you'd like to look at it—do you have time? You might have some ideas that could help."

"Sure. What's the situation?"

As they walked together she told him. After a look at

Chaser's specs, *Thunder's* engineering officer thought he
might be able to modify his own drive for greater Skip Factor.
"No question of full Krieger speeds, of course—he's shooting
for perhaps three hundred. But we've run into difficulties."

"Not enough power, or circuits too light to handle it? Has
to be one or the other."

Laroux shook her head. "We haven't investigated the two
aspects separately. Neither of us are any kind of designers—
we've just tried to beef up toward Krieger specs. But so far,
something's not right."

Remembering back to Nobody Home and his own crude
design work on *Star Flame*, Jay nodded. "No promises, but I
can give it a look—and a few computer simulations to check
possibilities."

"You do know design, then?"

"A little—enough to spot the bottlenecks, and maybe see
which ones can be cleared. Given the necessaries, of course."

Boarding *Thunder* they passed crew members who greeted
Shaida and looked at Jay with brief interest. In the drive
room the man who came to greet them was Jay's height, even
though stooped—and thin, a dried and weathered figure.
Shaida introduced him—"Skaen den Telmuk." The man's
handshake was dry also, the skin almost rasping. Below
sunken cheeks his thinlipped smile was that of a skull—but
the gray eyes were gentle. After Shaida explained, he said,
"You know the ins and outs of what makes Skip units tick?"

"A little," Jay admitted. "Could we sit down over a readout
of your original specs, and the changes you're making?"

"Sure—I was ready for a break, anyway. Let's go have
some coffee with our talk." He gathered up a pile of rumpled
drawings and led the way.

Besides coffee, Jay sipped with appreciation from a tiny
glass of den Telmuk's brandy. While he looked back and forth
from one section of the specs and modifications to another, no
one spoke. For nearly half an hour he studied, making notes
for questions he would need to ask. Then, before speaking,
he considered what he had learned.

Available power was a fixed quantity, but the two engineers—
copying from *Star Chaser's* design—had modified auxiliary
apparatus to improve utilization nearly thirty percent. They
had corrected the most obvious power bottlenecks—but had
overlooked two important ones. He estimated a possible forty

percent further improvement, no more. And that was by no means enough. Now then...

He saw it—the combination of multiple and cascade, *distributing* power automatically to various thrustor and Skip stages. *Thunder's* circuits were relatively inefficient—and the newer design used the same components. More of them, though, and arranged differently...

He pointed. "This section—the interface modules—you have spares?" Before den Telmuk could answer, Jay added, "What indicated Skip Factor have you reached, so far?"

"About a hundred and thirty—where at this stage we'd hoped for two hundred." Then, "Spares? How many? We've got some."

And Shaida Laroux said, "*Chaser* can afford a few—Chav's agreed to that, remember?"

Den Telmuk leaned forward. "What kind of Skip can we get?"

Jay shook his head. "No guarantees. But it *looks*—well, Shaida said you were after three hundred. I think we can come awfully close."

Back in the drive room Jay studied the Skip unit—he dismounted a connector and inspected its leads. "We have to rewire the framework anyway—I think we'd better use heavier stuff." Den Telmuk demurred—there wouldn't be room enough. Jay grinned. "Either cut and splice sections to expand the frame, or run all your low emission leads outside the shielding." When Jay went to *Search*, and Shaida with him, den Telmuk was busy with a welder and some scraps of bar and angle stock.

As Jay had hoped, all his computations for *Star Flame* were still available in the computer. He sent Shaida to requisition wire of the proper sizes—from *Chaser* or from the port's supplies—and took a revised readout, correcting the interface changes in his rough line sketch. Aloud he said, "I wouldn't have thought I knew enough—but it *should* work!"

He took the information to *Thor's Thunder* and discussed it briefly with den Telmuk before returning to the Tuang quarters. In their suite he found Raelle relaxing on a sofa, listening to a tape of chanted poems. Sometimes in unison and sometimes in counterpoint a man and woman spoke—

though they were not singing, their voices made shifting harmonies.

Raelle smiled at him—he waved, moved to bend and kiss her, and retired for his own turn in a hot tub. Then he rejoined her.

They were sipping wine—economically, from the same glass—when Setra Tuang's voice came from the intercom. "Dinner in about half an hour. Unless you'd rather eat alone—in that case just order when you're ready."

Jay reached for the comm terminal. "We'll be with you in a few minutes. Thanks." So they dressed and met the other two in the large dining area.

This room had a large skylight over the main table—now, reddened by high cloud masses, sunset glowered. As it dimmed, slowly, the room lights brightened. Automatically? Jay supposed so. The group sat and began eating.

Their hosts said little and seemed tense—talk concerned food, the expected weather, Jay's report on *Thor's Thunder*. To the latter, Setra Tuang showed interest. "Can you leave copies of all modification data, to help other older ships that may come here?"

"Sure, if it works." At her look, he added, "It should, you understand—but I haven't seen it *tried*, before."

Farig Mellieur spoke. "On Earth, don't they upgrade ships?"

"Of course. But that's a production job, handled by specialists. Except for retraining, to handle Krieger-range instruments, ships' personnel have no part in it."

"Naturally," the man nodded. "I should have thought."

Again conversation ceased. Troubled, Jay hardly noticed what he ate. At the end, with a minimum of asking and response, coffee and liqueurs were poured. Jay saw Raelle look to him, brows drawn down in puzzlement or anxiety. He had no answer—raising his liqueur glass slightly in her direction, he sipped from it.

A young man entered—a boy, really—stopping midway between door and table. "There's a call from South Port—it's Mr. Dardeen."

Tuang stood. "I'll take it." She left quickly; the boy followed. Mellieur held up crossed fingers. "Good news, I hope."

"So do I." Together Jay and Raelle said it, then looked at each other—out of the tension brief laughter broke. *As if we knew what it's all about!* The man seemed to find no fault with their reaction—he smiled and refilled their cups.

A few minutes later, Setra Tuang returned. She moved stiffly, all grace gone. Now her features made a blank mask—at the corner of each eye, a tear glistened but did not fall.

Mellieur rose and went to her. She gripped him tightly—her knuckles showed white. "Farig!" When she let go he helped her, as though she were aged, into her chair.

The two tears ran down her face. Another pair formed—but she blinked them away and shook her head, short hair barely rippling with the movement. "It's the slow death, Farig—Tom says there's no question. And it's not bad enough that we're already low on antigen! The damned thing's mutated again—what the child has, the stuff from Earth can barely stem, let alone cure!"

Mellieur gasped, "Poor Areyn!"

Between them, Farig and Setra explained. The disease, which afflicted only young children born on the planet, had the symptoms of a metabolic disorder—in some respects food ceased to nourish and the child dwindled, its rounded limbs shriveling to bony shanks and its torso shrinking to a skeletal appearance. Yet there was a seeming factor of contagion—perhaps some native virus, as yet unidentified, that acted to predispose or precipitate the malady.

At first the blight had struck seldom, a rarity that caused isolated grief but no widespread concern. Then, only a few years ago, the wasting sickness had swept an entire community. Two pitiful corpses, frozen, had been taken to Earth for study; the first Krieger ship to reach Waterfall had brought supplies of a curative agent. "Antigen, we call it," said Farig Mellieur. "That's not the full proper term, just what we use for short. Catch a child early and dose it for thirty days—complete cure. Start treatment later on, it may need the stuff for nearly a year."

"And the ravages *before* treatment," said Setra Tuang, "aren't reversible." On her fingers, she counted. "Muscle degeneration, coordination loss, partial paralysis, whatever degree of sight and hearing has been lost. Intelligence..." Face in her hands, she rocked back and forth; only small noises escaped her.

"They warned us," said Farig, "that the thing might mutate—that the antigen could be less effective or even useless against changed forms. We couldn't tell for sure—some cases seemed more resistant so we kept the children on treatment longer,

to be on the safe side. That's why we're running low, now."
On the table his hands clenched. "We're expecting—we were
promised—supplies of an improved agent, effective against a
wider variety of strains. But that ship's not due here for at
least six months. And Areyn..."

Jay found words. "Who—who is Areyn?"

Setra raised her head—now the tears streamed. "My sister's youngest—three years old. Sualna's daughter by Tom
Dardeen."

Rapidly, Jay asked questions. Raelle looked at him, frowning—
then her forehead smoothed and she nodded. The facts...

The slow death—roughly half a year from onset to ending.
But the first month was crucial—if treatment began much
later the result was at best a crippled child, and at worst a
human vegetable. Areyn! Perhaps a week into it, maybe
less—but the antigen was only marginally effective at all.
Areyn was only one of several in need of treatment from the
scanty stock, though the others, at least, were responding to
the curative agent.

Convinced, Jay nodded. But another question—"What happens if you slow the life process? Drastically."

Farig looked puzzled; Setra wiped her eyes and answered.
"It helps—but not enough. The death slows only about half as
much as the child's own metabolism. But—?"

Palm toward her, Jay signed for silence while he calculated.
Then he nodded. "Hypothermy's out—we have neither the
space nor facilities. With available drugs, what kind of ratio
can you get?"

Setra Tuang's eyes widened. "Five or six, sometimes, with
extreme dosage—four, easily. But—you say, *you* don't have
facilities. What?—I mean, your little ship can carry only two.
And—"

"Two adults, with a safety factor," Raelle said. She reached
and squeezed Jay's hand. "And we're not the largest people in
Courier work, by any means. If we don't have leeway for a
three-year-old child!—" And now Setra's smile reflected Raelle's.

"A minute, here," said Mellieur. "One question. You're
only a few days from Earth, you've said. What need to drug
Areyn?"

Jay shook his head. "A few days from *some* Earth. We told
you—high Skip increases Drift, makes it more likely we'll
find bigger differences. So we can't go at top Skip. What's the

point of taking Areyn to an Earth that's never heard of the problem?"

At first Setra nodded—then she sat bolt upright. "*An* Earth? I'd forgotten—if Areyn goes with you, we'll never see her again!"

Mellieur grasped her hand. "Do you want the child *here*, Setra—or alive?"

Aimlessly her head moved from side to side. "Farig—I don't know what to say. What can we do? I—"

Jay spoke. "Wait a minute—there's another chance." Quickly he detailed it—*Star Chaser* was nearly ready to leave. Departure might be accelerated; he, Jay, would stay and help complete the work on *Thor's Thunder*. Skipping at ten-third, *Chaser* was nearly ten weeks from Earth—but over this distance no ship had ever drifted at Skip twelve hundred, and at that rate the time was roughly eight weeks. By slowing the child's metabolism—"Well, it's a gamble. By your own figures, she'd be near the edge of the permanent-damage threshold. But you could be sure of Areyn's reaching the same Earth, the same people, that studied this problem, *here*."

Tuang looked to Mellieur. "Farig?"

He shook his head. "*We* can't decide. Put the matter to Sualna and Tom—she's their child. But have them bring her here immediately."

And, Jay realized, there was more to it. "If she goes with us, now—we *could* hit an Earth that doesn't know the situation at all. What data—medical studies and chemical formulations—do you have? Besides the antigen itself, we'll need copies of all that."

Tuang nodded. "Yes—of course." Lack of knowledge, she explained, was not the difficulty. Simply, the planet's medical people and their technicians were only partway along the path of making the tools to make the tools that could handle the necessary analyses and syntheses. "We knew it would take time—another year, maybe two—we counted on new supplies from Earth to tide us over. But for Areyn, the time's run out." She stood. "I'll go call Tom and Sualna. Probably they can't get all the data together this evening, but they should be here sometime tomorrow." She left, and her walk showed some return of grace and vigor.

Mellieur said, "Excuse me. I'll go see how fast *Star Chaser* could lift, given overtime help around the clock."

When he was gone, Jay said, "One thing about these people—they don't just sit on their hands. Any chance at all, for an answer, and they're up and moving."

"Yes, Jay—which gives the child her best hope? Us, or *Star Chaser*?"

He shook his head. "Drift only knows, Raelle. *I* sure don't."

Next day Dardeen flew in before noon. Jay, as he was entering *Search*, saw and heard the landing—but completed his chores before returning to the building. He arrived to find conference in session—Dardeen, face grave, stood to greet him. The woman alongside, who also rose, was neither so tall nor so thin as Setra Tuang. Her features showed resemblance but were less strongly accented, and her hair was worn loose, falling not far short of her waist.

"Sualna Tuang, Jay Pearsall," said Dardeen; his pride was evident. Jay shook the woman's hand briefly and then they sat.

"They've been telling me the alternatives," she said. Her voice was much like her sister's, but with a slight husky pitch. "Let me see if I understand them." And briefly she cited the arguments for and against sending her child on *Search* or on *Star Chaser*. "Do I have it correctly?"

Jay nodded. "What you've said, yes. What you left out— I'm not sure I made that clear last night, to the others." The perfect arches of her brows slowly lifted. He said, "You understand that on *Star Chaser* Areyn would reach *the* Earth that developed the antigen. There, the gamble is the time element." She gestured agreement and he decided that Drift had been explained to her, well enough. "With *Search*, time's no factor—we'll have it to spare. But—not only can your daughter never return to this timeline of Waterfall, but we definitely risk reaching an Earth that never heard of your problem and will have to tackle it from scratch, using the data you give us to take along. Did you know that part of it?"

As she shook her head, the long, glossy hair rippled. "I—I'll have to consider." She turned to the others. "What do you think, all of you?"

None, Jay saw—not even Dardeen, the father—wished to make the decision for her. Suddenly he saw the strength of the bond that joined this group family, long divided physically but not in thought or feeling. When Setra had spoken, and Dardeen and Mellieur, the choice was still Sualna's. She turned to Jay.

"If Areyn goes on the large ship she will assuredly come back here alive—but perhaps not all of herself?" Jay had to nod. "And if she goes with you, I'll never see her again. But—if I understand properly—either she'll be fully restored or—or else she will die. Is that right?"

Until he had swallowed something intangible, Jay could not speak. Then, "I'd say those are the most likely outcomes."

Her eyes closed—for a moment she could have been a statue. When she looked at him, Jay knew what she would say. "Areyn takes after me—and I was always of the gambling instinct. She goes with you."

The child was in another room, warmly bedded, drugged and fed through a vein in her tiny arm. When Jay saw her, her eyes were open. There was a kind of consciousness at such times, Sualna told him, but so slowed that no communication was possible. Dardeen had shown him a Tri-V sound picture of Areyn, taken before her illness—a happy child, filled with joy and vigor. Here, now, lay only the matrix of that child—eyes dull, cheeks sunken, mouth lax—most of the hair gone, since loss of hair was usually the first visible symptom. "If it weren't for that," Dardeen had said, "we might be another week or two, catching on to what's wrong." Looking at the pathetic little mannequin Jay could find no word of comfort—for any of them.

He did not want to eat with the group. Pleading necessity he went to *Star Chaser* and found Shaida Laroux sipping a last cup of luncheon coffee. "Can I grab a snack here, and a little later go do all I'm going to have time to do, on *Thunder*?" While he ate he told her—not in detail—why *Search* had to leave immediately. "But I'll get everything down on paper for you and den Telmuk. This afternoon. All right?"

"If it has to be, I guess we'll manage."

Even a small, comatose child requires a certain amount of space. Arranging this in *Search* was not easy. All right—Jay and Raelle could eat sitting in the control chairs or on the sleeping couches. The dining nook came out and the reinforced crib, with its supportive equipment and necessary supplies, went in. Fastened solidly, of course—and Jay insisted on full shielding all around, with insulated safety controls. "We *plan* to stay at or below Skip ten-fourth. But just in case—something could change, could happen—she has to be protected against high ionization."

Areyn's parents, her aunt Setra and Farig Mellieur all agreed. Tom Dardeen affected an air of cheer. "See how well she'll be cared for?" But his tone did not convince Jay—nor, to his eyes, did it reassure the others. Nonetheless, he felt, they all pretended well—each trying to keep the rest from sinking into pessimism and desolation. But Jay had attended funerals that were happier.

He excused himself for a last visit to *Thor's Thunder*, taking with him the notes and readouts he had promised Shaida. Aboard, the work was going well. Initial tests of the partial reconstruct validated the hopes he had given, and although the complete unit could not yet be tested under power he considered that the remaining changes were straightforward enough. Jay's confidence rose again. He shook hands with Skaen den Telmuk. The woman left the ship with him, and it was at the foot of *Star Chaser's* ramp that he bade goodbye to Shaida Laroux.

At dinner no one mentioned the child. The concerned family spoke of impersonal matters—overall progress of the colony, and the reports that *Search* would take to Earth. "Relevant or not," said Setra, "when you get there."

"That's right," said Jay. "The premise of Courier Service is that events in large tend to follow a pattern. Discrepancies make themselves obvious, so the reports are always of some value."

For coffee they moved to Setra's study. The conversation, it seemed, was not portable—Jay felt the strain of people avoiding a subject. Finally Sualna said, "I—I'm losing the will to follow my decision. I seem to have to talk about it—do you mind?"

Raelle, sitting beside her, took her hand. "Of course not, Sualna. What most disturbs you?"

Facing the child's mother, Jay saw that she stared past him.

"I can give up Areyn—for her life's sake I can do that. But—to *whom?*"

Raelle's head turned sharply; she gazed into the other woman's face. "Why—we hadn't thought! Just the medical aid—that's as far as I'd considered the matter. Jay?—"

He did not hesitate. "We'll keep responsibility for her, not pass it off to any impersonal agency—you can trust us. I don't know—I'm not sure—whether our circumstances would be suitable for foster-parenthood." He grinned briefly. "Or our qualifications, either. But Areyn won't wind up in a Care Center."

"I grew up in one, you see," said Raelle. "They're well managed, really—but they lack the close *personal* ties a child needs." Her smile was lopsided. "No—if we can't give her a home ourselves, and I rather share Jay's misgivings on that score, we'll make very sure she has a good one before we bid leave of her."

Jay said, "Do any of you have any relatives on Earth whose alternates might be well suited to raise Areyn?"

Dardeen, Mellieur and the two sisters looked at each other. Dardeen started to speak, then shook his head. "No. He and my niece—they're good kids, but they don't stay put in one place long enough for a child to get to know the neighbors."

Setra spoke. "Our aunt—if she were only younger . . ." And Sualna, shaking her head, almost smiled.

"Oh!" Raelle's exclamation startled Jay, and the others turned to look at her. "I—why are we looking for fosterparents? Sualna—in whatever timeline we reach, *you* will be here, won't you? Or perhaps on Earth? So—"

Sualna gasped, then turned abruptly to hug Raelle. Her shoulders heaved—but when she sat up again, wiping tears away and brushing hair back from her face, her quivering smile was broad. "Of course!" Her eyes closed. "Why—possibly *that* me will have a healthy Areyn and welcome her twin. Or it might be that she has lost hers, and to have her restored will be a miracle!" Now she looked around, from one to another. "Maybe—but only in my dreams will I dare hope it—from another timeline *my* child will be returned!"

The odds, Jay thought, were bad. But he did not say so.

The next morning, with Dardeen's help, Jay and Raelle moved their belongings back aboard *Search*. Waiting, then,

Jay was beginning his preliftoff checks when Shaida Laroux entered. "There's a problem," she said. "Could you give us a few minutes, over on *Thunder*?"

Raelle said, "Go ahead, Jay. I've nearly finished my part of the checklist—I'll have plenty of time for the rest of yours." He nodded, and followed Laroux off *Search*.

"Warm this morning, isn't it?" he said. Ground fog had not wholly lifted—the sun showed only as a spot of brightness in the haze, but he felt its heat.

The woman smiled. "Yes, and getting warmer. Not a bad climate here, though—nothing extreme." For a few steps she was silent, then said, "The trouble on *Thunder*—I don't think it's the equipment."

"Then what is it?"

"Either Skaen's misread your data, it looks like, or he's not trusting it. I think he's made changes on his own."

"What kind?"

She shook her head. "You look at it first. Maybe I'm wrong."

He shrugged. In silence they reached and boarded the ship. When they entered the drive room, den Telmuk had the Skip exciter humming on test—making adjustments, checking his meters and readjusting. Jay cleared his throat. "How's it coming along?"

The dried, stooped man looked up, then step by step cut power to the equipment. He shook his head. "Not too well—there'll be no three hundred out of this getup."

"Mind if I take a look?" Applying test power, Jay made a few routine checks. Den Telmuk was right—indicated performance was far below Jay's predictions. He disengaged enough connectors to be able to open the main unit and began checking major circuit layout inside the containing framework.

Yes—that was right, and that, and—*wait a minute! What the hell?* He had spoken aloud; den Telmuk said, "What do you mean?"

Jay faced the man. "Why didn't you follow the plans? It's a *balanced* design, damn it! You've hooked up a brute force feed—wasting half your power, fighting mismatches you've put in."

The older man hunched his head down toward the protection of his stooped shoulders. "It didn't look heavy enough—I was afraid of a burnout. I—"

"It's the *phasing*, I told you. We split the primary feed,

keep it balanced. You—" Short of yelling he stopped himself. "Den Telmuk—do you want this thing to work, or don't you?"

"Well, of *course*—"

"Then—" Jay shook his head. "I'm leaving today—I have to. I'll take time to change the strapping you've done, to what it should be." He picked up den Telmuk's tools and began shifting the connections. "For the sake of your ship, man, follow the design exactly as I've given it to you—all the way. Then test it—if you're not satisfied, do whatever you damned well please." He shook tension from his shoulders and began on the next tier of strapped terminals. "I'd hate to think I've been wasting my time here. But if you don't give the design a chance, before messing with it, I sure as hell have."

Blinking, hands spread, den Telmuk searched for words. "Now wait—I didn't mean—" He shook his head. "You're right. I don't understand it, the way you drew it, and I got scared. All right—I'll do it that way now—and hope it works."

"It should. To the best of my knowledge, it will." Finishing the wiring changes he set the tools aside. "And if it doesn't satisfy you entirely, on your static test runs, simply go back to your original layout. You *know* that will work. Right?"

Den Telmuk stood silent, then nodded. "Sure—I should have thought of that myself. It's just—this is *new*, and—"

"Trust your test procedures." Jay shook the man's hand. "I have to leave now. Good luck."

Out the corridor and to the ramp, Shaida Laroux followed. At the exit portal she grasped his arm to halt him. "Thanks, Pearsall. I think Skaen will be all right now. It was just—you were leaving, and he didn't know—"

"Used to having things handed to him all certified true and approved—is that it? And this time it wasn't, and he knew it."

Laroux grinned. "Something like that. And. Well—it's been good knowing you. Go safely back to Earth." He offered his hand but she moved past it to hug him. After a few moments they released each other. She stepped back; he nodded, turned and walked down the ramp to ground. On his way back to *Search* he thought, *sometimes you have to take new things on trust. He couldn't—can I?*

Sualna alone brought the child aboard. The woman's eyes were wide, her face solemn. Until she had Areyn placed in the crib and all the supportive equipment connected she spoke no unnecessary word. Then, straightening up, she said, "Setra, Farig and Tom—if they can't get here, they send their good-byes and best wishes. Another rush order from South Port—equipment failure and short of spares." She paused. "Barely, they had time for Areyn's last farewell. I—" She stopped, as if she had forgotten what she intended to say.

She looked from Jay to Raelle and handed Raelle an envelope. "Setra said to tell you, your friends at the university are away for a few days—you won't be able to talk with them before you leave. But here's the readout, their preliminary report analyzing Drift. You'll want to study it." Her voice trailed off.

Raelle went to her. "Sualna—is there anything we can do now?"

As though she had not heard, the woman said, "I've cut off the rest of Areyn's hair, you'll notice, so it won't make an untidy mess, falling out." She looked down at the child and stroked its pale cheek and forehead. "Now, if we could wait a little? I've stopped the drug—for a few hours, only—I'll set it back properly before I go." She looked up. "It's so she can be aware enough to hear me one last time. You see?"

"Of course." Raelle spoke; Jay could not. "Come sit down, won't you? We can have coffee or something."

"Tea?" Jay nodded. His hand at Raelle's shoulder signaled her to stay with Sualna. Though he would have preferred coffee he made tea for all three of them.

Then, sitting on the edge of the sleeping couch, he said, "If there's anything more you can tell us—what to watch for, what to do if there are any changes?—"

Sualna gestured toward the crib, with its panel of meters and control knobs. "Everything's there. Except for keeping her clean, just check the meters. If one starts drifting out of the indicated range, adjust the associated control. If that doesn't work, there's—there's nothing you can do. Nothing anyone can do." Her hand shook—Raelle steadied her cup and then took it as Sualna let go and covered her face with both hands. Her body shook once and then again, and was still. She lifted her head, looked to Raelle and retrieved the cup. "Thank you—I'll be all right now."

Like a statue she sat. Now and then she looked toward the crib, but said nothing. Jay's muscles began to ache—he felt inhibited from moving to relax them. His tea was cold; at measured intervals he sipped it anyway. Just as he decided to go make a fresh supply—anything to break out of this strange paralysis—Sualna stood, and moved to bend over the crib.

Raelle went to her. "Is anything wrong?"

"No." The taller woman shook her head. "She's coming awake—as much awake as I dare allow, even briefly." She put a hand to the small chin, and said, "I'll have to speak very slowly, and repeat a great deal. Please be patient with me."

Jay gestured to her. "Whatever you need—take your time."

Without answering, Sualna knelt, leaning over the crib, and began to speak. Her voice came low, its huskiness greater than usual—slowly she spoke, and as she had said, with much repetition. "Areyn. Areyn. Areyn . . ." Momentarily her brows raised, as if noting a response that Jay—from where he sat—could not see. "Areyn, I love you—always remember I love you—love you, Areyn, love you, I love you . . ."

On and on, ever repeating but constantly adding some new thing to what she had said before. ". . . so you can live, Areyn. You must go away so you can live, for I love you. Always remember, I only send you so you can live. Remember, Areyn . . ."

It was, Jay thought, like the phasing of the power feed he had adapted for *Thor's Thunder*—a blending of multiple and cascade. ". . . back to me, Areyn. Someday you may come back to me, because I love you. Remember—you go away so you can live, Areyn. Remember I love you, you may come back to me, I love you . . ."

The pattern of phrases grew; it went full circle. All the thoughts and wishes, all the love in Sualna's voice, became to Jay's ears a unity. Without volition he found himself standing, edging forward to see into the crib. And as Sualna's grave face relaxed into a tender smile he saw the child's mouth, lax until now, draw itself into firmness. The eyes half-opened, moved from side to side and fixed upon Sualna. One small hand twitched; the mother grasped it. Still she continued her litany—and now Jay saw, distinctly, that the little girl smiled. Then the lips moved—Jay heard nothing but Sualna nodded. "Yes, dearest—yes! I love you, too. So you will go and live, and remember, and—and someday come back and—yes, Areyn, oh yes!"

Her voice grew softer. She put one finger to the child's mouth, and Jay did not understand how or why she moved it.

For minutes more she repeated her phrases as in a ritual chant. Then, looking at a meter she said, "You can't hear me now—but I still love you." And nothing more.

After so long, silence came as a shock. Sualna stood. In matter of fact tones she said, "One thing I forgot to tell you. Every day, perhaps in the morning, test her front teeth with your finger. If you find them beginning to loosen, note the date—it's critical. You can't do anything about it but the doctors on Earth will need to know." She looked around her, then directly at Jay and Raelle. "Thank you for your patience, and your help. I know you'll do your best. Good-bye."

She turned to go but first Raelle and then Jay moved to embrace her. Tightly held together by all their arms, the three stood. Then slowly they relaxed their grips and were apart again. Sualna nodded. "Yes—it is the same for me." Then she walked, without haste, out and down from *Search*.

And Jay said, "If we fail her, she'll never know. But that won't make it any easier to live with."

Shortly before noon, *Search* lifted on a Krieger trajectory— not the standard one from the Can's own files but a higher-arching course obtained from *Star Chaser*. "That particle storm passing the Cluster," Chav Baedig had said. "It's still growing—there's *mass* building in there—but we don't know how fast. So they upped us a little, to be sure we'd miss it cleanly." After Raelle made the second course correction, the last needed for another forty hours, she and Jay checked the crib indicators and found Areyn Tuang's condition stable.

Then, safely committed to space, they had lunch.

As on their previous hop they leveled off at ten percent of Limit, with Skip Factor averaging ten-fourth. The fuel now entering the hellbox was still from the mined tailings on Nobody Home. Its composition varied—both Skip and percent of Limit were subject to unpredictable change. When the situation grew worse rather than improving, Jay and Raelle set up watch-and-watch procedures—at all times one sat as pilot, ready to compensate for the erratic power flow. Jay set the computer to integrate their varying progress, to give them position checks and the necessary timing for course changes. After a few watches the forced routine began to seem natural.

*   *   *

The second "morning," after checking Areyn's crib and finding the meters steady and the small teeth still firm, Jay sat to relieve Raelle at control. "I'll be glad when this freaked-up batch of fuel is used up."

She nodded. "Yes." Before she could say more, a deep rumbling behind them shocked both into silence. *The hellbox?* Jay made to rise, to go see what was happening—but *Search* bucked and shuddered, throwing him back hard enough to daze him.

Shaking his head he blinked, and looked—*the meters!* Thrustor drive was crowding half of Limit, and Skip Factor climbed—suddenly the needle jammed offscale! Raelle said "What?—"

As Jay reached for the steering level, blue ionization thundered, blurring sight. He pulled the lever—his other hand scrabbled for the power switch he could no longer see. Before he found it the Courier Can—all of it—shook and rang to titanic impact. The blue glow flared and collapsed, leaving his skin smarting raw—his lungs gasped for air that seared them. For a moment—how long?—vision darkened further and he could not move or think.

Gradually, sight returned—and a measure of coherent thought. Through the feel of overall aching bruise, he concentrated on understanding what he saw.

Arms around her head, Raelle lay slumped forward—he shook his head and looked to screens and meters. All right— *Search* was pointed safely toward Galactic zenith. But—he ignored the insanely flickering digital readout and compensated for the backup meter's bent needle—at only half the speed of light. Skip Factor read *one*—the unit had blown.

Raelle's breathing was shallow but even; conscience drove him first to see to the child. Areyn had curled—convulsed? —to the fetal position, but the indicators showed normal. Rearranging her, into a more relaxed stance, could wait.

Back to Raelle. Gently he pulled her up, leaned her against the control seat and drew her arms from their tight grip around her head. Her jaw muscles were knotted. Cords stood out in her neck, and veins at her temples—her eyes held shut, clamped, the corners twitching. Gently he stroked— slowly, patiently, massaging the tensions out. At her forehead some hair fell away—where it had been rooted he saw pinpoint burns. Under his hands he felt her head move slowly, then faster, from side to side. After a moment he held it still—her body jerked in a great spasm and her eyes opened.

"Jay? I—"

"It's over, Raelle—we're safe now." *If we can repair this.* "You, though—are you all right?"

She winced, then tried to smile. "I don't know. Probably. When I stop hurting." Then, "Areyn?"

"All right for now—needs some attention but it's not urgent. *You,* though—"

Raelle shook her head. "Let's worry about *me* later, too. What *happened*?"

"I don't know exactly. Some extreme irregularity in the fuel, I suppose—so hot it paralyzed the metering circuit. But how?—" He shrugged. "All I saw was Skip Factor going offscale—then the thrustor drive hit half of Limit and the exciter blew." *I hope that's all we've lost.* He told her their course and speed—she looked at him blankly.

He squeezed her shoulder, not hard. "Before I activate the spare exciter I'm going to pump some fuel through the works, with power off. Not much—only enough to be rid of this freak stuff, and there shouldn't be much more of it. But we can't chance another thing like this happening."

As though she had not heard him, she said, "Skip Factor offscale? Why—that would be ten-*seventh*." She looked at him. "You know what that means? At half of Limit—Jay, for a finite period of time we were moving at five million times the speed of light!"

He tried to soothe her. "Don't worry. I checked—we haven't got ourselves lost, or anything. We're not all that far off course."

"Not in space, maybe. But, Jay—how about *Drift*?"

First they saw to the child—gently rocking her contorted limbs and body into a relaxed position, caressing the small face until its tensions eased. "Slowed as she is," said Raelle, "imagine the jolt it took, to do *that* to her." Jay nodded. He hoped Areyn had taken no permanent damage—the odds against her were bad enough already.

Raelle insisted on evaluating and ministering to her own hurts. "You go see what's left of the drive, and tell me later. I'm going to unfold the bath cubicle and have a lot of steam and deep heat—then I'll report to *you*. All right?"

He had to agree. While she stripped for her chosen therapy he gathered his test instruments and began inspecting the drive for damage.

She was still in the cubicle, wisps of steam escaping, when he finished. Their troubles were not so bad as he had feared. As nearly as he could tell, his guess was correct—the catastrophe was due to passage of a concentration of high-energy fuel that was also intensely radioactive. It had ionized and incapacitated the metering sensors, overriding the control settings; suddenly both thrustors and Skip unit had overloaded past all safety limits. But aside from the Skip exciter—for which they had a replacement—nothing was damaged beyond repair.

He pumped fuel out, fruitlessly but harmlessly, until the Venturi chamber monitor showed radioactivity down to safe limits. The bin indicator informed him that fuel reserves were still well above the danger point.

After stowing the test gear, he set to preparing a belated lunch.

Raelle emerged from the cubicle and folded it away. She wore a towel over her hair and another around her hips. Jay saw a colorful bruise on her left shoulder and one more just under her breast. Otherwise she seemed undamaged and, he saw, moved well.

She looked at him a moment, then said, "I'm not hurt, really. My scalp feels like the middle of a tug-of-war—I had no idea electrostatic repulsion could be *that* strong! At the front I suppose my hair lashed out and got grounded. I've cut bangs to cover the burned spot—if it doesn't grow back I'll keep them." She moved to sit down. "Now can we have something to eat?"

Her air of belligerence startled him. Then she laughed, and he did also. "Sure," he said. "Coming up."

Together they installed the spare exciter, returned the overall Skip unit and then mutually adjusted exciter and normal drive for most efficient power exchange at the interface. Jay fought a stubborn reflective peak to no avail, until he found and corrected a loose connection. Sighing, he straightened up. "It's fine on test—let's locate ourselves and put the figures into Tinhead. Maybe we'll reach Earth yet!"

Raelle was at the screen controls. "Our trajectory's nearly

twice as high as we'd planned—but our vector isn't too far off. Extra time, I'd guess, less than ten percent."

Tinhead, the computer, agreed. In a few more minutes their course was reset, and *Search*—back to a conservative and now steady Skip Factor of ten-fourth—pursued its path toward Earth.

But Jay knew Raelle echoed his own thought—*which* Earth?

Well above ecliptic, with a minimum of ten days—by Sualna's guess—before Areyn's condition could become critical, they entered the Solar System. No outer planet held rendezvous with their course. Pluto wheeled almost in opposition—Neptune was angled to one side and Uranus near quadrature to the other. So it was not surprising that no signals from those beacons came through the hash of Solar static.

Jupiter, though—or rather, the drone-landed beacon on Big Jove's largest satellite—should have been heard. "It could be out of order," Raelle said. "The radiation belts—you know how often the units conk out, there."

"Maybe." Jay shrugged. "And it looks like the Guild won its strike, on this timeline—nobody's manning the old beacon ship in the Trojans, if it's still there at all."

From her seat beside him she reached to stroke his neck; he felt tensions ebbing. "What does it matter, Jay? It's Earth that's important—and we'll be there soon."

She was right, of course—*Search*'s Skip Factor was edging rapidly down to normal time, while thrustor drive gently brought the Can from ten percent of Limit down to five, then three and still slowing. Below their course Mars drifted—but even at the nearest approach no signal answered *Search*'s call.

Raelle scowled. Jay said, "We'll have to wait 'til we get there—all the way. That's all."

"Sure." But she spent more time at her remote instrument displays, tuning and adjusting. Screens and meters gave no response.

Now they approached Earth itself. Only a few million kilometers distant from the planet, the silence was not promising.

Jay clutched Raelle's wrist. "I think—let's circle in behind Luna. Just in case."

*   *   *

Well outside detection range for a vessel of *Search*'s mass they entered the ecliptic plane. Earth was to their right with Luna almost directly trailing in orbit—a little more than half full, seen from Earth, and waxing. Only when the satellite hid its primary, or nearly, did *Search* begin approach. And even from a distance they could see that the Farside installations they knew—well, those structures simply did not exist.

Raelle drew a shaky breath. "We've Drifted badly, Jay."

"Yes." Slowly now, even by the standard of training flights, Jay came near the moon and then around its right side. And there was Earth—left hemisphere sunlit, the other dark.

On the dark side, visible with the screen turned high, lights shone. Until he exhaled, Jay didn't realize he'd been holding his breath. *At least there's people—civilization.* "That's Europe, I think, having the middle of its evening."

"Then our port will be at midafternoon. Shall we go in?"

"If it's there, yes." For thought neither of them had commented, they had not seen or detected any other craft in space.

Raelle took *Search* downward. Jay began calling on standard ship-ground frequencies but the monitors showed no response. They dropped closer—five thousand kilometers, three, two—at one thousand she slowed to hovering and moved back and forth, parallel to the surface. "See anything, Jay?"

"No more than you do. The port area's somewhere in the middle of that cloud cover—without infra I couldn't even locate the coastline."

"All right. Down some more, then." At five hundred the monitors showed a pulsed signal at high power—it carried no intelligence, merely a uniform, repeated on-off pattern. Jay looked to Raelle and shrugged.

Just above one hundred kilometers the detectors showed sign. "Jay—a ship! And another—a whole squadron, it looks like! But—they're coming right at us. I—"

"Ships, hell—those are missiles! Get us out of here!"

While he still spoke, Raelle headed *Search* east at full power—normal drive only, for at those speeds Skip gave no advantage—then pulled up in a tight turn directly away from Earth, toward Luna. The missiles veered to follow—the leading one gained on them and came within fifty kilometers.

Then the distance began to increase, and the missile exploded—a fireball bloomed. *Search*'s radiation counter chattered briefly; Jay looked and said, "Bad stuff. A little closer and we'd be needing treatment we don't have aboard." Behind them, one by one the other missiles detonated— futilely, for distance gave safety; now at each sunburst the counter merely clicked a time or two. Then, its crew silent, *Search* drove outward.

Again they neared the moon. Raelle said, "What can we *do*? Even if food and fuel would last, there's no place to go. And Areyn! Jay—"

"I don't know, either. We've got to *talk* to Earth. Here—let me have control. You did a great job down there—but the lunar orbit I have in mind, it's easier to do it than tell it."

He set a polar orbit, temporarily parallel to Luna's direction of motion. Viewed from Earth it circled the moon counterclockwise, never out of sight behind the satellite. "This isn't really stable," he said. "Too many forces pulling on it. But with occasional corrections it should hold long enough."

"Longer than *we* can last, you mean?"

"I didn't say that." Raelle was out of her seat, getting some food from the space locker. Jay went to her—they clung together and kissed. "Unless Earth has gone completely crazy here," he said, "they'll *have* to welcome the technology we can give them." He shook his head. "What happened down there—it has to be some kind of mistake."

"All right—let's eat." She handed him a bag of space-frozen fruit. "Want to thaw and peel these while I do the other stuff? The Tuangs apparently like the rinds, but I can't stand them."

They ate leisurely, discussing what they would say to Earth—to anyone they might be able to reach. Then Jay checked Areyn again, to make sure the violent maneuvering had not disarranged her, and found nothing changed. Raelle sat at control, searching frequency bands for anything directed at *Search*. He joined her, but put his own efforts to transmission—he recorded a tape, spliced it into a loop and began beaming it Earthward on several wavelengths, occasionally changing one and then another.

"Calling LeGrave spaceport—calling *any* spaceport. Calling Earth, anyone who hears me. This is the Courier Can *Search*, out of LeGrave—oh, about a year ago. If that doesn't make sense to you I'll explain in full when somebody answers me. We need to land—but we can't if you're going to keep shooting at us. Come in, please—*anybody*—come in, please!"

The tape ran nearly four hours before it drew response. The intermittent beam they had detected earlier came again— but now the pulses varied in their timing, oscillating at frequencies in the audio range. Raelle looked at Jay. "Can we decode that?"

"I think so. Looks like pulse position modulation. Not very efficient for this kind of work, and we're not set up for it directly. But I think I can dude up a compatible feed, from the scanner circuit..."

The frequencies did not quite match—he had to maladjust his equipment to one extreme of its range before a distorted, gravelly voice came from the speaker. "...are you, anyway? You haven't come far, in anything that size. Where's the mother ship? Why's it hiding? No records on anything like that—let us have a look at you, if you're not some kind of alien monster." A pause, then the voice began again—soon they realized it was also a loop tape. Jay stopped his own and spoke directly.

"All right, I'm reading you. The first thing—before *I* explain ourselves—why the hell did you try to blast us, down there?"

Almost as soon as the signals could make the roundtrip, the other tape stopped in midphrase. The voice said, "If you don't know that, you can't be Earth human."

The man refused to explain further. "Not until I *see* you first!" Jay controlled his impatience and gave the parameters by which a receiver on Earth could get a viewscreen picture from *Search*. More than an hour later the man acknowledged reception. "Two of you, huh? Is that all there are? Step up a little closer—we want a good look." A pause—then, "You're human, I guess. Now then—where can you have *come* from?"

"From Earth," said Raelle, "by way of Nobody Home where we expected a colony and didn't find one, and a stop at Waterfall on our way back."

"If you're going to lie, you'll have to do better than that. Colonies? I doubt if any survived. There's been no contact for more than fifty years—and there'd better not be, either. Try the *truth*, now—though how we can believe you, I don't know."

Puzzled, Jay finally decided what to say. "The most important part of the truth *is* hard to believe—if you don't know it already, and I gather that you don't. The funny part—the trouble—is that if you could be aboard here, face to face, you'd be convinced in five minutes. But just to tell it—well, I'll try."

He began with the prime fact—the reality of multiple timelines. Knowing nothing of space progress on this Earth he detailed its history on Earths one and two—sublight travel, then Skip Drive, Krieger ships and finally the Courier Cans and the reasons for their use. "And that's how we're here. Things went differently with you, I take it?"

For a time he thought the other had cut the circuit, but on a 'scope he saw the pulses, moving only with the random push of noise level. Then the man spoke again. "For purposes of discussion I'll accept what you said. It makes no difference, because you can't land anyway. There's no way to authorize it even if I wanted to. And now I'll tell you—assuming you really don't know—why I couldn't possibly want to."

He told it well, Jay had to admit—briefly and to the point. This Earth knew nothing of timelines or Drift—its technology had not progressed that far. Through the eras of sublight travel and early Skip Drive its history was much the same as the ones Jay and Raelle knew. Exploration, the start of a few colonies, and then . . .

"The Plague, you see. That's what put us back in our bottle—and drove the cork in solid."

The clincher was that no one knew where the scourge had originated. Three ships had returned, each from separate missions covering a total of seven worlds, within hours of each other. The crews mingled and traded experiences among themselves as well as meeting with port personnel, newspeople and scientific inquirers. When the sickness appeared, no one realized it was serious until the deaths began—and by then it was spread among crews and groundies alike.

"In the next two years nearly half of Earth died—worse than that, some places. Every time we thought inoculations had it under control, the thing mutated. All that saved us was that the *survivors* were immune to the mutations.

"After that, six more ships landed. Most of their crews died, too. Then we—those in charge at the time, I mean—set up the Embargo. No admittance—no more landings. We put fuel and food dumps up on the moon—if there was any left, you'd be welcome to it. But it's all gone now, I'm afraid—the last two ships that came, there was nothing for them. So it was stand clear or get blasted. And it still is."

Raelle leaned forward. "You can't turn us away like this! We have a sick child aboard. She needs help—*now*."

Immediately Jay knew they had lost. After the three-second lag the voice said, "Sick? No, thanks—not another Plague. You—"

Overriding the voice, Jay ceased to listen. "*Not* Plague. It's a metabolic disorder—attacks only young children born on Waterfall. We have the data. Your facilities—"

He waited. Slowly the voice came again. "I'm sorry. Even if you're right, we can't take the chance. And neither can you! One thing I hadn't mentioned. All of us—Plague survivors and their descendants—we're carriers. You couldn't come down here and stay alive."

Poor Areyn! We tried, Sualna . . .

"You may wonder why we can't send you up fuel and food." *Without suits or airlocks, what good would it do us?* "Something we hadn't realized earlier—you see, like everything else, it'd be contaminated." Now that was ridiculous—no organism could live for long in close proximity to fuel, and irradiation could safely sterilize any food. This Earth's fear, Jay decided, had become pathological. "Anyway," the voice continued, "we disabled every spacecraft on Earth, all but the missiles to keep anything from landing."

They looked at each other. *There must be something we can say—but what?* Ten seconds passed, then the voice came. "No point in talking any more—it's all been said. It hurts to know you exist. I want to go and forget it."

"Wait a minute!" Raelle's voice went shrill. "We've got so much you can use—Krieger drive, our improved Skip units. Other things—your scientific community—"

When the man spoke his tone was totally impersonal. "You don't understand. Those things are no use to us—no use at all." Then on the 'scope the pulse pattern vanished; from the speaker came only background hiss.

Fuel and food—given those they could survive, and perhaps even save the child. "Head out just long enough to build our speed and Skip Factor—*ensure* Drift—then come back.

We have time enough to do that once—maybe even twice—before Areyn's condition becomes irreversible."

Jay made a new loop tape. He proposed that supplies be placed at an isolated location—a small island, perhaps. "We'd land there and nowhere else—land, load and lift, as quickly as possible. Then you could flame the site thoroughly. There's no risk, none at all." He finished by explaining how he planned to eliminate any possible contamination from Earth's gifts, and put the tape on beamed channels to Earth.

An hour passed with no response. Finally Raelle said, "They're still too afraid—of *any* contact. But what if—?"

Her plan was better, Jay agreed. She taped it herself. First she explained how *Search*'s space locker worked. "We'll open it in space, you see—it will be completely sterile. We land as proposed before, isolated—but we stay sealed. You have people in protective suits—the kind you use for working with radioactives—have them come and load food and fuel into our space locker. None of our air reaches you—none of yours reaches us. Back in space again, cold and vacuum kills any possible contamination that might have been introduced. It's *totally* safe—for you and us, both."

Again they began transmission. No answer came—none at all. After twelve fruitless hours, Jay made a fourth tape.

As he recorded it, Raelle shivered. "Please don't let it play on the monitor. Once is enough."

His brows raised. "You disagree?"

"No. It needs saying. But *I* don't want to hear it again."

So it was through a headset that Jay listened as his voice repeated his words—slow, cold and deadly.

"Cower then, Earth! Hide in your corked bottle—hide from the Plague you've already beaten. The lives you spent in that victory are wasted, because you behave as though you'd lost, instead.

"So hide! Live where you are, and die there. Leave the universe to somebody—some race—that isn't afraid of it!"

He heard himself twice through, then nodded and unplugged the headset. He turned to see Raelle watching him.

"Jay—do you think anyone is listening?"

"Probably not." He managed a grin. "But it makes me feel better."

For two days, hardly speaking except in the course of routine work and the gaspings of frantic love, they performed their duties as though those chores still had meaning. The trouble was, Jay thought, that there was simply no future for them—and yet he could not think to end their lives before starvation did.

And could Raelle? She did not speak; he did not ask.

The third day, when they checked pale, somnolent Areyn, Raelle said, "Jay! Her teeth—they're loosening. Not much, but you can feel it." He leaned over and put his own finger between the pallid lips. Yes—to his gentle pressure he felt the teeth move slightly.

He nodded. "You're right. I'll log it—Sualna said to."

"For *what*?" She screamed it. "We're all dead, Jay—you know it and so do I. The only question is—do we end that poor child before her body eats itself?"

"No." Without thought the answer came. "I have to admit, though—I don't know why."

Once again in his own mind he recited the parameters of hopelessness. Fuel—enough to take them perhaps a tenth of the way to the nearest colony—assuming they reached a timeline in which colonies existed—and then coast forever at four-tenths the speed of light, as dead there as they would be here. Food—a week, perhaps two, then slow starvation. And the child—what to do? He shook his head. "It's—Raelle, Areyn dies only when we see the wasting's gone irreversible. Or to avoid leaving her alone without us."

"Yes. I suppose that's all we can do for her, now."

On the fifth day Raelle would not speak at all, nor touch him or be touched. Ignoring the breakfast he had prepared she sat at the controls. He watched her run computer simulations—when he asked what she was doing she still kept silent. He looked at Areyn—was the child worse? He could not tell. He moved to sit beside Raelle, watching her and then toying with the screen controls to look at Earth—so near in time and distance, yet unattainable.

Rage, as it had done so many times before, came strong within him and then drained away. He could put *Search* to ground if he wanted to—not for the first time, he thought that. And perhaps he would, Plague or no Plague—if only to show that unknown voice what his silly missiles were worth if Jay Pearsall decided to challenge them. . . .

No. He shook his head. That was foolish. Leave *Search* here in orbit—a more stable one, rather—he'd have to remember to change it. Someday, perhaps, this Earth might regain its courage and look outward again. *Search*, left intact, could save the timeline many years of slow experiment. Yes—that was best.

He sunk into reverie, hardly noting what he saw. Childhood dreams came to mind, and his parents—then their childless counterparts on Earth-two. A flash thought of Reyez Turco and the abundant woman who waited for him. Nobody Home, the missing colony—sea devils—fighting them—the harsh life, the work of survival—Dolman Crait and his threats. Then Waterfall—Setra Tuang, Sualna, the others—and *Areyn*! Jarred into the present, Jay blinked and turned to see what Raelle's movements meant, that his peripheral vision had caught.

"What?—" For she was activating the Skip exciter, feeding it power. "Raelle! That won't do us any good—we'll just die out *there* someplace, instead of here. And here, maybe *Search*, someday—"

She faced him. Under her eyes the skin was pouched and darkened. Now she shook her head. "Jay—you didn't read the reports from the university on Waterfall. Neither did I, until now. But I thought—I thought I should understand why we have to die. Instead, I found—"

"But what are you *doing*?"

"Probabilities—sheafs of probabilities—they may duplicate themselves, or almost. We've Drifted so far—Jumped, really, with that burst at Skip ten-seventh. The old advice, to stay with a bad bet—it doesn't apply now, because if we stay, we're dead. So—"

"But we don't have *fuel* to go out and back!"

Wide-eyed, lips stretched to a caricature of her smile, she shouted at him. "Jay! Who ever said we had to *go* anywhere, to get up to high Skip Factor and its Drift?"

For a moment he could not speak. In his mind his training replayed itself—*when* you reach certain speeds you begin to boost your Skip accordingly. Of course. *When*.

Abruptly he broke into laughter and reached to hug her shoulders. "Why—you're *right*! Right to try it, anyway. Nobody ever—I mean, Drift was a by-product, something to avoid or put up with—no one ever considered the idea of building Skip Factor by itself, at rest. *How* did you think of it?"

Her smile had seen better days, but she said, "Because there wasn't any other way."

As Skip Factor built—odd, how differently *Search* resonated to the exciter alone without the thrustors' growl—Jay made small maneuvers, shifting *Search*'s orbit to Lunar ecliptic for the greatest stability he could compute. As he finished that chore he saw Skip pass five thousand—when he ceased drawing power the rate of increase curved upward. And they seemed to *race*, not coast, around Luna.

"Ten-fifth," said Raelle, "and climbing. Do you see any changes?" For a moment he didn't realize what she meant— then he studied Earth on the screen, near to passing out of view in the new orbit.

"Nothing yet. Except heavier cloud cover. Do you suppose—"

"Could be greenhouse effect, Jay. The timeline that rejected us—its Plague may have saved it from overpopulation that would have smothered in its own wastes."

"Possibly. I—" Now as Earth reappeared the screen showed change. *"Look!"* Gradually, orbit after orbit Jay saw Earth lose its vapor sheath, saw its oceans dwindle and vanish, then slowly reappear. For long moments he conceived these events as happening in time, in sequence—then he realized the changes were *across* timelines, in Drift. "Sheafs of probability, you said, Raelle! All those timelines where Earth's lifeless, uninhabitable—but it's looking better now. Maybe we should cut back on Skip and be ready to grab a viable line, if we can spot one."

"Yes. It's hard to understand, to know what to do—no one's ever *done* this before." The sound she made was between a laugh and a hiccough. "We don't even know—are we still Drifting *away*, or maybe swinging back toward where we started?"

He had no answer. "Just pull down some more—on our Skip, I mean." They went behind the moon again. And when they came around it—there, rising from Earth, *a ship*.

"Cut it, Raelle! Cut it dead!"

Twice more they circled Luna. At each opportunity Jay put the screen to high mag and studied Earth. On the third pass he said, "Let's try it."

"Land, you mean?"

"Maybe. Leave orbit, anyway—start down slowly, see if

anyone's willing to talk. And if not—now, thanks to you, we *still* have a choice."

This Earth fired no missiles. In short order its communication system put a picture on *Search*'s viewscreen. The woman facing them—Jay assumed their own picture was getting through—smiled and said, "You're the new shuttle, are you? From the Mars equatorial station?"

Raelle gestured for Jay to do the talking. He said, "This could take some explaining. My first question may give you an indication." He paused. "Do you have star travel?"

After the first shock, information came quickly—from both sides. For more than a century this Earth had launched sublight ships, but Skip Drive had never been developed. Jay's brief explanation quickly brought higher authority on the circuit—his screen split into two pictures, then four, then six. The last to appear—a tall black man, nearly bald—said, "I don't have to understand all this in detail to know you're the most welcome visitors we could have. Whatever we can do for you, just name it."

Now Raelle spoke. "We have a child aboard—" and quickly she told of Areyn's plight. "We've brought a sample of the basic medicine, and all the data available. If you—"

The man shook his head. "We don't have even a start on that kind of problem." Then he must have seen, as Jay saw, how her mouth compressed. For he said, "But we have *time*, you see. You say you've slowed the little girl's life processes by a factor of four or five—something like that." He smiled. "We can slow them nearly to zero—virtually suspend them, indefinitely—without harm. So bring her—our people will begin work with what you've brought, and sooner or later the child will live."

This Earth's port had the same location they had known, but a different name. *Search* landed, and a group—including the woman who had first spoken with them—brought a ground car to greet them. The woman—short, chunky and somewhat exotic to Jay's eyes—introduced herself. "Telia Hargan—since you can't know our customs, I'm to be your mediator." Jay wondered whether the butterfly design on her left cheek were tattoo or more temporary adornment.

He said, "Will you grant us Courier privileges as we know

them? Access to your computer data to see how your Earth compares with the ones we've known?"

"Give them *our* Earth-status sheets, too, Jay. We'll have to share."

"Of course, Raelle—next time we go aboard. I didn't think to bring them."

Telia Hargan brushed black, bushy hair back from a saw-toothed hairline. *That can't be natural—what's the purpose? And the method?* She said, "Plenty of time—we'll be a while, just adjusting to the concepts you bring us. Tell me—do your alternate timelines really trade back and forth between themselves? That's a fascinating possibility."

Jay realized his answer—that all interline contact was at random, that to his knowledge no one could control Drift or even calibrate it—would disappoint Hargan. And by the looks of her, it did. He added, "Keep in mind—to the worlds we've seen, the whole idea's barely a few years old. Hardly explored. There may be solutions we haven't dreamed of." Then her eyes glinted and she smiled.

A medical team brought Areyn Tuang off *Search*. Jay and Raelle conferred with the head of that team, gave her all the data they'd brought from Waterfall and a summary of the child's condition since leaving the colony, and received assurance that they would be kept informed of all developments. Then Jay wanted to get to a computer terminal and evaluate this Earth. But everyone else pleaded hunger—and to his surprise he found that for the moment he, too, needed food more than information.

Only Telia Hargan ate with them; the rest went elsewhere. Hargan said, "You've been isolated together—we know a large group might be a strain. Now—while we have time to relax, do you have questions?"

Jay shook his head, feeling that only the data banks, not any one individual, could have the facts he needed. But Raelle said, "Our overall question has to be, how closely related to the Earths we knew, is this one of yours?"

Grinning, Hargan shrugged. "Whatever comes to mind, ask away."

Raelle frowned. "Do you know a space office named Forgues?"

Telia Hargan scratched her cheek; an edge of the butterfly flaked away. After a moment, she nodded. "Sure—the big brain. Oversized head on a small body, almost deformed.

He's been gone ten years, in command of *Bear Trap*. Due back in another year or so, with luck. And the scuttle is that if his expedition has any good fortune and returns fairly near to sked, he's closely in line for command of the port."

Raelle gripped Jay's arm. "You see? Even here, where they don't *have* Skip Drive yet, Forgues is on his way to Admiral. And that could indicate..."

He patted her hand. "Yes—I know what you're trying to say and I hope you're right. But our hostess can't possibly know all the people we want to check on. So let's drink our coffee and go quiz the local computer terminals."

Hargan looked surprised, but she said, "I'm ready when you are."

In the booth, the keyboard closely resembled an outmoded model Jay had learned in school a decade ago. The anachronism bothered him—he made errors and irritably canceled them.

First he stayed with data in large—impersonal matters. And except for lack of Skip Drive he found that this Earth paralleled his own, remarkably.

What colonies had this timeline seeded, and how advanced were they? Waterfall, Mossback, and of course Second Chance— all the nearer ones he could remember were active and in good order. He paused to realize that these reports came from sublight travel. Expeditions might now be returning from worlds he knew about, that this Earth as yet did not. He nodded—the pattern boded well.

Raelle interrupted him; he deactivated the terminal. Arms around his neck, she said, "*I'm* here, Jay! Off Earth at the moment, training to leave on the longest expedition to date. But not lifting for another month or so—I'll have time to meet me again!"

He kissed her, then said, "If they have any sense, it won't leave until they've added Skip units."

And Raelle said, "Probably not. But it's the meeting that counts, not the length of it."

She left, then, to follow her own curiosities, and Jay carefully pursued his own. Setra Tuang was gone to Waterfall— her sister Sualna was also scheduled to go, but not soon. He recorded Sualna's location and access code; there was no reason to disturb this alternate of the woman—not yet, not while Areyn's fate was still in doubt. Though *this* Sualna had no such child . . .

And now he faced what he had been avoiding. He punched for data on Harwood and Glenna Pearsall—did his parents exist, here?

Yes. They had gone to space on a planet-hunting expedition. He scanned ahead—they had returned, and safely! The current data—he read it carefully and shook his head in wonder. As a result of time dilation in sublight travel the two were fifteen years short of their natural, chronological ages—and they had left the Space arm for ground duty. He read no more.

For a time Jay sat. Then he switched to the communication net and punched for the address code of Junior Commander Harwood Pearsall. Waiting, he wondered what he could possibly say to this man. For a moment his finger rested on the "Cancel" key—but he did not push it.

The screen lit. Jay saw the father he had known when he was perhaps six or seven years old—and thought, *he doesn't age much*.

"Yes?" The older man spoke without warmth, granting an unknown caller no prerogatives. Jay tried to think—how to breach that coldness?

Finally, "I—please be patient—but may I speak with your wife, also?"

On the screen, the face, puzzlement. "I don't recognize you."

"I know you don't—you can't—but it's important. Please . . ."

Woody Pearsall squinted. "There's a familiar look to you, somehow. I'll grant you five minutes. Wait, now."

"Of course." The man left the screen's view. Jay waited, and after a time Harwood Pearsall returned. With him came a woman from Jay's dreams.

Glenna—his mother as she *had* been—walked with assurance and pride. Her long bright hair bounced in the wild, leaping curls Jay remembered only from early childhood. Her smooth complexion bore a faint flush, as from recent exercise. She said, "The king of the mountain will be along as soon as he's washed his face and hands. Now, Woody—and you at the other end, who maybe I know and maybe I don't—what's this all about?"

Her husband said, "He's the one who called. You're not sure whether you know him?"

Her remembered gesture—one fingertip to the tiny mole beside her eye—melted Jay's feelings. All planning failed him; he said, "I know you—you don't know me. But at the port—*they* can tell you. Telia Hargan? And the black man— one of their top people—I don't remember his name."

"I know it," said Harwood Pearsall, "and I know Hargan, also. If you—" He turned to meet the rush of the small boy who came laughing and leaped into his arms. Pearsall grunted and caught his balance. "Well—whoever you are, meet the rest of the family. Our son Jay, age six. And isn't it about time you introduced yourself?"

Unable to speak, Jay stared at the three. *Now I understand what Raelle felt.* And then, *here I stay!*

He cleared his throat. "You're going to find this a little hard to believe . . ."

ABOUT THE AUTHOR

F. M. Busby's published science fiction novels include *Rissa Kerguelen*, the related *Zelde M'Tana, Star Rebel* and *The Alien Debt; All These Earths*, and the now-combined volume *The Demu Trilogy (Cage a Man, The Proud Enemy*, and *End of the Line)*. Numerous shorter works, ranging from short-shorts to novella length, have appeared in various SF magazines and in both original and reprint anthologies, including *Best of Year* collections edited by Terry Carr, by Lester Del Rey, and by Donald A. Wollheim. Some of his works have been published in England and (in translation) Germany, France, Holland and Japan.

Buz grew up in eastern Washington near the Idaho border, is twice an Army veteran, and holds degrees in physics and electrical engineering. He has worked at the "obligatory list of incongruous jobs" but settled for an initial career as communications engineer, from which he is now happily retired in favor of writing. He is married, with a daughter in medical school, and lives in Seattle. During Army service and afterward he spent considerable time in Alaska and the Aleutians. His interests include aerospace, unusual cars, dogs, cats, and people, not necessarily in that order. He once built, briefly flew and thoroughly crashed a hang glider, but comments that fifteen-year-olds usually bounce pretty well.